To my baby, who isn't a baby anymore.

I love you more, Ry.

1

Myles Redmond was annoyed.

Scratch that. He was more than annoyed. He was pissed and currently doing his best not to glare at the woman sitting in the chair next to him.

Dear God, he'd never resented anyone more in his life, and the fact that he was married to her made the nightmare they were living through one hundred times worse.

It would be fair to say their three-year marriage hovered on the brink of failure, and the outcome of this meeting might be what sent it plunging to its demise.

Myles clenched his jaw as he regarded Holly, taking in her unsmiling face and rigid posture. His wife's beauty turned heads everywhere they went but had failed to turn his since she'd demanded the DNA test.

"Would you stop looking at me like that?" Holly huffed, cutting a pair of ice-blue eyes at him. She sniffed and abruptly looked away, her chin notched a fraction higher as she presented him with her profile. "Whether you want to admit it or not, we're doing the right thing."

She'd worn a light blue dress for the occasion. As if she hadn't made her hopes for the outcome of the meeting clear enough. Blue was her *lucky* color. Her long manicured nails kept up a rhythmic tapping on the wooden arm of her chair.

"And what exactly is that?" he asked, his tone like shards of glass.

Exasperated, she rolled her eyes and flicked a wavy lock of platinum-blond hair over her shoulder. "God, I hate when you're like this. You know exactly what I'm talking about. I can't believe you don't want to know who she belongs to." She addressed the empty desk in front of them more than she did him.

"She," he stressed through gritted teeth, "has a name. Her name is Haylee, and she is our daughter." His voice was low and controlled while he seethed inside. It didn't matter what the DNA results revealed. Haylee was their child. After all they'd— *she'd* gone through to have her, how could she say otherwise? That was the thing he couldn't understand. His part had been easy. Hers had not—as she'd frequently reminded him.

Holly huffed out a sound of deep frustration, her narrowed gaze taking a glancing stab at his face. "She's not ours, Myles, and for the life of me, I don't understand why you refuse to accept it. It's as obvious as the nose on my face that she belongs to another couple."

"She's ours." He was the only father Haylee had ever known, and no test was going to change that.

"I'm sure her biological parents will have something to say about that." His wife had made up her mind and refused to be swayed.

Recognizing the pointlessness of arguing with her, Myles kept his mouth shut and averted his gaze. These days, it was impossible to look at her without feeling a profound sense of betrayal…and anger—so much anger. Feelings far removed from how he'd felt the day they'd exchanged their wedding vows.

"Myles, they have as much a right to know as we do. Wouldn't you want to know if you were in their place?" Holly said, her voice cajoling, indicating a switch of tactics. Good cop, bad cop, meet Holly the Bully and Holly the Sweet-Talker, the same woman employing two tried-and-true methods to get her way.

Well, it's not going to work this time.

The office door behind them opened, and Dr. Kelly Franklin walked in, saving him from more of his wife's attempts to convince him her motivation was altruism, not selfishness.

Small in stature at barely over five feet and clad in a white lab coat, Dr. Kelly had brown shoulder-length hair and carried herself with the confidence of the framed Harvard MD degree hanging on the wall.

"Good afternoon, Mr. and Mrs. Redmond. Thank you so much for coming in on such short notice."

The doctor's greeting was warm and respectful. More importantly, she didn't sound as if she was about to plunge a knife into his heart. That said, it was clear she hadn't come bearing tidings of joy either.

Myles made a move to stand, but she stayed the act of male courtesy—ingrained in him by his father—by motioning for him to remain seated.

Quelling his instincts, he subsided back into his chair and watched as she quickly took hers behind the desk.

"Sorry to keep you waiting."

She was nervous but doing her best not to show it. As a former defense attorney, Myles had learned to pick up on the subtleties of body language. She hadn't blinked once since she'd greeted them, and the distinct tapping sound that began shortly after she sat down was her nervously tapping her shoe on the floor. Holly's hands were on her lap.

"We were early," Myles said. Fifteen minutes, to be precise. Because this was important. The rest of his life hinged on what she was about to tell them. Despite vowing to himself that he'd remain calm, he felt tenser than ever.

For a beat, her brown eyes bounced between them. Then she blinked and said, "The DNA test confirmed that—"

"She isn't ours, is she?" Holly asked, cutting the doctor off midsentence.

Myles turned and narrowed his eyes at his wife. Why not put up a billboard? *I don't want her. Give her to someone else.*

As far as he was concerned, Holly had checked out of motherhood and their marriage before she packed her bags and took off to San Diego to stay with her mother after telling him she needed space.

What kind of parent needed "space" three weeks after the birth of her daughter?

His wife, that was who.

Look, he got it. They had hired a surrogate, so Holly didn't get to bond with Haylee the way mothers usually did, but she'd known that from the outset. They'd both gone into this with their eyes wide open…and then some. Furthermore, parents didn't walk away just because their child didn't turn out the way they wanted or expected. That wasn't the way parenting worked.

At the end of the day, though, he had to face some hard truths. He was just as much to blame for what was happening. While he might be successful in other parts of his life—he was a loving father, son, brother, and uncle and a loyal friend, and had been elected president of the California Bar Association two terms in a row—he *sucked* when it came to romantic relationships.

How did he know?

Because he already had one failed marriage under his belt, and it looked like he was coasting for divorce number two. In sports terms, he'd soon be 0–2.

Dr. Franklin tentatively cleared her throat before continuing. "Unfortunately, your case is a little more complicated."

"Complicated? What does that mean? Either she's ours or she's not." Holly turned and looked at him as if expecting him to echo her demand for clarity. "Although I think it's obvious she can't be." The latter she muttered as an aside meant to be heard—just in case the good doctor didn't know where *she* stood on the matter.

Myles's jaw locked. According to his wife—who'd gone from being the top-producing female real estate agent in Southern California to self-ascribed geneticist—Haylee couldn't be the product of two white, blue-eyed parents. *If she has a drop of Nordic ancestry in her, I'm the Queen of England*, Holly had said in reference to her parents' Swedish heritage and Haylee's slightly darker complexion, dark brown curly hair, and brown eyes.

Never mind that he was a quarter Sicilian on his mother's side, and his hair was dark and wavy. In her summation of their daughter's parentage, it was clear Holly hadn't factored his genes into the equation.

"Would you mind elaborating?" he said, his brow furrowed in concentration.

Dr. Franklin inhaled and treated them to another unblinking stare. "It means that you're right. There was a problem, but not what I assumed. The error occurred during the egg selection portion of the fertilization stage, not the implantation stage."

For the first time since they walked into the office, Holly appeared genuinely confused. "Are you saying that—" She broke off, as if unable or unwilling to give voice to whatever conclusion she'd drawn in her mind. Unusual for her.

The doctor met Holly's puzzled stare. "I'm sorry to have to tell you this, but you aren't your daughter's biological mother." Her gaze then shifted to him. "However, you are her biological father."

Holly's gasp cracked the air like a thunderclap. The deafening silence that followed was just as loud.

Myles was too stunned to speak, his heart pounding so loud in his ears that, for a few moments, it drowned out all possible thought or comprehension.

"No, no. That can't be right." Holly turned to him, her eyes wide with shock and disbelief.

If he could speak, he didn't know what he would say, given the state of his mind. Completely blown.

The doctor's composure—which had remained relatively calm thus far—began to show cracks. Based partly on the dates on her diploma, he guessed Dr. Franklin was in her early forties, but the depth of the lines now bracketing her mouth and fanning out from her eyes spoke of the toll this must be taking on her and made her look years older.

Swallowing visibly, she continued. "We had the test run by two different labs. The results are the same."

Accompanying his wife's cry of dismay came the realization that his claim to his daughter was as solid as any father's could be. Haylee was his. Relief began to seep into every part of his being. Seconds later, it washed over him in a flood. He could breathe again.

Dr. Franklin regarded them, self-reproach stamped all over her face. "I'm sorry. I'm so very sorry. I don't know how this happened. It's never happened to us before. But I promise to get to the bottom of it and do whatever it takes to make this right."

Coming into the meeting, Myles had prepared himself for only two possibilities. Either Haylee was biologically theirs, or she wasn't. And in the latter's case, he'd been fully prepared to fight to keep her even if his marriage would be one of the casualties of any battle he'd have to wage.

The one thing he never imagined was discovering he had a baby…with a woman he'd never laid eyes on.

2

Whitney loved acting. She loved it as much as she did her music career. It was all the necessary other stuff she could have gladly done without.

That was the main reason she relished a day like today. For the first time in months, she didn't have to wake up at the ass crack of dawn and sit in a makeup chair for hours, only to hurry up and wait for her scenes to be called. The movie she was costarring in had wrapped last week, and she was temporarily free to wake up whenever she wanted on the days she wasn't going into her company's headquarters in Culver City.

Today, she'd gotten up at eleven and had a leisurely breakfast of coffee and a fruit cup before settling down on the sofa in her office to start reading the script she'd been sent a week ago. She was a third of the way through it when Kennedy called.

"Hey, girl, what's up?" Whitney said, tapping the screen to put the call on speaker.

"I'm good. What's up with you?"

"Right now, I'm on vacation from two of my three jobs," she said, laughing. "I'm going into the office tomorrow, but only because April'll be there." April was a senior women's evening wear and bridal designer at Oasis, Whitney's fashion company. She was also a good friend.

"Other than that," Whitney continued, "I plan to catch up on some sleep and fly out to Jersey to visit my parents. I told you my dad's having back surgery, and it'll be nice for my mom to have another pair of hands around to help out."

"Oh good. We can hang out when you're here."

"Absolutely. How are things with Nate?"

"He asked me to move in with him, and I said yes," Kennedy stated, breathless excitement in her voice.

Whitney snorted a laugh. "So when's the wedding? I'm going to need to block out the time on my calendar at least six months in advance."

"You must not have heard me right," Kennedy replied with a laugh. "He asked me to move in with him, not tie the knot."

"Sweets, he asked you to move in with him last year. What's new is that you finally agreed. And let's face it, you were practically living with him anyway. You're only making it official by letting USPS and your landlord know what's what. I'm talking about the wedding. And don't even pretend that won't be happening sooner rather than later."

Not only did Whitney know it, she could feel it in her bones. Her friend had found the love of her life and basked in the before, current, and aftereffects of it. As well she should. Nate was one of the good ones. It also didn't hurt that he was fine as hell and rich with a capital *B* for *billionaire*.

"You need to cool your heels," Kennedy said, a smile obvious in her voice. "We're taking it one step at a time. First step, live in sin. If the sinning continues to go as well as it has been, *then* we can talk marriage."

"Oh, I bet you're sinning the hell out of each other every night and are loving every second of it." Whitney snorted.

She shot an absent glance down at the script open on her lap. "And don't give me that. You know damn well you're marrying this one."

"*Maaaybe,*" Kennedy said, drawing out the word. "Okay, fine, I would say the odds are good. But we've only been dating for six months. We have lots of time to think about marriage."

"Just don't make him wait too long."

Kennedy made a sound, a mixture of amusement and exasperation. "What do you mean, wait too long? Six months is nothing."

"You've got to be kidding. That's as long as three of my relationships."

Dating in Hollywood was a crapshoot, and so far, luck had not been on her side—and it wasn't because she was too picky, as way too many of her friends claimed. If anything, she wasn't picky *enough*. She was becoming convinced that some malevolent being had put a hex on her love life.

"Speaking of relationships, how are things going with Daniel? Any better than the last time I asked?"

"The romance part is as good as dead," Whitney replied matter-of-factly.

Things between her and Daniel had barely gotten off the ground before the coasts and then oceans had come between them, effectively grounding their relationship for good. Not only did he live on the other side of the country, but his professional tennis career sometimes had him flying internationally more than she did on a world tour. Although to call what they had a relationship was being generous. They'd been long-distance sometime lovers. Now they were strictly phone and FaceTime friends.

"That's too bad." Kennedy let out a rueful sigh. "You know Nate'll be disappointed. When you guys started dating, I think he seriously thought about hanging up his keyboard and going into matchmaking. Give old Tinder a run for its money."

Whitney chortled at that. Her friend's significant other was the founder and CEO of the third largest tech company in the world. Had Kennedy not dragged her to the US Open quarter-finals (Nate's company was a longtime sponsor), she and Daniel probably wouldn't have met.

Their attraction had been immediate, and he'd quickly followed up their introduction with a dinner invitation. Two days later, he sliced and backhanded his way into the finals.

After a picture of them dining together made the front page of every New York and national tabloid, the paparazzi descended on them like shoppers at Walmart on Black Friday. When Daniel won the Grand Slam, the press—determined to cast her in the role of one half of the new Hollywood and sports power couple—had credited her with being his lucky charm.

"Nate needs to stick with what he does best, which is giving you multiple orgasms."

Her friend's gasp collapsed into wheezing laughter. While they were giggling like two Catholic schoolgirls at their first all-male revue, another call came through. Glancing down at her phone, Whitney saw *Special Blessings* light up the screen.

At the sight of the name of the fertility clinic, her stomach didn't so much as drop as it seemed to tumble down a long flight of stairs, each contact a reminder that she hadn't yet reached the bottom. An ominous feeling of dread turned her blood the consistency of treacle.

Because if and when the time came, she was supposed to be the one calling them, not the other way around. This wasn't good.

Not good at all.

"Shit."

"What's wrong?"

Whitney started at her friend's voice, and it was then she realized she'd cursed out loud. "Do you remember me telling you that I froze my eggs because of my endometriosis?"

"Yes, of course, I remember."

Suddenly, the voicemail icon on her phone appeared. Her heart tumbled another step.

She gulped before continuing. "Well, someone at the clinic where my eggs are stored just called. They left a message."

"Go ahead and listen to it," Kennedy urged.

She didn't want to, but it wasn't as if she had a choice.

"Okay, hold on." Whitney clicked the voicemail icon. She read the message transcript aloud: "'Hi, Ms. Richardson. This is Dr. Franklin at Special Blessings Fertility Clinic. I need to speak with you as soon as possible. It's urgent. I'll be in the office until 6:00 pm. Please call me at your convenience at 555-908-9863, extension 13665. After office hours, you can contact me at 555-898-8473.'"

"What do you think the doctor wants?" Kennedy asked when she was finished.

Full-blown panic overtook her. Her heart felt as if it were tripping over itself. Whitney inhaled slowly in an attempt to calm her nerves.

"I don't know. I think something must have happened to my eggs. My gut says they accidentally destroyed them." Her gut rarely failed her.

"You can't know that for sure. It could be something else." Kennedy sounded as if she was trying to convince herself that there was some benign reason behind an *urgent* call from the fertility doctor responsible for keeping her precious eggs safe in their liquid nitrogen home.

"What else can it be? It's the only thing that makes sense. Which means I'll be forced to do it all over again." Her stomach roiled. The injections. The misery of being pumped full of hormones for weeks on end. Her body, twenty-five years old at the time, had barely tolerated it. Lord only knew how it would handle the regimen five years later.

Whitney's eyes slammed shut as she prayed, almost certain the odds were against her.

Please, don't make me have to go through that again.

"Listen, I'm going to call her back now. I'll talk to you later." No use putting off news that wouldn't get any better with age. It wasn't wine.

"I'm leaving work now, but I'll be at Aurora's for a bit. Call me and let me know, okay?" Kennedy said, her voice laced with concern.

"Yeah, I will. Bye."

"Bye."

Whitney hung up and quickly called the first number in the message since it was just past four. The doctor answered as if she'd been sitting waiting for her call. Not that she didn't value promptness, but in the scheme of things, this didn't bode well at all.

"Ms. Richardson, thank you for calling. I know how busy you are, so I appreciate the speedy response." After a nerve-wracking pause, Dr. Franklin said, "This isn't the sort of thing I wanted to have to tell you over the phone, but I'm afraid it couldn't wait."

Oh God. I'm right. My eggs are gone.

Would you calm down? Things could be worse. Think of all those women who don't have IVF as an option. It's not the end of the world. You'll survive.

Inhaling deeply, she slowly exhaled and braced herself for the words that would confirm what she already knew to be true.

"I don't know how to tell you this—"

For God's sake, just say it and get it over with. Say it so I can start making plans.

Although she had no idea when she'd be able to carve out the time to go through the process again. In three months, she'd be on a press junket promoting her upcoming film—a coveted theatrical release in a sea of movies made for streaming services. And after that, she'd be in England filming her first period piece. And then the press tour for the movie she just wrapped. And then she had to record her next album after that.

Ugh. Her calendar was her enemy.

"—but there's been a mix-up at the clinic. DNA testing confirmed that you're the biological mother of a baby born via a surrogate of one of our other clients. A married couple."

Wait, what?

Whitney's breath caught in her throat, causing a brief paroxysm of coughing. "Wait. I—I don't understand." Stuttering, she desperately tried to make sense of what the doctor had just said. Then it hit her, the four words that loitered in her memory bank, and she strived to make sense of all the other words.

There's been a mix-up.

Whitney feared she was going to throw up. Or pass out. Or both, which could be deadly. But she didn't do either, and since dying wasn't an option, her mind tried to sort through the mess. What surrogate? Which couple? And why *her* eggs? Her eggs were supposed to be fertilized with the sperm of her future husband—whoever that turned out to be—not some stranger's.

"I don't know how, but somehow, your eggs were used in the fertilization process instead of the wife's." Dr. Franklin relayed the information in a voice too calm for the situation. Because if ever a situation called for freaking the fuck out, this was it.

Tossing the script aside, Whitney turned in her seat, planting her bare feet on the polished hardwood floor. In as coherent a voice as she could muster, Whitney reiterated everything her mind had managed to absorb. "So that I understand you correctly, are you telling me that one of your other clients—a married couple—used a surrogate to have a baby, and due to a mix-up, you fertilized my eggs with the father's sperm, implanted that in the surrogate, and now I'm the biological mother of the couple's baby?"

"Yes, that's it."

It must have been due to brain overload or the farfetchedness of it all, or both, that her mind shut down completely. Because seriously, if this were a movie script, she'd tell her agent to stop wasting her time because the plot stretched credulity.

She, Whitney Richardson aka Sahara, had a child with a man she didn't know. A man she'd never laid eyes on. A child she hadn't carried and was being told about after the fact. Nightmares didn't come scarier than this. This couldn't possibly be true. The chances of something like this happening had to be one in a million. Or more.

Whitney took back what she'd wished ten minutes ago. If she had to choose now, she'd rather suffer through another *ten* rounds of the egg retrieval process than have her life resemble a damn *Black Mirror* episode.

She wasn't ready for a baby. That was the reason she'd frozen her eggs. Her acting career had only just hit its stride. Oasis had become a success beyond her wildest dreams and required more of her time than she could have imagined when she'd launched the venture. A child wasn't in her current plans, and she certainly wasn't going to take on that kind of responsibility without a committed partner.

Nope, there'd be no baby daddies for her. Single parenthood wasn't a joke. It was serious business, no matter how much money she had or how many nannies she could afford. As much as it was in her control, she wanted her children's father to play a positive and critical role in their lives, preferably by her side as her husband.

"I understand this must be a lot to digest," Dr. Franklin said in the same tone her obstetrician used when instructing her to relax before prying her open like an oyster with the cold steel of a speculum. "But I assure you, Ms. Richardson, I'm going to get to the bottom of what happened."

"I'll need to contact my lawyer." At a minimum, what the doctor had confessed to was gross negligence. But Whitney would have to discuss that with a medical malpractice lawyer who handled infertility cases. She'd ask her cousin to recommend one. Cheyenne practiced family law in San Diego.

"Understood." The doctor sounded clear-minded and sober. No doubt she'd already contacted her insurance company. The consequence of the clinic's mistake was going to cost them all.

Whitney rose to her feet and crossed the room to her desk. There, she opened her laptop. "I take it the baby's living with the couple?"

"Yes."

"And they intend to raise the child?"

"That's my understanding. Mr. Redmond seems particularly eager to do everything they need to establish permanent legal custody."

Since he was the biological father, that made sense.

"Is it a boy or a girl?"

"A girl. She's six months."

Her heart clenched, and it was a physical pain in her chest. A baby girl. She'd always wanted a girl.

Whitney gave her head a hard shake. Why even ask? The less she knew about her, the better. A child deserved parents who loved, wanted, and possessed the financial means to care for them. As long as she was satisfied the couple met those criteria, the best thing she could do for the baby was to take herself out of the equation.

"There's one other thing," the doctor said before ending the call.

What more can there possibly be? Whitney wanted to scream. Instead, she listened with a fatalistic sense of calm.

"The couple—the Redmonds—they're white."

3

"You've got to be shitting me!" Aurora exclaimed upon hearing Whitney's bombshell news. Her blue eyes swiftly sought out an equally stunned-looking Kennedy, who occupied a seat on the couch next to her in Aurora's Upper East Side brownstone in New York.

The three women FaceTimed via two large-screen TVs, Whitney in the family room of her Hollywood home.

"This is a joke, right?" Aurora prompted, desperately clinging to the only probable explanation for what she'd just heard.

A defeated sigh accompanied a slow shake of Whitney's head. "I wish it were. Believe me, this is something I would *never* joke about." Before making the call, she'd taken some time to sit with herself. To try and decide what she was feeling besides shock.

Hurt? Anger? Betrayal?

It must have been pity, because *why me* was still running through her mind on repeat.

"*Oh my god! That's* what the doctor called to tell you?" Kennedy asked on a sharp intake of breath.

Whitney nodded. "Yep. That was it."

"What the hell, Sar." Aurora's expression had gone from gobsmacked to dazed. "This is nuts."

"Tell me about it," Whitney muttered with feeling.

"And here you thought they'd destroyed your eggs," Kennedy reminded her.

Whitney huffed at that. "Yeah, no such luck." She'd never thought that her eggs being destroyed would be the lesser of two evils, yet here she was. "And get this, the couple is white," she added as the coup de grâce.

Her statement elicited twin gasps of shock.

"I know." Whitney knew exactly how they felt. The hits just kept coming. "Crazy, huh?"

Yesterday, she'd been single and childless. Today, only one of those statuses applied. She was the biological mother of a *biracial* daughter. Not in a million years or the fever swamp depths of her dreams could she have imagined something like this happening when she woke up this morning.

"How do you feel about that?" Aurora asked, tucking her long honey-blond hair behind her ear. Clad in a white graphic tee and frayed jean shorts, with her pretty face scrubbed free of makeup, her friend was often mistaken for a college student.

Whitney simultaneously shrugged and shook her head. "I'm not sure. On the one hand, I'm glad they want to raise her, especially the wife. The news must have absolutely crushed her. But on the other hand, I worry about the child. What happens if they have more kids? I don't want her to feel…you know, like she doesn't fit in."

"I think they'd have to be living under a rock not to realize that she's going to need to know both sides of her identity. I'm sure they'll do whatever they can to make sure she has positive Black influences in her life," Kennedy said.

"I would hope so," Whitney muttered, shifting to tuck her

feet beneath her butt. "Luckily, your future children won't have to deal with this. They'll have your and Nate's families."

Kennedy gave her the *you're jumping the gun* look.

"No, you stop," Whitney chided before Kennedy could put words to the look. "You can't tell me you and Nate haven't talked about children."

"They have," Aurora piped up. "Nate says they plan to have lots."

"If lots means two, maybe," Kennedy said, her tone dry.

"Hey, if I marry Cam, so will mine," Aurora joked about Kennedy's drop-dead gorgeous older brother, who, like his sister, had inherited their father's gray-blue eyes.

Kennedy snorted and rolled her eyes. Whitney had met Cameron Mitchell shortly after she started dating Daniel, instantly relegating him to the friend zone. A really good friend, mind you, but they would only ever be that. The man preferred playing the field to committed relationships, which would have made for a wildly incompatible coupling if the chemistry had been there.

"Never mind me and Nate and our future children. The only way you'll know is when you meet the couple yourself. By the way, who are these people? What do they do? For all we know, they could be serial killers."

"Way to make her feel better, Ken," Aurora chided, giving her friend a shoulder bump.

"The clinic runs background checks, so I think they're safe," Whitney said. "And the couple is Myles and Holly Redmond."

After Dr. Franklin revealed their identity, Whitney had requested a meeting. She couldn't very well relinquish her biological child to people she'd never met.

And since the last thing she wanted was to be spotted at the fertility clinic, the doctor had made a quick call and arranged for her to meet the Redmonds at the husband's office. No one would think twice about her presence at a law firm.

"Did you google them?" Aurora asked.

"If you want to know the truth, it didn't occur to me." Wherever she was in the discovery process, she was still reeling and had yet to enter the *take action* stage. Googling required action.

Aurora bolted off the couch and disappeared from the screen, only to return seconds later carrying a laptop.

"Here, I'll look." She began tapping away on the keyboard. Kennedy watched, looking over her friend's shoulder.

Suddenly Aurora's eyes widened. She shot a quick look at Whitney before returning her attention to her laptop. "'Myles Redmond,'" she read. "'President of the California Bar Association.'" A dark blond eyebrow inched up. "Hmm, not bad for an older guy. What do you think?" She turned the computer to face the camera.

An image of Myles Redmond's face filled half the screen. He looked to be in his mid- to late fifties. Maybe even early sixties. He was handsome in a distinguished way. Having a full head of salt-and-pepper hair undoubtedly helped with that.

Whitney's shoulders slumped. "I thought he'd be younger." By a good twenty to twenty-five years.

"Me too," came her friends' staggered responses.

"His wife's probably a lot younger. You know how some of those older, well-to-do men can be."

Whitney made a face. "You say that as if it's a good thing. As if I want an old lech raising my daughter."

"Now, now, now. It's not for us to judge how, when, and with whom two consenting adults find love." Aurora tsked like a Sunday school teacher and returned to tapping on the keyboard.

Whitney wasn't surprised at her friend's defense of age gaps in general, given her ex was widowed, in his forties, and had a college-aged daughter.

"I think I found the wife," Aurora crowed. "Holly Redmond. She's a real estate agent."

"She's beautiful," Kennedy remarked.

Again, Aurora presented Whitney with her findings.

"She is," Whitney concurred upon seeing the picture on the woman's professional website. Blonde, blue-eyed, and young, especially in comparison to her husband. She had a bit of a Blake Lively look to her and couldn't have been much older than Whitney and her friends, who were all thirty.

"At least she has a young mother," Kennedy said. "And hopefully she'll keep her father young."

Whitney wasn't sure about that, but she'd table her opinion until she met the man.

"So, what's next? Are you going to meet them, or do the lawyers take it from here?" Aurora asked, closing the laptop, and placing it out of sight of the camera.

"I'm meeting them tomorrow. Dr. Franklin said since they're going to raise her, they want me to sign some papers to make everything legit. But that was before I knew he was my father's age."

"So, what are you going to do?" Kennedy asked.

Whitney lifted a shoulder. "I don't know. All I know is that I want to do what's best for her." She paused. "Damn, I don't even know her name."

"That might not be such a bad thing." Kennedy was never one to mince words or not say what was on her mind.

Whitney gave an absent nod. "You're probably right. She already has a mother and a father. It would be selfish of me to interfere, right?"

Her friends looked just as torn as she felt.

"If you don't want any sort of custody and don't want to be a mother right now because of your—"

"I want to be a mother someday, just not right this second," she said, cutting Kennedy off. She had a lot on her plate. Geez, she barely had time to date, and even part-time parenting was no walk in the park. She'd be in over her head if she tried to take it on.

"That's what I mean. Don't let this force you into accepting a responsibility you can't handle."

"Right," Whitney replied, chastened.

"I'm only saying that it seems you've already made up your mind." Kennedy's voice was soft and her tone understanding.

Logically, she was on firm ground, but emotionally, there was quicksand everywhere. "Yeah, but what if I change it? What if sometime down the road, I want to see her—I want to be in her life? I'll have closed the door to that if I sign away my rights."

Regret was a dish best never served. Someone had said that, and if they hadn't, they damn well should.

"Oh honey, did the thought ever cross your mind that when she's an adult, she may come looking for you?" Aurora asked, ever the optimist in search of a silver lining.

Whitney had, but it brought her no solace whatsoever, as it wouldn't be for another eighteen years.

"Or maybe," Aurora continued, "you could have one of those open adoption arrangement thingies? They can send you pictures and let you know how she's doing. You know, on major milestones and other occasions like that?"

Kennedy didn't appear as enamored with the idea. "I don't know. First, you have to have the parents' buy-in, and a lot of adoptive parents don't want the biological parents hovering in the wings. Second, what happens if pictures and updates aren't enough? Third, you're famous. If the media ever gets wind of her, that kid's life will never be the same. Hers or the whole family's."

Of course, her friend was right. What had she been thinking?

"Maybe as a condition of you signing away your rights, you make them promise to do the things that concern you most about them raising her," Aurora suggested.

"That's not a bad idea." If that was all the leverage she had, it was better than nothing. The goal was to ensure that her daughter grew up loving herself, knew the history of her people (both sides), and had a healthy respect for everyone who paved the way before her. That wasn't much to ask.

Aurora placed her empty wineglass on the table beside her. "So, you're good?" she asked, stretching out her legs.

"As good as I'll ever be, I guess," Whitney replied, her voice bone-dry.

A phone rang. Kennedy smiled when she looked down at her lap and quickly answered, holding her finger up in the universal sign of *hold on* before disappearing from view.

"Ken is about to jet," Aurora said. "Nate had to work late, which is the only reason she's here on a workday."

Kennedy reappeared. "You mean it isn't enough that we see each other every day at work?" she said, addressing Aurora.

The two—who'd been best friends since high school—co-owned Token, a PR agency that specialized in helping companies diversify. Currently, they had more business than they could handle. Nate had been encouraging them to open an office in Southern California, and she had been the first one to champion his idea. LA could use a PR agency like that.

"You didn't used to think that before you started dating my brother. As a matter of fact, now that you're living together, you should want to spend more time with me, not less. Don't forget that you were my friend first," Aurora said with a mock pout.

She then turned her attention to Whitney. "Back me up here, Sar. Who would you rather hang out with, me or my brother?"

"You, of course," Whitney replied, fighting back a smile. She playfully added, "Plus, Ken got to him first."

"I'm way more fun than my brother," Aurora said, wrinkling her nose.

"I think it all depends on the kind of fun you're talking about. Right, Ken?" Whitney winked at her friend.

Aurora groaned and covered her ears. "Now I wish I'd never brought it up."

The beep of an incoming message sounded. Kennedy glanced at her phone and then promptly rose to her feet. "My ride's here. I've got to go." Turning to Whitney, she said, "Let me know how it goes, and if you need to talk, I'm here like always."

Kennedy didn't need to tell her. She knew.

Before Aurora walked her friend to the door, she motioned for Whitney to stay on the line. In less than a minute, she was back, this time sitting on the edge of the couch, slim legs pressed tightly together, looking much more subdued.

"Hey, before you sign anything, I think you should see what you're giving up. Ask for a picture."

"Do you really think that's a good idea?"

Aurora grimaced. "*Ugh*, I don't want this to come out the wrong way, and I'm not trying to be a Debbie Downer, but all I keep thinking is that you froze your eggs for a reason. What if…" Her voice trailed off.

"What if I can't get pregnant? What if I can't have a child of my own?" Whitney finished the question for her without flinching. She'd always known that was a possibility.

"Although I'm sure you'll be fine," Aurora hastened to add. "But *what if*? Would you regret signing your rights away without seeing her?"

Whitney sighed and shook her head. "I don't know. I haven't

thought about it." At least not in depth. Frankly, she hadn't had time.

"Kennedy wishes I'd never gotten involved with you-know-who. She hates that he broke my heart. But do you remember what you told me?"

Whitney gave her a rueful smile. "I said loving him was part of your journey, and now you'd never have to wonder *what if* because you know." She'd only discovered Aurora was seeing the lieutenant governor of New York days after the idiot had broken up with her.

Lesson learned? Don't get involved with politicians. They suck.

"Don't you think you owe it to yourself to at least see her, even if it's just a picture? I don't want you to wonder *what if.*"

Whitney didn't want that either. Right now, her daughter was an abstract. She had no face and no personality attached to her. Maybe that's what she needed to feel confident about the decision to let her go.

"And you may also want to have a thorough background check run on them just to be sure," her friend added.

Aurora was right. A picture wouldn't hurt, and a background check would go a long way in putting her mind at ease.

4

What does a woman wear to her first meeting with the father of her child (a child she hadn't known existed until twenty-four hours ago) and his wife?

Normally, Whitney would have gone with her trademark look that Kennedy had affectionately coined chic casual. Whether appearing on a late-night talk show or meeting with corporate executives, she liked to keep things on brand and typically rocked a pair of skinny jeans with high heels and a top that offered a tantalizing glimpse of her taut midriff. This meeting, however, called for a different look, so she'd opted for a pale champagne single-breasted pantsuit, one of her favorites from Oasis's Classique line.

"This way, please, Saha—I mean, Miss Richardson," Mr. Redmond's paralegal self-consciously corrected herself.

Whitney flashed a friendly smile. "It's okay if you call me Sahara. I don't mind." It was what everyone called her. She was only Whitney to her family and the friends who knew her before her debut album came out.

"I wish Mr. Redmond had told me his appointment was

with the biggest female performer on the planet. No wonder he didn't want you to wait in the lobby," she said with a nervous laugh.

Her name was Shannon, and she'd come down to personally escort Whitney up to the fifth floor and had been sending her furtive glances since they boarded the elevator.

"Biggest? Not even close." Whitney was both amused and flattered. "But it does have a nice ring to it. I'll be sure to pass the news on to my manager, though. She'll get a kick out of it." Stacy, her manager of six years, assured her it was going to happen. Just give it three more years.

"If I knew Whitney Richardson was you, I'd have brought my T-shirt to work for you to sign. I went to your concert in LA last year. The show was fantastic," she gushed. "And you were great in *Land of Riches*. I had no idea you could act."

That makes two of us.

"Thank you. I'm so happy you enjoyed the concert and the movie." Whitney opened her purse, a small oval clutch the exact shade of her suit, pulled out one of her business cards, and handed it to her. "As for the shirt, here's what we'll do. Take my card, and if you leave your name, address, and size with my message service, I'll have one autographed and sent to you."

Her offer was met with a gasp and hazel eyes flaring in happiness and gratitude, a look she'd never tire of seeing or eliciting. The look of pure joy on people's faces was half the satisfaction she got from doing what she did for a living.

"Oh my goodness, thank you. Thank you so much. You have no idea what this means to me," the paralegal said, her eyes glittering with excitement as she accepted the black-and-gold embossed card and clutched it in her hand.

By the time they stepped off the elevator, Whitney knew Shannon was two years out of college (and she looked it). Her parents and older brother were lawyers. She'd been working at

Redmond & Williamson for a little over two years and would be starting law school in the fall.

As they approached the corner office, Shannon's steps slowed, and she turned to her. "I just want you to know that you're in good hands with Myl—Mr. Redmond. He's a brilliant attorney, and no one knows IPO law better."

His specialty is IPO law? The background check she'd had run—which had come back clean—hadn't included that tidbit. It had only listed that he'd been a defense attorney for a reputable law firm in LA before striking out on his own. Whitney filed that in the back of her mind under services she might need if her CFO got her wish to take the company public. It would also give her a reason to contact him again. Maybe get news about her daughter.

Stop it! she quickly admonished herself. Here she was plotting future contact before she'd even met the couple. As things stood, she was there to assure herself that her daughter would be in good hands before relinquishing all claim to her.

No, great hands.

No, the best hands in the world.

"That's why I'm here." Whitney lied through a beaming smile. "I heard he's the best."

"You won't regret it." Shannon then turned and gave a brief knock on the office door before pushing it open. "Myles, Miss Richardson's here."

Myles Redmond stepped out from behind a large executive desk.

"Buzz me if you need anything," Shannon called out before retreating and closing the door behind her.

Whitney could only stare wide-eyed at the man advancing toward her, his hand extended in greeting. He wasn't Myles Redmond, president of the California Bar Association. He couldn't be. This man had to be at least twenty-five years younger, *and* he was *fine as hell* if one's tastes ran to dark, slicked-back hair, light eyes, square jaws, and thousand-dollar suits. Hers did not (musicians and athletes were more her speed), but that didn't mean she didn't understand the appeal.

"Ms. Richardson, it's nice to meet you."

A tiny shiver ran up her spine. He had the kind of low, masculine voice that was music to a singer's ear. In her professional opinion, she gave his nine-and-a-half on a ten scale.

Whitney blindly shook his hand. "*You're* Myles Redmond?" It was pointless to try to hide her shock.

"I was the last time I checked," he said with a grin.

"I'm sorry for staring, but the picture on the internet...isn't you."

A hint of amusement lit his cobalt-blue eyes. "Don't tell me. You searched for Myles Redmond, and the internet spit out a picture of a man who looks old enough to be my father."

"It sounds like this has happened before." It was nice to know that she and her friends weren't the only ones misled by Google's search results. The people at Google really needed to fix that.

"It used to happen a lot more when my father was still practicing."

"Wait, are you saying that was a picture of your father?" Well, that was a twist she hadn't seen coming. She struggled to remember exactly what the man looked like apart from the fact that he had blue eyes and a full head of salt-and-pepper hair. Aurora had said he was good-looking for an older man, but she'd been too stuck on the *older man* part of it to give the image a closer look.

He nodded. "He retired three years ago."

"So your father was president of the California Bar, too?" Whitney shouldn't have been surprised. She'd worked with sons, daughters, and other family members of bigwigs in the music and movie industry. Why would the law profession be any different?

"Do you think I took the pledge of walking in his footsteps too far?" he asked with a droll smile.

"I didn't realize the position was passed down from generation to generation," she teased.

Whitney didn't know if it was a trick of the light, but what looked like irritation flashed across his face. When she blinked, it was gone.

"That was meant as a joke," she mumbled, feeling uncomfortably gauche. And it wasn't as though she believed this applied to him. For all she knew, he was the best lawyer ever to walk the earth, and his father had been a lightweight by comparison.

Myles Redmond dismissed her apology with a wave of his hand. "No, you're fine. Believe me, it's not the first time I heard that either."

Whitney winced inwardly. *Way to put your foot in it, smart-ass.*

"If it makes you feel better, I've only heard good things about you." Once she realized how her compliment could be taken, she hastily added, "As a lawyer."

Great. That sounded even worse. As if it could've been anything else.

His gaze narrowed fractionally. "And by everyone, I assume you're talking about Shannon? The woman whose checks I sign." He said it in a voice so dry it could have kicked off a sandstorm in the Mojave Desert.

Whitney's face warmed in embarrassment. It was clear he'd heard his paralegal singing his praises. "It must be gratifying to have the complete confidence of someone who works for you. Who looks up to you."

He let out a short, self-deprecating laugh. "I guess it's better than if it had come from my mother."

The tension in her shoulders eased. She'd told a bad joke. He'd countered with something wry and witty, and now she was back on solid ground. There was still time for her to make, if not a great first impression, then at least a favorable *second* first impression.

"Sit, please. Make yourself comfortable." He gestured at the guest chairs in front of his desk.

Whitney did as instructed, placing her purse on the empty chair beside her.

After he resumed his seat behind his desk, his *let's get down to business* face was in place. "It's hard to know what to say. I'm sorry you got dragged into this mess."

"You don't have to apologize. None of this was your or your wife's fault." It was at that moment it dawned on her that what should have been a meeting of three was only two. "Speaking of your wife, will she be joining us?"

"Unfortunately, she wasn't able to make it today," he said, his expression inscrutable. And apparently, that was it. No explanation as to why she wasn't there or what was keeping her from meeting the biological mother of the child she was raising. Had their positions been reversed, Whitney would have arrived early with bells on.

"You must have been shocked when you got the call." He continued as if the topic of his absent wife was never raised.

Whitney huffed a laugh. "To say the least. I certainly didn't have it on my bingo card." What happened to them was a once-in-a-million kind of mix-up. Screwup, really.

"Is there anything you'd like to ask before we go over the papers?"

What was the hurry? He hadn't even offered her a drink and expected her to sign away the rights to her child.

No, not so fast.

"I do have some questions."

"Of course. Ask away," he said, glancing at the clock on his desk for the second time in as many minutes.

"What's her name?"

"Her name is Haylee, spelled H-A-Y-L-E-E."

And just like that, she was struck by a pang of wistfulness. "That's a beautiful name. What is she like?"

Whitney thought it was a perfectly normal thing a mother would want to know. However, the father's eyebrows rose at that.

"She's a good baby. Happy. Sweet. We love her."

The way his features softened when talking about his daughter suggested he was a doting, loving father. Which didn't compute with him not having a single picture of her proudly displayed in his office.

"Do you have a picture of her? I'd love to see her." If the man didn't have at least one on his phone, the man didn't deserve to raise any child of hers.

Again, he reacted as if the question came out of left field.

"Do you think that's a good idea?" he asked. "I'm sure this can't be easy for you, but I think seeing her would only make things harder, and I don't want to do that."

Whitney's heart melted a little. He sounded like Kennedy, and she found his concern for her endearingly sweet.

"I think you're looking at this situation in terms of an adoption where the mother has carried and bonded with the child during the pregnancy and then has to give it up. In that case, I would agree with you. But that isn't the case with us, so you don't need to worry about me getting attached. I'm fully aware that Haylee already has a mother."

Myles Redmond didn't look entirely convinced, his expression turning wary. There had been a definite shift in his mood since she'd started asking questions about her daughter.

Whitney sat quietly as he regarded her. Actually, it was more of an inspection, his gaze never once leaving her face. She assumed she passed when he slowly opened the top drawer of his desk and removed a picture frame. After a discernible pause, he leaned forward and handed it to her.

Whitney took it before he changed his mind, as she feared he might. Then she looked down and let out an involuntary gasp. A wave of emotion washed over her, so strong that she experienced a moment of lightheadedness.

The word *adorable* must have been invented with her baby girl in mind. Accompanying the word in the dictionary was Haylee's beautiful little face. And Whitney refused to believe she was viewing her through the prism of a mother's bias. Staring back at her were brown eyes so large they practically swallowed her face, a full head of dark brown hair that was beginning to curl, full rosy cheeks, and a Cupid's bow mouth. Whitney wanted to eat her up.

"How old is she here?" she asked, sparing him a glance and unable to wipe the besotted look off her face. Not even his guardedness could dampen her joy of the moment.

"Three months."

"Do you have any more? Anything more current? Dr. Franklin said she's six months."

Was she pushing?

Yes.

Did she care if it made him uncomfortable?

Of course she did. As a recovering people pleaser, she was only four years into the *take me as I am* stage and at constant risk of relapsing. Was that going to stop her? Hell no. Recovering meant she'd learned to assert herself.

He withdrew a dark green cell phone from the open drawer, held it up to his face, and then began tapping on the screen. Pausing, he stared down at the phone before offering it to her.

With the framed picture in one hand, she eagerly accepted the phone with the other.

Whitney made the sound someone makes when something steals their breath, grabs a tight hold of their heart, and refuses to let go. What else was she supposed to do? She was human. This child was a part of her.

Haylee's cheeks were chubbier in the new picture, and she had two little teeth protruding from her bottom gums.

Tears pricked the backs of her eyes, but for the life of her, Whitney couldn't put what she was feeling into words.

"Her hair is getting curly," she whispered to herself, forgetting for a moment that she wasn't alone. Forgetting that her daughter's father was watching her as closely as she was staring at the breathtaking result of this accidental collaboration of theirs.

After one last look, she reluctantly returned his phone and the framed picture to him. She wondered if he'd mind sending her the pictures. It would be as easy as a text message or an email. Even better, if he and his wife agreed to send her a picture maybe once or twice a year, she could watch her daughter grow up from afar.

Intuitively, she knew he wouldn't go for it.

Then she remembered Aurora's words. *"I don't want you to wonder what if."*

"I would love to meet her," Whitney blurted out before she lost her nerve.

5

Fuck.

This whole situation was out of control. Before it was all over, the woman would have partial custody, his daughter would have a room in her Beverly Hills mansion, and his life would be turned upside down.

Dr. Franklin had given him the distinct impression Ms. Richardson was coming there to sign the papers and dash. Instead, not only was she swooning over pictures of Haylee, but she now wanted to meet her.

No. This time, he was putting his foot down. "I'm sorry, but—"

"Please."

Dammit. He could see who his daughter got her eyes from. Her beautiful mother. They were big and brown, and framed by long, thick lashes that curled at the tips. Currently, they pinned him in place with a look of entreaty, making her extremely hard to resist.

"As you just said," she continued, "this isn't easy for me. I didn't know how I'd react, but after seeing her, I have to meet her—see her in person. Because in my heart, I know that if I don't, I'm going to regret it for the rest of my life."

Jesus H. Christ. What the hell was he supposed to say to her? What was he supposed to do now? She didn't seem the type to take no for an answer.

"I promise," she said, dogged in the face of his lack of response. "It'll just be the one time. And Haylee is still so young, she won't even remember me."

Myles didn't frighten easily. In his prior life as a criminal defense attorney, fear had been a luxury he couldn't afford in order to do his job right. But the prospect of Whitney Richardson meeting Haylee scared the shit out of him.

As sure as he was that the world revolved around the sun, he knew the woman who'd been staring at his daughter's picture with her heart in her eyes wouldn't be able to walk away after she met her. Not after she held Haylee in her arms. She was going to want her, full stop. And she had the means to make that a reality and, in turn, engage him in the fight of his life.

I'm damned if I do and damned if I don't. It doesn't get simpler than that.

No matter how he looked at it, he had no choice but to agree to her request. She'd *pretty please* him to death while simultaneously digging in her heels. And he wasn't talking about the delicate, expensive ones encasing her slender feet right now. No, he was talking about the boots with the steel toes meant for stomping an adversary into submission.

Despite her appearance, Whitney Richardson wasn't one of the *beautiful with very little brains* kind of star. He'd read about her meeting with The Snyder Group that detailed how she and her all-female team had walked out because there hadn't been a single Black person at the table on the other side.

A pushover she was not.

"And it'll give me a chance to meet your wife," she added

with dogged persistence, taking a blowtorch to a life that suddenly felt as if it was built on ten acres of dry grass doused in diesel fuel.

After the meeting at the clinic, Holly had given him an implicit ultimatum: Haylee or her. It had been the easiest decision of his life. She'd packed up the rest of her things and moved out the next day, and he hadn't seen or heard from her since. He'd heard from her divorce lawyer, though. She'd filed, and their divorce should be finalized in six weeks since she'd technically moved out weeks after they'd brought Haylee home from the hospital.

"I bet most people have a hard time saying no to you." He did his best not to sound confrontational.

The second Dr. Franklin called with the identity of the biological mother—he'd been vaguely familiar with her music and had no idea she'd taken up acting—he'd hung up and cursed up a storm. Then he'd gotten on the internet to learn everything he could about the woman whose name and face were instantly recognizable worldwide.

She was Sahara, like the desert.

Thank goodness for Wikipedia. Everything he wanted to know about her had been there on her page.

Whitney Louise Richardson, thirty years old, five-foot-six, attended Rutgers University before dropping out in her third year. Six months later, she landed her first record contract. Her first album sold over four million copies, earning it double platinum status. At twenty-four, she won her first Grammy for best song and best new female artist.

Then she surprised the world by setting her sights on an acting career, and three years after her Grammy wins, she became an Oscar-nominated actress for her supporting role in the movie *Land of Riches*. She lost out to a seasoned two-time Oscar-winning actress. Not satisfied with a singing *and* acting career, she founded Oasis, a fashion company, and launched her own clothing line at the age of twenty-seven.

As for her personal life, she'd recently been dating Daniel Woodson, the second-ranked male tennis player in the world, but their relationship appeared to have ended last year. The current status of her love life was unknown. Despite being seen out in public with various men, if she was seeing one in particular, she was keeping it well under wraps.

A quick look at IMDB revealed her next movie, *Sinner*, was currently in postproduction and would be in theaters on Christmas Eve. The woman had more balls in the air than a juggler in a traveling circus. No matter what his gut was telling him, there wasn't room for a child in her life.

"Is that what you want? To say no?" Her question was as direct as her stare. So direct and unwavering he had to force himself not to look away. For reasons he couldn't explain, the woman made his skin itch.

Instead, he cleared his throat. "I don't want to complicate the situation any more than it is already."

Which was the truth. All he wanted was to protect his daughter. She needed stability and normalcy, something a celebrity parent couldn't provide. Haylee deserved parents who wanted and loved her, and as the status of his marriage plainly indicated—divorce: pending—the only person she'd get that from was him.

"It won't. I promise it won't." She leaned forward, her hand gripping the arm of her chair, a silent plea in her beautiful brown eyes. "I just want to meet her. And I won't stay long. Just tell me the place and time, and I'll be there."

Fuck. Why did she have to be so...not what he expected? He'd come prepared for one of those *"Do you know who I am?"* Hollywood types, her vanity and ego covered in beauty a millimeter deep.

Or maybe that was the woman he hoped he'd be dealing with.

Unfortunately, Whitney Richardson's beauty wasn't airbrushed or Photoshopped, and if her vices were vanity and ego, she was a magician at hiding them. Maybe that meant he could take her at her word.

"What about this?" He tapped his finger on the ten-page document on his desk that would grant him sole legal custody of his daughter. "Would you like to go over this now?" He was hopeful but not holding his breath.

"Before I sign anything, I'd like to go over it with my lawyer. You don't mind if I take it home, do you?"

Yes, he minded, but then again, what choice did he have? It was a legal document. Of course, she wanted *her* lawyer to look it over. She didn't know him from Adam and had zero reason to trust him. Buried in all that legalese could be a clause that stipulated she pay eighteen years of child support. But he knew he wouldn't be able to breathe easy until he got her signature on the dotted line.

"That way, we can finish it up at our next meeting," she said when he was slow to respond. "Please."

The softly spoken one-word plea finally got her what she'd been pushing for the past five minutes. Not that he could refuse, given the choice appeared to be no visit, no signature.

"How about Saturday at one?"

A smile broke out across her face, and if he thought she was beautiful before, she was positively breathtaking now.

"Thank you so much. You have no idea what this means to me," she said, her eyes bright with emotion.

Oh, he had a good idea. He just hoped the visit was going to be what it took to bring their association to a close. Then Haylee and he could go on with their lives.

6

When Myles and his soon-to-be ex-wife had started down the IVF and surrogacy path to parenthood, never in his wildest dreams had he imagined he'd be raising the child alone. Yet here he was, very much alone as he had been since her birth, trying his best to comfort his crying daughter.

Haylee was teething, and it was fair to say they were both feeling her pain. She'd woken up three times last night, so father and daughter were operating on less than five hours of sleep. After over a month of this, he should have been used to running on fumes.

He wasn't.

Law school and studying for the bar hadn't been this taxing. It was a good thing he would gladly lay down his life for his child, or he might do something stupid like run out and find a wife to help shoulder the parenting responsibilities.

And *stupid* was what he'd have to be, because he was never getting married again. That ship had sailed twice. The first had been the *Gloucester*, and the last one the *Titanic*.

Cradling Haylee in his arms, Myles held the teething ring

to her mouth as she gnawed on it between plaintive wails of misery. He paced the length of the kitchen and then circled the island, waiting for her bottle to warm.

"I know you're hungry, princess. Don't worry, Daddy's going to feed you. Your bottle will be ready soon." He spoke softly to her as she stared up at him with large, tear-filled brown eyes. Big dark curls surrounded a face flushed almost the same color as the strawberry-adorned dress she had on.

Today would be the first and last time Whitney Richardson would see Haylee, and then, when the time was right, when his daughter was old enough to understand, he'd tell her about her biological mother.

Suddenly, Haylee gave her head a violent twist, wrenching the teething ring from her mouth. Her cries began to escalate in volume and pitch. If he didn't do something soon, they'd become full-throated cries of bloody murder.

Grabbing the bottle from the warmer, he quickly tested the temperature on the inside of his wrist. Satisfied it wasn't too hot, he touched the nipple to her lips. Emitting a wild, desperate sound, she latched on and began inhaling the milk.

"You're a greedy little thing, you know that?" he crooned, smiling and lightly stroking the small fingers that gripped the bottle as if her life depended on it. Any week now, she'd be able to hold it on her own.

His words were met with starved sounds of feeding. He placed the abandoned teething ring on the counter, able to breathe a little easier for the first time since he woke up this morning to his daughter's cries. It took about a minute, but eventually her sucking became less ravenous. She took a deep breath and then fixed her gaze on him, her tear-filled eyes dominating her little face.

"See, disaster averted," he said, his tone soothing. "It looks like you're not going to starve today, isn't that right, darling?"

The buzz of the motion detector had his eyes darting to the refrigerator door that lit up and displayed the security app. He observed Whitney Richardson walking toward the front door attired in pink shorts and a white sleeveless top, her hair hanging in dark waves down to her elbows.

It seemed in every picture he'd seen of her on the internet and in print, she had her hair styled differently. Whether in braids, cornrows (he'd had to look up the name for that one), various ranges of curliness, wavy, or straight, each style complemented her.

Myles watched her a few moments longer. She looked young for her age. The dimples helped shave a few years off, he imagined.

Dimples. Myles glanced down at his daughter. Another thing Haylee must have inherited from her, because they damn sure hadn't come from his side of the family.

She reached out and pressed the doorbell. When it chimed throughout the house, Haylee instantly became alert, her eyes darting to the left. She knew what that sound meant: visitors. Myles took his cue from her and made his way down the hall to answer the door.

A dazzling smile wreathed the star's face the moment her gaze landed on his daughter after tripping briefly over his.

"Hi," she said, barely sparing him a glance. "I hope you don't mind me coming a little early."

Given he hadn't wanted her there in the first place, yes he minded. Her mere presence felt like a threat to the life he'd come to know. The sooner they got this over with, the better.

"No, you're fine," he lied, stepping aside to allow her to enter.

The only thing he wanted from her was her signature on the papers that would grant sole legal custody of his daughter. In return, she'd leave with the assurance that Haylee was being raised by people who loved and wanted what was best for her. The same thing she said she wanted. He hoped to God she'd be true to her word.

Once inside, her gaze swiftly returned to Haylee. And there it was again, that look of wonderment.

"I usually have her fed by now."

His voice appeared to snap her out of a daze. She gave him another fleeting look. "That's okay. I don't mind."

If Whitney Richardson looked besotted, Haylee appeared fascinated as she stared at the star, smiling around the contoured nipple of the bottle. Except for her tear-streaked cheeks, no one would know she'd been crying up a storm less than five minutes ago.

"She's beautiful," Whitney whispered, her eyes glistening with unshed tears.

Her hand opened and closed at her side as if she was having a hard time controlling her need to hold her. Myles observed the movement, and the dread he'd experienced when she'd asked to see Haylee returned tenfold.

Fuck. She wasn't supposed to fall in love with her.

Whitney took a step closer, her hand tightly clutching the strap of the pink purse slung over her shoulder. "I think she looks a bit like me, don't you?" She glanced at him as if seeking confirmation.

Myles had seconds to determine whether admitting he could see the resemblance was wise or foolhardy.

"She does," he said, deciding the truth would work in his favor. "She also looks like my sister when she was a baby."

"Hey, sweetie." Whitney cooed, lightly stroking the back of Haylee's hand. "Aren't you just the sweetest baby ever."

Haylee responded by latching on to her slender finger.

Such a look of profound joy sparked in Whitney's eyes, Myles wouldn't have been surprised if she burst into tears. He watched their interaction with a growing sense of foreboding.

After another awkward moment of silence, during which Whitney savored the contact with the child she'd only known about for less than three days, he said, "Why don't we go to the family room? It's more comfortable."

"Yes, of course," she was quick to reply.

But as he turned, his daughter refused to release her hold on Whitney. Her finger or her heart. And it was clear that Whitney wouldn't have it any other way. She stayed close enough to his side that her bare arm lightly brushed his as they made their way to the back.

"Is your wife home? Will she be joining us?" As they passed the staircase by the kitchen, she looked up as if expecting to see Holly descending.

"Unfortunately, she had to go out of town. Family emergency." Myles had decided that a family emergency sounded important enough to justify her absence without raising suspicion.

"Oh, that's terrible. I'm sorry."

Myles felt a stab of conscience at what appeared to be a look of sympathy and concern on her face. But he couldn't tell her the truth without jeopardizing his goal, which was sole legal custody. Then no one would be able to take his daughter from him.

"No one's sick or dying, so it's nothing like that," he reassured her.

The sympathy in her eyes dimmed but didn't disappear altogether. "Well, that's a relief." Her mouth curved into a ghost of a smile. "That said, I was really looking forward to meeting her."

"She's sorry to have missed you too." Afraid she'd suggest they arrange another meeting, he diverted her attention with an offer he knew she couldn't refuse.

"Would you like to hold her?"

"I thought you'd never ask," she said happily.

Myles turned and led her to the family room. Then he purposefully steered her to the couch located directly in front of the coffee table where the papers were laid out, awaiting her signature.

He didn't appreciate the way his body reacted to her dimpled smile. To her obvious pleasure. He resolved to ignore it. She'd be out of his life after today.

Whitney quickly sat, tucked her purse next to her, and looked up at him, arms extended.

He removed the now-empty bottle from Haylee's mouth before she ingested too much air. "You arrived just in time to burp her."

Whitney appeared game for anything. He was certain she would've looked just as excited if a bomb had gone off in Haylee's diaper and he'd asked her to change it.

"A bunch of my cousins have kids, so I'm a pro at this. You can trust me."

It would just be the one time, Myles told himself as he handed her his daughter. Whitney placed her against her shoulder, handling her with care.

"Oh, aren't you just the sweetest," Whitney whispered.

"Here, you may need this, although I don't use it as much anymore." Removing the yellow burp cloth draped over his shoulder, he silently transferred it to hers, careful to minimize contact between them.

Since Myles had someone come to the house to care for Haylee while he worked, she hadn't been exposed to many strangers. But she let this strange woman hold her without making a fuss. She let her rub and pat her back. Let her kiss her temple and the crown of her head.

You have a sweet and friendly kid. Don't go overthinking it too much.

In no time at all, Haylee let out a healthy burp, and one would think she'd taken her first steps or won a baby genius award, given the amount of praise Whitney heaped on her.

"You knew what to do, didn't you, sweets? That's because you're the smartest baby in the whole world, aren't you?" She lovingly kissed Haylee's chubby cheek and said, "Let's see if you have any more left in your tummy."

The doorbell chimed, and this time, Myles couldn't see who it was since the security monitor was in the kitchen. The only person he'd been expecting was sitting in front of him, cuddling his daughter, and his family and friends typically didn't show up unannounced. He thought about ignoring it, but the expectant look on Whitney's face said, *Aren't you going to get that?*

"If you'll excuse me, I'll be right back."

"Take your time. We'll be fine by ourselves, won't we, sweets?" Whitney cooed, gently rubbing Haylee's back.

"You can take her out back if you want. She loves being outside." He pointed to the patio doors leading to the covered sun porch.

"Good idea. I could go for a bit of fresh air too." She slowly pushed to her feet while balancing Haylee in her arms.

The doorbell chimed again, the caller's impatience evident by the subsequent knock on the door.

Whitney looked at him. "I think you'd better get that. Haylee and I will be in the back."

Myles gave a brisk nod before doing as she instructed. As he proceeded down the hall, he heard the jiggling of the knob that sounded like someone trying to open the door. That was when his low-key annoyance turned to anger.

"Myles, I know you're home," came a familiar voice through the door.

Shit. Fuck. Shit. Holly was the last person he'd expected.

He opened the door not because he wanted to but because he had to.

To get rid of her.

It had been roughly a month since he'd last seen his estranged wife. During that time, she'd cut her hair. Now she sported a blunt shoulder-length bob. Other than that, she looked her usual fashionable self, dressed in a cream linen suit. It was the kind of outfit she commonly wore when meeting with clients, suggesting she'd stopped by between showings.

Their gazes clashed, hers shimmering with irritation as the hand holding a key dropped to her side.

"What are you doing here?" he asked coldly. They hadn't parted on good terms, making the chances of this being a social visit slim to none.

"If you ever returned my calls, you'd know." She quickly breezed past him, knowing damn well he'd had no intention of inviting her in. But she also knew he wouldn't risk making a scene by physically barring her entry.

"When did you change the locks?"

She casually tossed the question over her shoulder as she dropped the key into her purse.

Myles had no choice but to follow her, managing to get in front of her before she made it past the living room, subtly blocking her path to the rest of the house.

His mission was simple. Keep the two women apart.

"I told you to have your lawyer call mine."

Slamming her hands on her hips, Holly glared at him. "I need to talk to you, and my lawyer doesn't work weekends."

"Would you keep it down? You're going to wake up Haylee," Myles said, his tone hardening.

That should keep her visit short. The last time they'd spoken, she'd told him that seeing his daughter—because Haylee wasn't hers—was a painful reminder of the end of their marriage, which was why he was surprised she was here now.

Holly's mouth formed in a scowl. "Can we at least sit down?"

Oh, for fuck's sake.

He motioned to the living room and muttered, "Okay, but make it quick." The odds of his two worlds colliding and blowing up increased with every second she was here.

Despite insisting they sit, Holly sauntered over to stand in front of the credenza she'd bought after she moved in. She'd wanted to put her mark on the house, and he'd been happy to oblige, wanting her to feel like this was her home, too. She redecorated to the tune of eighty grand.

"You haven't changed anything," she commented, her gaze idly surveying the room.

Myles didn't have time for idle chitchat. "What do you want?" he asked, his tone brisk.

Her gaze narrowed, and her mouth thinned. She wasn't used to him treating her like the stranger she'd become to him.

"Why do our papers say that we've been separated for five months? I moved out a month ago."

Ah, so that was her deal. "Holly, you moved out three weeks after we brought Haylee home from the hospital."

"I did not!" she exclaimed, indignant. "I went to take care of my mother."

Myles mentally rolled his eyes. There had been nothing wrong with her mother. Why she continued to pretend the four months she spent in San Diego at her mother and stepfather's guest house had been anything other than her shirking her responsibilities was ridiculous.

Their situation hadn't been ideal by any stretch of the imagination, but running away wasn't the answer. Children did that sort of thing, not parents.

"Why does it even matter? The faster this divorce goes through, the better. I thought that's what you wanted."

"For the love of God, Myles, I may have filed, but you're the one who wants the divorce. You know that better than anyone," she snapped.

"Would you keep your voice down? I told you, you're going to wake Haylee."

His soon-to-be ex-wife huffed. "That's right, because she's the only one you care about anymore."

"Jesus Christ, Holly, she's a baby, and she's my daughter. No one is more important to me than her." He spoke through gritted teeth, but his voice was low and very controlled.

"Fine, have it your way. You want the divorce to go through as quickly as possible, go ahead. I'm done trying to reason with you."

"Reason with me? The only thing you've tried to convince me to do was turn my daughter over to a stranger."

Holly made a scoffing sound. "You can't tell me they haven't found the biological mother yet. It's been over a month."

"They found her, and she doesn't want her." That wasn't a lie.

Holly's eyes went round. "What do you mean she doesn't want her?"

Somehow, she'd convinced herself that a lovely Black couple was ready to claim Haylee as theirs. That unlike her, the husband would happily raise another man's child.

"No. She's single, and she's not ready to start a family. She froze her eggs because of a medical condition that makes it difficult for her to get pregnant."

After a long pause, Holly opened her purse and retrieved a tube of pink lipstick and a compact mirror. She quietly reapplied it to her lips before snapping the mirror closed and returning both to her purse. She then squared her shoulders and lifted her eyes to his, a plastic smile on her face. "Then I guess that's that," she stated flatly.

"Yes, it is." And hopefully, this would be the last he'd see of her.

"Okay, I guess I should get going."

She paused as if expecting him to say something to stop her from leaving. Stop her from walking out of his life.

For months, he'd been mad at her. Mad that she'd abandoned their daughter not once, but twice, the last time permanently. Mad that she'd had the gall to demand he choose between them. Now he felt nothing for her. Not anger or sadness. Definitely not love.

All he wanted was to clean the slate and start over. The only demanding female he wanted in his life right now had dimples and big brown eyes, and wasn't old enough to walk.

Silently, he accompanied her to the door. She turned and regarded him. "I hope you realize what you're taking on. Haylee may be half white, but to the rest of the world, she'll be Black. Raising her won't be easy. And don't think your money will be a panacea for all. It'll only be able to do so much."

Myles knew better than to respond. He wasn't born yesterday. He knew enough to know what he didn't know.

"I know *I'm* making the right decision for Haylee," she continued. "I just hope *you* know what you're doing."

Myles clenched his teeth so hard his jaw ached. "Goodbye, Holly."

He nearly recoiled when she came up on her toes and brushed a kiss against his cheek. "Goodbye, Myles. I'll have the divorce papers signed and sent to your lawyer next week."

Myles watched as she walked to her car. Once she slid behind the wheel, he closed the door and breathed a big sigh of relief. Finally, she was gone.

One down, one to go.

Turning, he started visibly when he saw Whitney standing in the hallway, holding his sleeping daughter.

"Do you want me to take her?" He was more than a little unnerved by her stillness and the quiet intensity of her stare.

Instead of answering him, she posed a question of her own. "Did she say you're getting a *divorce*?"

7

"I'll have the divorce papers signed and sent to your lawyer next week."

That was what the woman said. Whitney was sure of it. And it didn't take a rocket scientist to figure out who the blonde was, because *she* looked like her picture. She was the wife he said was out of town on a family emergency.

Lying son of a bitch.

"I'm sorry, what?"

Whitney's eyes narrowed in warning. Oh, she'd make him sorry, alright. As smart as he thought he was, he'd never be able to play dumb enough to fool her.

"That was your wife, right? The woman who just left," she said, her demeanor having undergone a dramatic change from just five minutes ago. "I heard her say something about signing divorce papers and sending them to your lawyer."

Instead of fessing up as anyone with an ounce of integrity would, Myles Redmond continued to stare at her as if debating his life choices, not knowing that when it came to Haylee, he no longer had one.

And to think she was beginning to like him. Disappointment had her swallowing down the lump that had formed in her throat. He'd had her believing she'd be leaving her child in the care of two loving parents.

But that was a lie.

After what felt like an interminable amount of time, he inclined his head in a nod. "Yes, that was Holly."

"And you're getting a divorce." She wanted to hear him say it, the treacherous, lying rat.

Sighing heavily, he ran his hand through his hair, briefly looking away. A beat later, he finally came clean. "Yes, we're getting divorced."

Whitney was tempted to say, *see, that wasn't so hard, was it?* but knew the momentary satisfaction she'd get from the dig would be short-lived and would do nothing to get her the answers she needed. But boy, was she tempted.

"You weren't ever going to tell me, were you?" She was more furious than hurt but hated that the hurt came through in her voice.

"Here, let me put her down," Myles said, sidestepping the question. He then firmly but gently took Haylee from her.

Short of engaging in a tug-of-war with the man, there was nothing she could do but relinquish her daughter without a fuss.

"I'll be right back." With that, he started toward the stairs.

The second Myles and Haylee disappeared from view, Whitney returned to the family room and picked up the papers she'd left untouched on the coffee table. The termination of parental rights agreement he was expecting her to sign.

How could she now that she'd seen her? Held her? After watching Haylee fall asleep in her arms? How could she when she didn't know what was going on with Myles and his wife, except that they were getting a divorce?

Whitney was still reeling from the discovery. Had she not been in the kitchen rinsing off Haylee's pacifier, she wouldn't have heard their fateful exchange on the security monitor and would have remained in the dark.

Why were they divorcing? Was his wife unwilling to raise another woman's child? Or was it because that woman was Black? Myles wanted his daughter. Whitney had no doubt about that. His wife, however, was a different matter altogether.

She was trying not to jump to conclusions, but she didn't think she was too far off the mark with that one. Why else would a couple so desperate for a child of their own hire a surrogate and then file for divorce not even a year after the baby was born?

When she heard his footfall on the stairs, she turned, ready to get to the bottom of whatever game he was playing.

"She'll be down for a bit," he announced upon his return.

"Good, now we can talk," Whitney said with a crisp assertiveness to let him know things had changed. He wasn't running the show anymore.

"Why are you getting divorced?" No point in beating around the bush. She wanted answers. More to the point, she deserved to know what the hell was going on. Not that anything he said was going to change what she'd already decided.

Myles halted in front of her. His six-foot-two frame seemed to loom larger over her than ever before. "That's none of your business."

The distance in his voice was more daunting than his words. It was a good thing she had an exceptionally high intimidation tolerance level. She'd dealt with enough men like him in her years in the entertainment business.

"Anything that has to do with my daughter is my business," she said just as forthrightly. "Does she have anything to do with your divorce?"

His jaw firmed. "I deal in legalities, and legally, Haylee is *not* your daughter. She's mine and my wife's."

"You mean the one you're divorcing?" Her voice was heavy with sarcasm.

"Holly's name is on the birth certificate."

"That sounds like a very lawyerly answer."

He quirked an eyebrow. "Would you rather I not deal in facts?"

She held the papers up in front of his face. "If you're so sure about your rights, then why do you need me to sign this?"

"Because I'm a lawyer, and we generally like to cover all our bases."

"Fine, then cover this base," she said, crossing her arms over her chest, the once smooth papers wrinkling between her fingers. "Why did you lie and tell me your wife was out of town?"

"Because I knew it would complicate things."

He didn't even have the decency to look the least embarrassed at having been caught in such a blatant lie.

"Complicate things how? Are you and your wife planning to share custody? Didn't you want me to know that my daughter was going to be raised in *two* single-parent households? What is so complicated about the truth?"

To her string of questions, Myles responded with a blank look.

She made a point of slowly placing the papers back on the table while holding his gaze. "Well, I certainly won't be signing *this*."

A muscle in his jaw ticked, and his eyes became frosty.

Let him chew on that.

"Alright, since you refuse to answer my questions, I'll tell you what I think. I don't think you and your soon-to-be ex-wife will be sharing custody of Haylee. Do you know why I believe that? Because she was here and didn't see *her daughter*. And I think the reason you're getting a divorce is because she doesn't want her. Am I right?"

Myles remained silent, his expression giving little away, evidence she'd not only struck a nerve, she'd landed on the truth.

"Never mind. I have my answer."

"Haylee has me." His statement came out defensive.

"And now she has me," she countered. "You know, the only reason I was willing to sign this—" she waved a hand at the papers "—is because I thought it was the right thing to do. For Haylee, you, and your wife. As far as I was concerned, she had a nuclear family. I didn't want to be an interloper in her life. But I *needed* to see her, and I needed to see for myself that she was being well cared for and loved."

"Nothing about that has changed," he stated stiffly.

Whitney pursed her lips. "Are you telling me that your wife wants her? That you plan to co-parent Haylee with the woman you're divorcing?"

"Haylee has everything she needs."

She was starting to believe his inability to answer direct questions was caused by the condition commonly known as *you're not the boss of me*. A condition associated with five-year-olds.

"You don't get it, do you?" she huffed, exasperated. "Haylee doesn't have a *mother*."

"She has my sister, who lives twenty minutes away and loves her like she's one of her own. You don't have to worry about Haylee lacking a mother figure or a female role model. She'll have both."

Does he even hear himself?

"I'm sure your sister is a wonderful aunt, but that's what she is, Haylee's aunt. Haylee deserves to have a mother, and I am that mother. Me," she said, tapping her palm against her breastbone. "Haylee is also half black, so she's going to need someone who understands the challenges she'll face growing up. I think it's fair to say your family won't be able to help her in that respect."

Myles's gaze narrowed. "Are you suggesting that *you* raise my daughter?" He sounded insultingly incredulous.

It wasn't as if she was demanding physical custody, and he should have been damn happy she wanted to be a part of her daughter's life. And truthfully, even if he and his wife hadn't been in the process of divorcing, Whitney couldn't bear the thought of never seeing or holding Haylee again.

"I'm willing to be whatever she needs. I just want to be involved. I'm not sure what that looks like or entails, but I'm willing to do whatever it takes to make it happen. To make it work."

"Look, I just want what's best for her," he bit out.

"And you don't think having me in her life would be good for her?"

He met the challenge in her voice with another cold stare. "You act like you're a regular person. Hell, you're not even a regular celebrity. When are you going to have time for her? In between movies and tour dates?"

"You're a fine one to talk," Whitney fired back, not appreciating the dismissiveness in his tone. "You can't tell me being president of the California Bar isn't a demanding job. I bet you work a lot of long days and plenty of nights too." No one could convince her that workhorse wasn't part of the job description.

"I'm not juggling three careers. You, on the other hand, have your acting and singing, and if I'm not mistaken, you appeared on the thirty-under-thirty list of female entrepreneurs as CEO of your fashion company two years in a row. And then there's the press. Do you honestly think I want my daughter raised by a woman who's constantly being stalked by fans and paparazzi?"

Ouch, that hurt.

"I'll be able to shield her from that," she insisted. Her house was equipped with the security of Fort Knox, and although she'd never required full-time bodyguards, she'd hire them if it would make him happy. Haylee would be safe whenever she was with her.

"Yeah, well, don't mind me if I don't want to chance it."

She'd always done her best never to issue ultimatums or threats, but when the stakes were this high and everything she'd tried had failed, they were all she had left.

"Look, whether you like it or not, Haylee's my daughter, and I'm going to be part of her life. If you insist on fighting me on this, the only place we'll end up is in court."

Myles's nostrils flared, and he became ominously still. He pinned her with a look. "Is that supposed to be a threat?"

After years of having men treat her like a doll with her namesake's—the great Whitney Houston—vocals (sing, look pretty, speak only when told to), she'd finally summoned up the courage to stand up to industry execs who'd tried to intimidate her with that same look and tone. She landed her first role because the casting director said she possessed the perfect combination of sweet innocence with a sexy undertone, and some people made the mistake of believing that was all she was. Well, Myles Redmond was about to learn that she had a lot of steel in her spine.

"It's only a threat if you take it as one."

Boy, she would hate to have been the prosecutor taking him on in his defense attorney days. He had that whole piercing stare down. Not enough to weaken her resolve, but it did suggest if she took him to court, it would be a no-holds-barred fight. If there was one thing her parents taught her, it was to pick her battles carefully. Not all of them were worth fighting.

And since it looked like she'd be dealing with this man for the foreseeable future, it wouldn't be in Haylee's best interests to alienate her father right out of the gate.

"Honestly, I'm trying to be reasonable," she said, softening her tone and taking a big mental step back.

He quirked an eyebrow and continued to stare at her, grim-faced and silent.

Whitney's hopes wobbled and faltered. He wasn't making any of this easy. "Look, I'm not terminating my parental rights, so that discussion is closed. And I get this situation is rare and all kinds of messy, but I'm pretty sure in the eyes of the law, a mother should be afforded some rights to her biological child."

Watching the mix of helplessness and anger flit across his face, Whitney could almost sympathize with him. He hadn't selected her to be the mother of his child, and there was nothing he could do to change what was. But how did he think she felt? She was as much a victim of this as he was. They were in this together, whether he liked it or not.

Myles made a frustrated sound in his throat. "If that's all you have to say, I think you should leave."

Whitney blinked, taken aback by the finality in his voice. She couldn't believe he was kicking her out with everything up in the air. Nodding stiffly, she retrieved her purse from the couch and then turned to face him, back straight and chin raised. "My lawyer will be in contact."

Myles rubbed the nape of his neck before dropping his hand to his side with a weary sigh. "Could you give me a few days? You just dumped this on me, and I have a lot to think about."

Dumped this on him? Seriously, the nerve. He was the one who hid the fact that, for all intents and purposes, their daughter was motherless. But one of them had to be the adult, and clearly, the task had fallen to her.

Pasting a smile on her face, she informed him, "If I don't hear from you by Monday, my lawyer will be in touch… Tuesday morning."

Now, if *that* sounded like a threat, then mission accomplished.

That gave him five full days to get used to the idea that he was never getting rid of her. She was going to be in his life for as long as Haylee was.

8

When Whitney arrived home, she made a beeline for the kitchen and poured herself a large glass of lemon iced tea. Then, wide-brimmed hat in place and glass and cell phone in hand, she made her way to the backyard, where she planted her butt on the lounger by the pool.

Since she had planned to terminate her parental rights, she'd thought it best not to tell her parents about Haylee. What would be the point? She was their only hope for grandchildren, and it would have devastated her mother not to have a relationship with her only grandchild.

But all that had changed.

Now it was time to make some calls, starting with one to her favorite cousin, affectionately designated by the family as Legal Central.

Cheyenne answered with a cheerful, "Hey, I was just thinking about you."

After how she'd spent the last hour and a half, the friendly greeting was like a soothing balm on a stinging burn. "Don't tell me you didn't like the dress I wore on *Kimmel* last week?" Whitney teased.

Years ago, her cousin complained the dress she wore for an Oprah interview made her look like an escapee from a flamingo sanctuary. Too bright. Too much color. Too much everything. But the day after the interview aired, the blouse had sold out at every store in the country.

And rightly so. It was super cute.

"I recorded it, but I haven't watched it yet. But as long as you limited yourself to no more than three colors and your nails don't look like the girl from *The Exorcist* threw up on your toes, I'm sure you look fine."

"Excuse me, but I'll have you know mustard–green nail polish is extremely popular right now. I'm actually thinking of putting out pants that color in the summer line."

Cheyenne snorted a laugh. "No, you are not."

"Of course I'm not," she said, smiling. Her cousin knew her too well. "Listen, I have to tell you something, but you have to promise not to tell a living soul, especially your mother."

Their mothers were identical twins, lived in the same city, talked every day, and wouldn't be able to keep a secret from the other if you paid them. Unlike their mothers, she and her cousin didn't look a thing alike—save their height. Cheyenne was five years older and resembled their mothers, which in celebrity terms equated to a taller version of Janelle Monáe. Whitney, on the other hand, could have been Aaliyah's twin— something people in the music industry wouldn't allow her, or anyone else for that matter, to forget.

"Whitty Girl, have I ever spilled any of your tea?"

Before answering, Whitney took a sip of her drink, savoring the combination of freshly brewed sweet tea and lemon. Although a splash of vodka wouldn't have hurt, given the day she was having. "Alright, are you sitting down?"

"Oh wow. So it's that kind of news," Cheyenne said in a hushed, conspiratorial voice. "Hold on. Let me get comfortable. Sounds like I'm in for some piping hot tea."

Whitney heard the sound of cupboard doors closing, followed by muffled footsteps.

"Okay, I'm sitting down. You don't have to worry about me falling and splitting my head open on something sharp. And if I do, I promise I won't sue you," her cousin said, employing lawyer humor.

"So, this happened. There was a mix-up at the fertility clinic where I stored my eggs, and now I have a daughter, and I need you to tell me what rights I have as her biological mother."

"What!" her cousin exclaimed loud enough for her nearest neighbor—who lived a quarter mile away—to hear it.

Whitney winced and jerked the phone away from her ear. As soon as her hearing returned, she calmly told her everything that had happened, from her conversation with the doctor to her visit with Haylee and her President Lawyer father.

To her cousin's credit, she only interrupted once, and that was to say, *"No, that MFer did not,"* when Whitney told her how she found out the Redmonds were getting a divorce. Beyond that, Cheyenne kept her reactions to soft gasps without verbal commentary. When Whitney finally concluded the tragic retelling of the last three days, there were several moments of silence.

"Chey, you still there?" she prompted.

"Are you being for real?" her cousin asked in disbelief. "This isn't the plot of a movie you're auditioning for, is it?"

Whitney harrumphed a humorless laugh. "You know the shock you're feeling right now? Well, multiply it by a thousand to get an idea of how I felt when the doctor told me. Sometimes, I still can't believe this is real." Lowering her foot to the pool, she poked her toes in the water. The cold felt nice against the heat of the day.

"Oh my god, Whit, you're a mother."

The awe in her cousin's voice perfectly captured her own sentiment. She'd become a mother without lifting so much as a finger. Well, except the part where she'd been pumped full of hormones and had her eggs surgically extracted while under sedation.

"I know, right? Crazy." She shook her head. "What are the chances?"

"I'd say one in a million."

Whitney let out a derisive snort. "Try one in a bajillion or bazillion, whichever is larger."

"I don't think *bajillion* is a word."

"It doesn't matter. Let's just say it's rare and call it a day. Anyway, I need your advice. You deal with this family stuff all the time."

Chey had been practicing family law since she moved to San Diego after graduating from UC Berkeley ten years ago.

"I don't know, Whit. I've never handled anything like this, but I sure hope you're going to sue the damn clinic. What they did amounts to gross negligence."

"I intend to, and I'm sure the Redmonds will too." The estranged couple had probably already started the ball rolling on that front.

"I will say this, though. Their divorce will definitely help your case. Courts typically do whatever they can to keep children with their biological parents. You're not together, no, but after his divorce goes through, he'll be a single white father raising a biracial child. Add in the fact that it's a girl, your request for visitation or even partial custody strengthens your case. At the very least, you'll be granted visitation."

Whitney breathed a little easier, a weight lifted.

"But as I tell all my clients, unless the child's well-being is at risk, do whatever you can to keep this out of the court system. Especially someone like you. It would be a media bonanza, and you don't want all your business out on the streets because they'll try to dig up as much dirt on you as they can. They'll talk to all your exes and go through your trash. And you know how nasty that could get. If you can't come to some kind of agreement with the father, then try mediation. Going to court should be a measure of last resort," she advised.

"Believe me, I don't want to have to take him to court either. And I'm not trying to take her away from him. All I'm asking for is visitation." And they'd go forward from there, one step at a time.

"Okay, then just make sure he knows that. He has custody of your daughter, and he's the freaking president of the California Bar, so try and play nice."

"I am playing nice," she whined. "He's the one who double-crossed me. But I get what you're saying, and I promise I will." Things had gotten a little heated before she left, so she'd give him time to cool down and realize she was right. Haylee needed a mother, and luckily, she had one desperately wanting to take on that role.

"Hey, you okay?" Cheyenne asked, concern in her voice. "I can't imagine what you're going through. This has to be a lot for you to deal with."

"What doesn't kill you makes you stronger." She splashed the water with her toes. "It's funny. Last week, I didn't even know she existed, and today, I feel cheated. Like I've already missed out on six months of her life. But don't worry," she said before her cousin had a chance to respond, "I'll survive. I'm trying to look on the bright side. I had a baby without having to go through labor and missed the joys of swollen feet, leg cramps, morning sickness, and stretch marks."

Whitney glanced down at her perky B-cups, narrow waist,

and flat belly and wondered how much her body would change when or if she gave birth. Would it ever look like this again?

Probably not.

Chey snorted a laugh. "I can't disagree with you on that."

"What about you? Anything new going on?"

"I'm not dating anyone since the last time you asked, *two weeks ago*, if that's what you're asking."

"If I was specifically asking about that, I would've simply asked if you were dating anyone. Although it does sound like you need to get laid." Whitney was only half joking. There was probably some projection going on there as well.

"Tell me about it. It's been six months," her cousin lamented.

Chey had been up-front with her ex, telling him that she didn't want children, and he'd been fine with it. Or at least, that was what he'd said. But after two years together, he'd finally called it quits when it became clear he wouldn't be able to change her mind. Chey recently learned he'd gotten engaged—after dating the woman for a whopping three months.

Honestly, men! They weren't ones to let grass grow under their feet.

"Why don't you come to LA this weekend? I'm hosting the cast party at my place. It'll be fun. And you'll finally get to meet Kennedy's brother, Cam." If anyone could get her cousin out of the man rut she was in, it was Cam Mitchell.

"The hot one with the blue eyes?" Chey asked with more than a note of interest in her voice.

"Yes, that one. Come up early if you want. April, Troy, and Max will be here Friday, so there'll be a few familiar faces."

Whitney introduced the two women two years ago, and whenever April was in town on Oasis business, they would all hang out, which was typically two or three times a year.

"I probably won't be able to make it Friday night, but I'll definitely be there for the party," her cousin said.

They went on to chat about the hecticness of their respective careers and their pitiful dating lives before Chey circled back to the reason for Whitney's call. "Don't forget what I said. Try to make nice with Mr. President Lawyer. Like it or not, you now have a *baby daddy*, and he has custody. The two of you getting along is what's best for your daughter."

"I know. I know. It's just that he—"

"He's your child's father, which means he's the last person you want to be at odds with," Chey cut in. "Come on, Whit, you're gorgeous, talented, and super easy to get along with. Charming the man should be a cake walk for you. He'll have to be blind not to see that any child would be lucky to have you as their mother."

Whitney sighed. "How about this? I won't sic my lawyer on him if he doesn't get back to me by Monday, and I promise to be at my charming best the next time I talk to him. Will that do?"

"That's all he can ask for."

Whitney just hoped it worked. As for now, she had major baby shopping to do.

9

"So, what's she like?" Natalie asked the second Myles dropped onto the bench opposite her at the kitchen table. "As gorgeous in person as she is on TV? Tell me she has pores like everybody else, because there's no way her skin is that perfect."

With Whitney Richardson's threat hanging over his head, he'd found it impossible to concentrate and left work early. Which was how he found himself at his sister's house. He needed someone to talk to. Someone whose opinion and judgment he valued, and he could think of no one better than his twin. It also helped that she was at home in the middle of a weekday.

Natalie's question sent Myles's eyes skyward. As if he gave a rat's ass about Whitney Richardson's "perfect" skin. He hadn't come there for his sister to fangirl over the woman threatening to take his daughter from him.

"She's a pain in the you know what." He tried not to curse in the vicinity of the kids. Currently, his four-year-old niece, Sophie, and twenty-month–old nephew, Jonah, were watching TV in the family room. Sophie had recently gotten into the habit of repeating words she'd heard when you least expected it…as her parents had learned in the middle of a dinner party where his brother-in-law's boss had been in attendance. *"Uncle Myles, Daddy said* asshole *to the man in the car. That's a bad word."*

"Ah, come on. You know what I mean. Is she stuck-up or anything like that? She seems so sweet in all her interviews."

"Nat, she's an actress. How do you expect her to act? She has a public persona to protect," he scoffed. She was sweet when she got her way. When she didn't, she resorted to threats of litigation.

"I mean, she comes off as authentic, you know, genuine, and not everyone does."

"Well, Miss Authentic genuinely wants Haylee." A fact that continued to both anger and scare the shit out of him.

Compassion lit her eyes. "She's her mother, Myles. Of course she's going to want her."

"Whose side are you on?" he asked, stung by her betrayal. They were twins, although they didn't look alike. His sister was slight, had light brown hair and hazel eyes, and looked like their father. He'd taken after his mother, except for the blue eyes.

Growing up, he and his sister had been thicker than thieves. High school and college changed that, but they'd grown closer than ever after Haylee's birth. It also helped that they lived a stone's throw away from each other. Nat was a lifesaver in too many ways to count.

"I'm on your side. I'm on my niece's side."

"Do you understand the kind of mayhem that will follow her if she's in Haylee's life? Our lives? Is that what you want for your niece?" He hadn't been lying when he told Whitney Richardson that his sister treated Haylee as if she were her own. Natalie filled the void Holly's absence had created, and he trusted her with his daughter's life.

"Would you rather it be Holly?" his sister asked, irritation rife in her tone.

"It doesn't have to be either. The woman is nothing but an egg donor. A week ago, she didn't know Haylee existed."

"That's not her fault."

"I didn't say it was. I'm simply saying that I'm the one responsible for bringing her into this world. I wanted her. It's only due to a mix-up she's even involved."

"Haylee wouldn't be who she is without her. Remember that." There was a sharp edge to her tone. "Now my niece can have a mother who actually wants her. And in case you've missed the memo and a slew of child psychology books, a child needs a mother." His sister was as adamant about that as Whitney Richardson herself.

"A child needs a *good* mother. Someone who is going to be a positive influence in their life."

"And you don't think she will be?"

"I think her life is full enough already. She's not going to have the time to be the kind of mother Haylee deserves."

"Myles, you haven't even given her a chance," his sister scolded. "She may surprise you and turn out to be the mother of your dreams."

That wouldn't be the kind of dream he imagined she'd be starring in. He then irrationally resented her for that being the first thought that came to mind. *His* mind.

Myles let out a long breath, wearily shaking his head. "I don't know."

Nat reached across the table and patted his hand, her expression one of sisterly concern and compassion. "Don't know what? Whether she'll surprise you or whether you're going to give her a chance at all?"

"I don't know if I can trust her, *and* I think she doesn't know what she's getting herself into."

"First-time parents usually don't."

"It won't always be sunshine and roses," he said, thinking of the two a.m. feedings, the teething, and the sheer amount of *stuff* he had to cart around whenever he took Haylee out.

Yeah, sunshine and roses, alright.

Natalie let out a raucous laugh. "When is it ever? Because I must have missed that stage with both of mine."

"Which is exactly what I mean. She isn't the one who's up with Haylee at night or has to take her to her doctor's appointment. She'll sweep in and out like Haylee's fairy godmother." She'd be the rich, glamorous, beautiful, *fun* parent, while he was the one who'd have to discipline her and deal with the fallout.

"That's all going to depend on the agreement you two come to. She can have as much responsibility for Haylee as you're willing to give her *and* she's willing to take on."

From what he'd seen of her so far, he was afraid if he gave her an inch, he'd end up losing his daughter, and not through the courts.

"She said that one of the reasons Haylee needs her is that she's going to experience things in her life I can't relate to." As much as he wanted to deny it and wish it away, it was the truth. Haylee would experience racism, and there wasn't a damn thing he'd be able to do to prevent it, even if he stood vigil over her twenty-four hours a day. And it wasn't something he'd be able to relate to with her in any meaningful way. Not really. Life as the son of a lawyer of his father's stature and influence had come with a private school education and his pick of law firms after he'd graduated from Stanford. Doors had always been open to him, granting him easy entry to elite spaces.

His sister's features softened. "True, but you'll do the best you can because you love her with everything in you. And you can always talk to Eve. She's Asian and Black, so she knows all about growing up biracial."

"You haven't said anything to her, have you?" His question coming out sharper than he intended. Eve was her friend and neighbor and had a son Jonah's age.

Natalie gave him her *what do you take me for* look. "After you explicitly told me not to, what do you think?"

"Right. Sorry," he muttered. "This whole thing has me stressed."

"I understand." She gave his hand another sisterly pat.

He treated her to a tight-lipped smile.

"You're not going to lose her, and you have to stop worrying over who Haylee is going to love more. Parenting isn't a competition. You're going to be as much or more a part of the person Haylee becomes. Always remember that."

Myles laughed gruffly. "Dad did say you could always read me like a book."

"That's because we have that telepathic twin thing going on."

"I want you to meet her. You've always been a good judge of character, and frankly, after Holly, I don't trust mine. I don't want to fight this out in court, but just say the word and I'll let a judge decide." And he was acquainted with a few family court judges he wouldn't mind presiding over a potential case.

"Stop beating yourself up about it. At least this time, you got out early."

What went unsaid was the five years he'd stayed with Amy, determined to make the marriage work. His sister hadn't thought either woman was a good match for him, and she'd been right. As usual. Call it a twin's intuition.

"Let's not even think about settling this in court. As good as you are, and as many cases as your firm wins, that woman is worth over a billion dollars. Only an idiot would want to go up against that, and you, my dear brother, are no idiot."

Certainly not when it came to the law. Unfortunately for him, wives were another matter.

"Hey, who do you think the filthy rich call when they need the best law services money can buy?" Myles possessed no false modesty when it came to his professional abilities and the attorneys employed at his firm. They were all top-notch in their specialty.

His sister snorted. "Alright, alright, I'll meet her and give her a mental pat-down before you find yourself in court squaring off against one of your own lawyers because she was able to snap them up from right under you."

Myles shook his head. "Never gonna happen. The lawyers on my team have it too good where they are. Trust me, I know."

Last month, he'd convinced one of the female attorneys at the firm to go part-time instead of quitting. Jen had wanted a lighter workload after returning from her company-paid six-month maternity leave. She was the best patent attorney the firm had, and he hadn't wanted to lose her. After a bit of haggling, she'd gladly accepted a workload cut clean in half and a part-time paralegal. So instead of a grueling fifty-hour work-week, she now worked twenty-five hours and only came into the office once a week. She claimed her new schedule came as close to the perfect work–life balance as she'd ever be able to find.

"Good. I hope you make sure it stays that way. Brad's always complaining about his boss. Last night, I told him to stop complaining and finally do something about it. He needs to get another job."

"How many times do I have to tell that husband of yours that his talents are wasted at a state university? When he's serious about leaving, tell him to give me a call." Pushing to his feet, Myles said, "Now it's time for me to go home to my daughter."

He kissed his niece and nephew goodbye. They were so wrapped up in *Dragon Tales* that he was as good as forgotten by the time he exited the room.

Nat accompanied him to the front door. "Are you still bringing Haylee over this weekend? Sophie asks about her every day."

When his sister had gotten pregnant, his niece had made it crystal clear that she would only tolerate a sister. She'd met her brother's arrival with tearful sobs and a four-year-old's recriminations. Although she'd quickly grown to love her baby brother, Haylee's birth had made up for some of her disappointment.

Myles chuckled. "You can tell my little munchkin that Haylee will only come over if she's been a good girl for her mommy."

"Let me know about the meeting with Sahara, and I'll clear my schedule. But don't make it this Saturday because—"

"Soph has her ballet recital. I know, I know." Last week, she'd talked his ear off about it and had demonstrated, in her knee socks, why she was the prima ballerina among the four-year-olds.

Laughing, his sister hugged him before sending him on his way.

10

In the three years since Whitney started Oasis, profits had tripled, and the number of fashion lines had increased from three to five. Currently, she and her management team were debating the pros and cons of expanding their offerings to include home furnishings, starting with bed linens. Something she and April had been discussing for several months.

If they decided to go that route, Whitney wanted a line that specifically catered to the middle- to lower-income market. Mariah Johnson, VP of marketing and product development, was worried a move like that would diminish the Oasis brand.

Whitney understood her concerns and posed her next question to April, who'd be the lead designer of the new line.

"What do you think? I love your idea, but can we get the quality we're striving to achieve for the cost? None of this nonsense of sheets and pillowcases disintegrating in the wash after a few spin cycles," Whitney said with an irritated huff.

Seated around the table in the conference room at Oasis's headquarters were Mariah, April, Ellen Sato, the CFO, Sarah Torres, the sales director, and her. April was also the founder and owner of the aptly named April Rose Designs, and to this day, Whitney still couldn't believe she'd been able to coax her friend into giving up a bit of autonomy to sign a three-year contract with the company.

April insisted that Whitney was taking just as much of a chance on her. She was wrong. Her friend was wickedly talented and could have worked for any of the top fashion houses in New York or Europe, but she'd been determined to strike out on her own.

Although she'd come to the table with a huge platform and a sense of style a sizable number of her fans were eager to emulate, Whitney knew next to nothing about fashion design, much less how to run a clothing company. She'd definitely gotten the better part of the deal, because April would've been successful regardless.

"Would you be willing to take reduced profits on the line?" April asked, and Whitney couldn't tell if she was kidding or not.

"We'd have to cut it by twenty to make it work," Mariah said. Whitney could tell by her pained expression that she wasn't exactly overjoyed at the idea. "And if we're planning to go ahead with an IPO, we need to decide whether to do it now or after."

Whitney gave a contemplative nod of agreement. She still wasn't one hundred percent sure it was a good idea to take the company public. She loved the current profit-sharing model they had in place. IPOs were extremely expensive but would also provide the funds needed to grow.

Realize its full potential, as Ellen often said.

Sarah believed they needed to establish a presence in Europe in order to make a dent in the international market, which was going to take a considerable amount of money.

"I think we can take a hit." Bedding was notorious for its ridiculous markup anyway, so it wouldn't necessarily *hurt* the bottom line. Plus, it would just be one or two lines. Whitney directed her attention to Ellen, eyebrow raised in question. *What do you think?*

She shrugged. "If you're willing to reduce the margins on those lines, I don't see a problem. It's not that it won't be profitable, just not as profitable as the others."

Because her clothes weren't cheap, Whitney insisted they offer a budget line in every clothing category.

"Do you have the numbers for last quarter?"

"You're going to love this." Her CFO wore a pleased smile on her face. She then went on to say that net revenue went up a whopping twenty-five percent because of a drop in operating expenses.

"Why the big drop?" Sarah asked, beating Whitney to the punch.

"Nick says they switched factories."

Nick Cavanaugh was their main contact at ECO Apparel, the clothing manufacturer she'd partnered with when Stacy suggested she start her own clothing line.

After the music video for her Grammy-winning single had been released, Whitney's unique style exploded in popularity. Whatever she wore sold out within hours of her appearing in it, whether she was photographed walking down the street or posing on the red carpet. Fashion brands flocked to her and began bombarding her with their products. It had never occurred to her to capitalize on her fame that way.

How she'd become a fashion trendsetter, she would never understand.

Despite some bumps along the way—namely, the email hack that nearly ended their contractual relationship—so far the partnership had been an all-around success, boosting ECO's earnings by sixty percent and revitalizing their growth.

"That's some kind of savings," Whitney remarked, surprised

it was that much. Not that she didn't like making more money. She was all for that, but not at the expense of worker safety. She was a conscientious, by-the-book kind of CEO.

"Sarah, can you check with Kayleen over there and make sure they're not cutting corners? The factories have to meet ISO standards." Most of the manufacturing for their lines was overseas, but last year, ECO began talking about moving it. Nick had serious questions about the working conditions at the factories.

"Will do," Sarah said with a brisk nod.

"Good. And if that's all, I'll let you get back to your work." Pushing the chair back, Whitney stood, signaling the end of the meeting. Everyone collected their tablets and phones and quickly dispersed.

April followed Whitney back to her office, which was much smaller than those of the other executives. Since she wasn't there full-time, a large corner office would have been wasted on her. She was perfectly fine with hers, which consisted of a desk, a small round table, two chairs, and a single metal file cabinet.

"What time did you finally get in?" Whitney asked as April set the book of swatches she'd brought from New York on the table along with her purse.

It must have been late or her friend would have called her. And there hadn't been time for them to catch up before the meeting. They usually went over new design ideas and swatches whenever she was in town.

"Last night at ten. Our flight was three hours late, and we didn't get checked into the hotel until close to midnight. And then, with the three-hour time difference and the fact that Max slept on the flight over, he didn't fall asleep until close to three."

Max was her four-year-old son. April frequently bookended her business trips with a family vacation if her husband was available. The timing was perfect since her husband was currently on break until football season started next month.

"Where are they now, Troy and his Mini-Me?" Whitney wasn't exaggerating. Except for the dark curly hair Max inherited from April, he was the spitting image of his daddy, beautiful hazel eyes and all.

Smiling tenderly, something she often did when their names were invoked, April glanced down at her phone. "They should be on their way to breakfast. When I left this morning, Max was still sleeping. Troy promised to take him to IHOP, and then they're going to the children's zoo."

"You're still bringing the senator's son and his family to the cast party with you on Saturday, right?" April, Troy, and US Senator Elizabeth Carver's son Scott, and daughter-in-law Rebecca were all friends from back in their college days.

April rolled her eyes and gave her the *do you seriously have to ask* look. "Rebecca wouldn't miss this for the world. She's been dying to meet you since *forever*, and I told you, Grant Musgrove is her celebrity crush. They're flying in tonight, and we're taking the kids to Disneyland tomorrow."

"I can't wait to see Max. He's getting so big."

"Honey, he can't wait to see *you*. Then he can go back to school and brag to all the kids he went to Sara's house."

Whitney got a kick out of him calling her Sara, as Sahara was too much of a mouthful. Max's tongue handled his *H*s like they didn't exist, just like the French. She also found it amusing that he bragged about knowing her while his father was a Super Bowl champion.

"He gets so excited when he sees you on TV."

Whitney chortled. "His dad's on TV all the time." Troy had garnered several big endorsement deals. The country got to see his handsome face just as much if not more than they did hers.

"Yes, but his daddy isn't in movies and doesn't dance and

sing onstage like his Sara, silly," April chided, pooh-poohing her husband's NFL star status. "I told you, my son thinks football is boring."

"Ah, the innocence of children. To them, parents are never a big deal, just like I was Whit the Witless all through middle school," Whitney said, rolling her eyes at the horrid nickname a boy had christened her with. To her shame and embarrassment, the damn thing had stuck like glue.

"*Witless* is the last word anyone would ever use to describe you," April said, appearing offended for her. "Honestly, kids can be so mean, and unfortunately way too many of them don't get better with age."

"Were kids mean to you?" Whitney asked. When April's expression turned inquisitive, she continued. "I mean, you said you grew up in a white neighborhood and went to predominantly white schools your entire life. That couldn't have been easy."

"It wasn't too bad when I was young, but those teen years… Let's just say it helped when I started modeling."

Tall, slim, and beautiful, April was biracial—Black father, white mother. She'd followed her older sister into modeling at the age of ten and only stopped after she graduated from FIT with a degree in fashion design.

"Is there anything you wish your parents had done differently in raising you?"

April's green eyes narrowed. She looked downright suspicious now. "If I didn't know better, I would think you were asking for yourself."

Apparently, her questions hadn't been innocuous or general enough. If she hadn't promised Myles she wouldn't tell another living soul until he gave the go-ahead, Whitney would have told her the second they were alone.

"I'm asking for a friend."

"I'm sure she's a very close friend." April snorted, not appearing the tiniest bit convinced. "By any chance, does your friend think she'll be raising a biracial child because she's involved with a man of a different race?"

Myles Redmond's face immediately came to mind, and it was disconcerting to realize the thought of being intimately—sexually—involved with him made her feel...warm. Good Lord, she hoped she wasn't so shallow that a handsome face would cause her to overlook the obvious flaws in his character. Okay, so she had to make nice with him, but it didn't mean she had to like it. And it wasn't as if good-looking men were a novelty to her. There was an abundance of them in Hollywood, and she was around them all the time.

"She doesn't know for sure, but she wants to be prepared if something like that happens."

A secretive smile slowly crept over April's face. "If this man is anything like Troy, you—I mean your *friend*—will be fine. We're raising Max like my mother raised me, my brother and sister. She made sure we kept in close contact with my dad's family. We visited them a lot growing up. And she always made sure we had dolls that looked like us and that we were represented in the books we read and the shows and movies we watched."

"Your mother sounds wonderful."

"She is. And so was my dad." April's tone was wistful, and the look on her face nostalgic. Her father died when she was four. "My stepdad is pretty good too. But what I appreciated most about my mom was her honesty. She tried to shield us as much as she could, but she also wanted us to be prepared for... life, I guess."

Another wistful smile. "We were all preteens when she had a biracial friend of hers talk to us about her experiences of racism and colorism, and the benefits and drawbacks of being biracial."

"Did it help, the talk with her friend?"

April gave an emphatic nod. "You have no idea. She kinda validated things I felt about myself and made me realize it was completely normal. She also helped me to better appreciate the advantages I was given in life."

Beauty being one of them, she was certain. Also known as *pretty privilege*. Whitney had been told to her face that without it, she wouldn't have achieved the success she had thus far.

"Well, it must have worked, because look how wonderful you turned out."

After they exchanged smiles, April leaned forward, propped her elbows on the table, rested her chin on her interlaced fingers, and abruptly asked, "So, who's the guy?"

"What guy?" Whitney pretended not to know who or what her friend was talking about.

April smirked. "The guy that has you asking about raising biracial children."

Defeated, Whitney sighed and abandoned the *I'm asking for a friend* lie. It didn't work nearly as well as it must have when it was first used seventy years ago. "I can't tell you, but I promise I will when I can."

April sat up straight, her eyes glittering with excitement. "Okay, I won't ask." She made a zipped lip motion with her hand. "I've heard that sometimes studios make actors hide their relationships from the public if they think it will help the movie's box office."

"Yeah, something like that," Whitney agreed, eager to grab on to any excuse except the truth.

"I have one question and that's it, I promise," April said. "Since you're talking about raising children with him, could he be the one?"

"Definitely." Seeing as they'd be raising Haylee together, right now, he was the one and *only*.

April's beautiful smile broadened from ear to ear. "Oh, Sar, I'm so happy for you. I hope he's the one and that you have as many babies as your heart desires."

If only she knew the half of it.

But she would soon enough.

11

"That's him?" Cheyenne asked on a sharp intake of breath. Her cousin looked at her in utter disbelief before her gaze ricocheted back to the man under her slack-jawed scrutiny.

It was like Myles had undergone a makeover. The corporate lawyer had left the building, and in his place was an even yummier version clad in tan board shorts, a short-sleeve button-up, and open-toed leather sandals. It was just as Whitney had both feared and suspected. The body hidden under those Tom Ford suits was anything but soft.

"Yep, that's him," Whitney replied with feeling. "I couldn't believe it when I first saw him. I've only ever seen him in a suit, and you know how a good suit can give the illusion of broad shoulders and muscles and hide other stuff." Like a spare tire, which wasn't necessarily a bad thing.

"The only thing I want to see him in now is his birthday suit," Chey declared with a feminine growl of lust. "Because there is no illusion to what's underneath. That man doesn't need to hide a thing."

Chey wasn't lying. Someone could have knocked her over

with a feather when he'd called from the gate and minutes later stood at her door looking like a Calvin Klein underwear model out to wreak havoc on the female populace. No lie, the sight of him had effectively stolen the air from her lungs—the smash-and-grab kind. And she still wasn't sure whether she'd gotten it all back.

"I was in the neighborhood and decided to take you up on your offer."

Whitney had been proud of herself for managing the task of inviting him in without tripping over her tongue. It was ironic, though. For someone who didn't have any qualms about flaunting what she had, for some reason, she'd been self-conscious greeting Haylee's father in a sheer cover-up and a skimpy red bikini. Which was ridiculous. She'd performed onstage in front of tens of thousands of people wearing just as little.

Although it could've been the look on his face when he'd given her a quick once-over. Not a spark of interest or appreciation flickered in his eyes. But then again, there hadn't been disinterest or revulsion, either. She hadn't known what to make of his reaction to her scantily clad body.

Regardless, she'd been all smiles as she'd ushered him to the backyard and introduced him to everyone. *"Hey everyone, say hello to Myles. He's a lawyer, so mind your p's and q's. Myles, say hello to my forty closest friends…and Grant."* Everyone laughed, no one louder than Grant, who'd said in his proper British accent, *"I'm not worried, mi amor. I know you love me the most."*

More laughter had ensued, but her costar's teasing response had drawn a raised eyebrow from Myles, who probably thought they were more than just costars. It didn't help that Grant, *People*'s Sexiest Man of the Year, had a well-earned reputation for sleeping with his female costars.

She'd left him chatting amicably with Troy and Scott to go inside when Cheyenne's I'm here message popped up on her phone.

"Okay, he's hot. I get it. Now would you stop staring?" Whitney chided. "He's going to know we're talking about him." He was outside on the deck, and they were inside a good forty feet away, but the French patio doors were made of glass, and the man did have eyes, for goodness' sake.

"Now I get why you feel cheated. It isn't just about the baby, is it?" Chey teased with a playful jab of an elbow to her ribs. "Because if I had a baby with that fine specimen of a man and didn't get to enjoy the fruits of all that delicious labor, I'd be upset too."

Whitney couldn't help but laugh. "You're too much. Who knows if he's even good in bed?" Although he looked it. Large hands, big feet, and a nice, full bottom lip. It would be a shame for all that to go to waste and for him to be a dud in bed.

Her cousin gave her a sly side-eye. "Let me know when *you* do."

"Look, I'm not going to lie. If things were different, and I *had* to have a baby with him, it would be nice doing it the old-fashioned way," she half joked.

"Nice is vanilla. Sex with him has got to be next-level. I mean, just looking at him is making me hot." She fluttered her hand like a Southern belle catching all the vapors. "The man is a thirst trap, and I bet he gives good hard rides."

"Since I won't be having sex with him, I'll never know." No matter how appealing she suddenly found the idea. Alright, maybe not that sudden.

"Why not? I don't understand what's the big deal. He's getting a divorce, and you're not seeing anyone."

"Do I really need to state the obvious?" Whitney asked, expressively wide-eyed. "Because he's my daughter's father."

"Which only means you're more than halfway there. It's not yours or his fault the baby carriage came before the baby-making," Chey said with a wink.

"I barely know the man. And none of it matters because he isn't interested in me like that," Whitney said as more of a reminder to herself.

Cheyenne harrumphed as she looked her up and down. "Says who?"

"Says *me*. He's made it clear what he thinks of celebrities." Specifically, the one juggling three careers who was now the mother of his child.

"Yeah, okay. I'll check back with you in six months and see if you think he feels the same way."

Sputtering, Whitney shook her head. Her cousin didn't get it. "Chey, he doesn't want me in my daughter's life. Do you seriously think he wants to have sex with me? Have you forgotten I told him I was going to take him to court if he didn't agree to let me see Haylee?"

She didn't possess enough feminine wiles to get him to see her as anything other than the greatest obstacle to the life he had planned. She was simply the woman he endured because of their daughter.

"Okay, so, sex is off the table, and I don't know what I'm talking about," Chey said, rolling her eyes. "Now, c'mon, introduce me to the man. He's going to get spooked if he looks over here one more time and catches me eye-fucking him."

"Honestly, you're too much."

Pushing open the patio door, Whitney was immediately hit by a hot summer breeze. It was the perfect day to be outdoors enjoying the pool and soaking up the rays. Between the gardenias in the winter, the lilacs in the spring, and the heliotropes, she couldn't pick a favorite flower. What mattered was that regardless of the season, her backyard always smelled divine.

"Sahara, love, you coming in?" Grant shouted from the pool as they made their way to the deck.

Whitney smiled and waved at her *work husband*, as he'd been calling himself during filming. "Give me a few minutes."

When she turned her attention to the task at hand, Myles's gaze was darting between her and her costar. Now she was *positive* he thought something was going on between them, while she couldn't help thinking how hot he looked. Unfortunately for her, he was the worst type of guy. Easy on the eyes and hard on the libido. And sadly, it had been a hot minute since her lady bits had been this revved up and raring to go. Too bad he was her daughter's father, and he didn't like her so much.

"Hey, guys. I hope you're having a good time," she said, smiling widely at them. "This is my cousin, Chey. Chey, this is Scott and Myles. Scott is Rebecca's husband," she said gesturing at the handsome sandy-blond-haired man—and Myles, respectively. "You already know Troy."

Everyone exchanged friendly greetings, but of course her cousin had to take it up a notch when she shook hands with Myles. "Whit was just telling me that we have a lot in common."

He arched a brow. "Really? How so?"

"I'm a lawyer, and I heard you're president of the California Bar. That makes us kindred spirits, so to speak," she said with a teasing grin.

Chey was seriously getting her flirt on today. Except he was off-limits to her for the simple reason that Whitney was family. Her dear cousin wasn't allowed to mess with her child's father, no matter the circumstances. This followed the same rules as hooking up with a friend's ex. Absolutely forbidden.

Myles smiled in response, and it was then that Whitney realized she'd never seen him smile like that before. With his mouth and his eyes. It was so dazzlingly white and perfect, she was forced to look away or risk being blinded. She then took a moment to calibrate her breathing.

"Oh yeah? Which firm?"

"Dalton & Pritchard."

"I've heard of them. What kind of law do you practice?" He took a drink of his beer.

"Family law."

If Whitney hadn't been so finely attuned to their exchange, she might have missed the way his expression briefly shuttered and been oblivious to his guard going up. But through it all, his smile remained in place, easygoing and relaxed.

He nodded. "If you're ever in the market, we're always looking for good family lawyers."

Interest flared in her cousin's eyes. "If I'm ever looking, I'll certainly keep that in mind, although it would take a lot to get me to leave San Diego."

"Hey, you never know. Shit happens," he said, shooting a brief look at Whitney.

Mix-ups in fertility lab clinics happened, and they were living proof of it.

"Do you handle divorces?" Troy asked.

"Why, is April looking to get one?" Cheyenne treated him to a cheeky grin. "Tell her to give me a call when she's ready to free herself from the old ball and chain."

Laughing, Troy turned and gazed at his wife, who stood with a few of the other mothers—Rebecca among them—supervising their children playing in the ever-popular inflatable bouncy house. As if sensing her husband's regard, April turned and spotted him. A huge smile broke out over her face. After blowing him a kiss, she returned her attention to their son.

Boy, that was some serious spousal telepathy they had going on. Whitney wondered if she'd ever attain that kind of emotional connection with a man. In all her years of dating and her two serious relationships, it had yet to happen.

Troy turned back to Chey. "Does that look like a woman

searching for a divorce lawyer to you?" he asked with the confidence of a man who knew his marriage was rock-solid and built to go the distance.

"Hey, you were the one who brought up the subject of divorce, so you can't fault me for asking," Chey said, laughing, her hands up in surrender.

Whitney couldn't help but notice that Myles was the only one in the group not laughing. She imagined he was thinking about his soon-to-be ex-wife and the demise of his marriage.

"I hope everyone came with their bathing suits, because Marco Polo's in an hour," Whitney announced in a bright voice. "The kids picked it, so everyone plays. No excuses."

"I can't play in this," Chey said, glancing down at what she was wearing. Her cousin was a little curvier than her, and currently those curves were displayed to their best advantage in the black-and-white-striped bikini she wore under a white cover-up.

"Sure you can. I am, and so are Margo, Trish, and Jess," Whitney said, with a pointed look at three of her castmates sunning by the pool.

At her words, Myles cast a glance down the length of her body, showing a bit more interest than he had previously. But there was something almost clinical about his appraisal, Which dealt an uncharacteristic blow to her ego, forcing her to acknowledge that she wanted him to find her not only attractive but sexually desirable, too.

Suddenly, a child's wail split the air. Whitney turned with a start.

"Daddy, Charlie hit me!" Scott's daughter, Samantha, squirmed out of her mother's arms and took off, barreling toward her father in aggrieved three-year-old histrionics.

"Here we go again," Scott muttered under his breath as he handed Troy his drink. He descended the stairs to the deck just in time to catch her up in his arms. At the scene of the crime, his wife was speaking to their son, the five-year-old culprit and tormenter of his little sister. His friend quickly joined him.

"She hit me first," Charlie cried to his mother, who was on her haunches in front of him, lightly holding his hands.

Everyone had stopped what they were doing to watch the scene play out in front of them, most with amused smiles, while others shook their heads as if recalling the trauma of incidents in *their* pasts. From the side of the pool, Grant caught her eye and mouthed *thank God* while making a hasty sign of the cross across his bare chest. Her costar was the Jake Gyllenhaal of Leonardo DiCaprios and vowed never to cave, as he believed George Clooney had.

Whitney couldn't help but return his smile.

"I'm going to say hi to April," Chey announced. "Be back in a bit, Whit."

In a flash, she was gone.

And then there were two.

"What's that all about?" Myles asked, suddenly right there beside her, only inches separating them. So close she could smell him. As the global brand ambassador for Dior, Whitney had a nose for scents, and whatever he had on smelled amazing.

When she peered up at him, he tipped his chin toward Grant, indicating he'd witnessed their exchange.

"Grant has this thing about kids."

"He doesn't like them?" Myles asked.

"Oh no, he adores them as long as he can give them back to their parents. He just doesn't want any of his own." As one of the most eligible bachelors in Hollywood, Grant wanted it known that when it came to marriage and children, he was the confirmed kind.

"Hmm," was the total sum of Myles's response.

"So, you got yourself a lawyer," he said in a musing, nonconfrontational tone, but his words were not. He knew precisely what he was doing.

"I did not get myself a lawyer," Whitney replied with a smile and a touch of grit in her teeth. "My cousin happens to be a lawyer."

"A family lawyer who mostly handles custody cases?"

"As you of all people should know, we don't get to pick our families. Sometimes you win, and sometimes you get really lucky. I got both." Whitney flashed a thinnish smile.

"We had an agreement."

"I know, and I haven't done anything to break it."

"Are you sure?"

"Are you accusing me of lying?" She should have been surprised or offended. She was neither.

"I just want to make sure we're still on the same page."

"Nothing's changed on my part. Has anything changed with you?" she asked, all wide-eyed innocence. "I assume you haven't hired outside counsel."

"I have no reason to."

"Good, then neither have I." Out of the corner of her eye, she caught a glimpse of Cam making his way down the stone walkway toward the backyard.

Upon spotting her, Cam cheerfully returned her wave.

"If you'll excuse me, Myles, it looks like my last guest has arrived." Whitney then made a move to leave.

Myles shot a quick look at Cam. "We're still on for tomorrow?"

"Of course," she said. "I wouldn't miss it for the world."

12

"Nat, where the hell are you? You said you'd be here in twenty minutes *an hour ago*."

Myles was more annoyed than anxious. At least, that was what he told himself as he played lookout by the window in his living room.

It wouldn't be the crime of the century if Haylee were late for the second visit with her biological mother. But he felt under the microscope as it was, his role as Haylee's father and only parent already found wanting. He could do without the judgment. And his sister knew the position he was in and had easy access to the time, weather, and maps. She could've at least called to let him know that she was running even later. It was now quarter to twelve, and Whitney would be here in fifteen minutes.

"I'm sorry," his sister said, sounding breathless. "But your nephew broke the crystal vase Brad's grandmother gave us for our fifth anniversary, and I had to clean it up."

"Why couldn't Brad do it?"

"Because Jonah had a meltdown when I wouldn't let him play with the broken pieces. The choice was either I clean up the mess or deal with your screaming nephew, because I sure as hell wasn't going to do both. I decided I'd rather walk on the broken glass and let his father deal with him."

His nephew wasn't just a handful, he was two handfuls and a half, and had yet to officially enter the terrible two stage, which was said to be worse. He prayed to God his daughter would be more like his niece. Then he remembered Sophie's penchant for picking up curse words from adults and repeating them back at the most inappropriate times. Yes, even better.

"But don't worry, I'm on my way. We should be there soon."

Frowning, Myles switched the phone to his other ear. "I should have come and gotten her myself," he muttered.

"What sense would that have made? You asked me to meet Sahara and give you my opinion, and that's what I'm going to do today. Anyway, I shouldn't be that late."

"Alright. I'll see you in—" He broke off when he saw an unfamiliar metallic-blue Mercedes turn onto his cul-de-sac and slow to a crawl. "Damn. I think she's here," he said when it stopped in front of his house. "I gotta go. See you in a few."

Keeping his eyes trained on the car, Myles watched the passenger door open and Whitney Richardson emerge, looking like she was on her way to a photoshoot instead of a child visitation appointment. The uniformed driver, who rushed to open the door for her, arrived seconds too late. Myles couldn't hear what she said, but she smilingly dismissed his assistance with a careless wave of her hand.

He wasn't sure why, but he hadn't expected a chauffeur. At least not for personal trips like this. Whitney Richardson seemed the kind of person who valued her independence and guarded her privacy too much to have someone privy to her whereabouts every minute of the day.

But that just went to show how little he knew about her. The mother of his child was still very much a stranger to him.

Myles moved away from the window and waited for the doorbell to ring before making the short walk to the front door. Couldn't have her mistaking his promptness for eagerness.

"Hi. You're early." He stated it as a fact, not a criticism, or at least, that was his intention.

Speaking of eagerness.

Whitney treated him to a dimpled smile. "I hope that's okay. I didn't want to be late, and you know how traffic can be around here."

"Right." Myles stepped aside. "Come in. My sister's running late, so Haylee isn't here yet, but they shouldn't be long."

A fleeting look of surprise crossed her face as he closed the door behind her. "Oh, okay."

Then, as if realizing she was going to be alone with him for who knew how long, she motioned behind her. "I can wait in the car if you want," she said, making it clear ten minutes alone with him was probably nine minutes too long.

"I think your chauffeur is already gone."

"He can't have gotten that far," she said, already riffling through her purse and pulling out her phone.

Myles's brow furrowed. She couldn't be serious. "Put that away," he said, gesturing at her phone. "Why don't we wait in the family room?"

Whitney stilled and tentatively regarded him. "Are you sure?"

"Sure about what?"

"It's just that you look like you don't want me here," she said matter-of-factly.

He didn't, but it wasn't supposed to be obvious. Or better yet, she wasn't supposed to call him out on it.

"What gives you that impression?" he found himself asking out of curiosity. He'd like to think he was being cordial, if nothing else.

Myles hated to admit it, but Whitney Richardson intrigued

him. She looked younger than her age, she was the head of a billion-dollar company, she had an incredible voice, she could act, she was fucking gorgeous, she hadn't asked for any of this, and yet here she was. At his house, waiting for his daughter. The cynic in him was convinced there had to be an angle, and he needed to find out what it was.

"First, I think you're still upset about me speaking to my cousin about our situation, even though you're a lawyer too, and one with an entire law firm at your disposal."

He hadn't become a lawyer to thwart her eleven years later, but she had a point.

"Second, you refuse to call me by my first name, which is silly since I have two to choose from."

Okay, he'd start calling her by her first name, and again, she was right. His reluctance to do so bordered on childish.

"And last, it was the way you said *your chauffeur*. As if you're judging me for having one." She paused before saying, "You're going to find out eventually, so I may as well tell you. I can't drive."

They hadn't moved beyond the entryway and stood facing each other, his bare feet to her wedge sandals.

Myles blinked. "You can't drive?" He'd never met an able-bodied, fully functioning adult who couldn't drive. It was almost impossible to get around the LA area without a car.

Whitney shook her head.

"But why?" he asked, still incredulous.

At her rueful laugh, Myles felt the tension between them all but disappear.

"Because where I grew up, I didn't need a car to get around, and we only had one car, which my mother used to get to work. Since my dad worked in the city, he took the train into New York. Plus, adding me to their insurance would have raised the rates sky-high."

"Okay. So when the cost of insurance wasn't an issue, why didn't you get it then?"

"I don't know," she said, her slender shoulders lifting and falling in a shrug. "Between recording, touring, and everything else, there never seemed to be enough time in the day. And on a list of priorities, learning to drive didn't crack the top ten. Plus, my record label always made sure I had transportation to get where I needed to be. Then, you know how it goes. After a while, I just forgot about it."

"So it's not that you have a fear of driving or anything like that?" She didn't sound as if she'd been involved in a life-changing car crash.

Whitney shook her head again. "Nope, nothing like that. I guess you could say at this point, I haven't made it a priority. But I plan to learn…one day. Actually, now that we're talking about it, I probably need to get it done sooner rather than later."

"Why, because of Haylee?"

Tilting her head to the side, she studied him, her expression thoughtful. "I get the feeling you wouldn't want Haylee being chauffeured around. Hell," she said, a hint of teasing in her voice, "you made it pretty clear that you don't approve of it for me either."

"That's not it at all," he lied, trying not to come across as petty and judgmental, both of which he was guilty of when it came to her. "I just think a driver's license is a good thing to have."

"You're right, it is. And since it seems to be so important to you that I get mine, I promise I'll get it by the end of the year."

Before he could respond, the front door suddenly swung open behind them. He turned to see a startled Natalie staring wide-eyed at him and Whitney, holding his sleeping daughter.

Noting a slight family resemblance, Whitney ascertained that the woman, who looked a bit like Natalie Portman, must be Myles's sister. The siblings had identical smiles.

Upon seeing them, she froze, and a look of surprise flashed in her hazel eyes at nearly tripping over them at the door. The look was quickly followed by a breathless, "We're here." A smile curved her lips as her gaze met Whitney's. "Hi, I'm Natalie, Myles's sister. Sorry we're late."

Whitney tore her gaze from her sleeping daughter and returned the woman's friendly greeting. "Hi, Natalie, I'm Whitney. It's nice to meet you."

Jumping into action, Myles gently lifted Haylee from his sister's arms. "Here, let me take her."

When he made a motion to relieve his sister of the diaper bag, Whitney intercepted, grabbing the strap as it slid off Natalie's shoulder. "I'll take that."

As Haylee's mother, she might as well make herself useful. It looked like she wasn't going to be holding her anytime soon as Haylee's father was busy asserting his paternal rights.

As if reading her mind, Myles looked at her and said, "Don't worry, she'll be up in a few minutes. She always falls asleep in the car."

Whitney knew that about babies. "That's okay. I have nowhere else to go today. I can wait her out." That was probably what he was afraid of.

"Natalie, why don't you entertain Ms. Ri—Whitney while I take care of Haylee." He and his sister exchanged a meaningful look.

"It would be my pleasure," Natalie said, beaming. Unlike her brother, she looked genuinely happy to get to know her.

Myles was still in the *fake it until you don't have to fake it anymore* stage, but he appeared to be making an effort since he'd learned that for her, having a driver was a matter of necessity. And for the first time *ever*, he'd called her by her first name. Hopefully one day soon, he wouldn't have to fake it with her.

While Myles took Haylee upstairs, Whitney accompanied

his sister down the hall and into the family room, where they made themselves comfortable on the sofa and armchair.

"It's so nice to finally meet you," Natalie said, grinning. "You're just as gorgeous as your pictures. And I'm not going to lie, I did ask my brother about that," she confessed, her tone affectionately conspiratorial.

Whitney couldn't help but warm to her. How could she not? Myles's sister was friendly and engaging and didn't treat her as a threat to everything she held dear.

"I can see where my niece gets her looks."

Whitney's face warmed with pleasure. Until those words, she hadn't realized how much she'd been seeking some validation that Haylee was part of her. "After meeting you, I can't take full credit. I can definitely see you in her." Myles hadn't been lying about that.

"You should see my baby pictures. My mom swears Haylee looks more like me at that age than my own daughter," Natalie said, and in her eyes, Whitney could see the love she had for her niece.

Not that she hadn't believed Myles when he'd said his sister loved Haylee as if she was one of her own, but seeing it for herself allayed many of her concerns.

In the next beat, Natalie turned serious. "My brother is afraid you're going to try and take Haylee from him. Are you?"

Surprised, mostly at her frankness, Whitney gaped at her. "Wh— No!"

"I didn't think so, but I had to ask. You understand that, don't you?" she asked in a way Whitney found endearing. The woman loved her brother and her niece and was understandably protective of them.

"I love Haylee," Whitney said, "and it's obvious he does too. I would never try and take her away from him. All I want is to be a mother to her…if your brother lets me."

"He will," Natalie said with the confidence of someone who loved him and had more faith in him than Whitney did. "Right now, it's hard for him to trust—" After a pause and a hard swallow, she continued, "—since things ended with Holly." Her expression became tentative. "He told me you know about that."

"Yes, that they're getting divorced." Whitney wondered if she knew he'd intended to keep her in the dark. She highly doubted it.

"Give him time. As long as you're there and make Haylee a priority, Myles will come around."

"She is a priority," Whitney assured her. "She couldn't be higher on my list." The moment she made the decision to *be* her mother, she'd been all-in, and time had only solidified her commitment to her daughter.

That appeared to satisfy Natalie, whom Whitney was certain had come here specifically to render judgment and report back to her brother. It was something she and Chey had done to prospective boyfriends before.

"Which is all anyone can ask for," Natalie said.

With the super serious part of the discussion over, the women were chatting like long-lost friends when Myles returned with Haylee. She was awake now, her eyes wide and alert.

"Coming through," Myles said. "I got a hungry princess on my hands."

Whitney came eagerly to her feet, her arms itching to hold her, but she kept them at her sides as he approached. "I can help. What do you want me to do?" She'd show him. She was going to be the best damn mother he'd ever seen.

After shooting his sister a look Whitney couldn't decipher, he addressed Whitney. "Would you mind holding her?"

The way he said it, it could have been a throwaway line in a scene, but she was well aware of its importance. He was trying.

"I would love to," she replied softly, giving her daughter

her undivided attention. "Hey, sweetheart," she cooed. Hay-lee stared up at her, her eyes round and curious.

Slowly, Myles eased her into Whitney's arms, giving her plenty of time to pull away if she wanted, and there was lit-tle Whitney could do but hold out her arms, hold her breath, and pray.

Haylee's gaze sought her father's as if seeking his assurance. Once again, Whitney had to remind herself that to her daugh-ter, she was a stranger. Who even knew if Haylee remembered her from the first visit?

"It's okay, princess," he said in encouragement.

Watching the naturalness and the intimacy of their interac-tion made her heart ache in a way Whitney had never experi-enced before. That Myles loved and adored Haylee was obvious. Whitney, in many ways, stood on the outside looking in at the child who, in a matter of days, had captured her heart, and the man with the power to grant or bar her entry.

Today, he was granting her entry, and for that she was grateful.

With a gurgled sound of delight, Haylee stretched her chubby little body toward her. Whitney practically snatched her from him and cuddled her close. Haylee immediately grabbed her diamond teardrop earring.

Between laughter and winces, Whitney carefully extricated the diamond from her tight grip. "You like my earrings, huh? Don't worry, sweetheart, Mo—I'll buy you a pair when you're older."

She'd almost said it. *Mommy.* If either sibling caught the slip, neither let on. But what did she call herself when she was with her daughter? She snuck a peak at Myles and found him star-ing at her. Whitney hurriedly looked away.

The next hour went by too quickly. Playtime started with the bubble maker and ended with too many rounds of peekaboo to count. Whitney's heart was full to overflowing with love for her daughter, savoring every cuddle and smile like a recently unearthed hidden treasure. The final game of peeka-boo ended when Haylee crawled into her lap and fell asleep.

Whitney looked up at Myles from where she sat cross-legged on the family room floor. "It must be naptime."

"Here, give her to me. I'll put her down," he said, rising from the couch where he and his sister had been observing the interplay between mother and daughter, joining in at times.

Whitney's arms involuntarily tightened around her. She didn't want to let her go. He had Haylee all the time.

"I can do—"

"Myles, why don't you let Whitney do the honors?" Natalie said, cutting Whitney off and treating her brother to a pointed look.

Myles froze, his gaze flicking from his sister to her. "Sure. If you want to."

"Of course she wants to, Myles." Natalie's tone was mildly chastising. "She's her mother."

At that moment, Whitney elevated her daughter's aunt to sainthood, because it was clear the woman had been put here to do God's work.

Whitney sent her a grateful smile as she hoisted Haylee to her shoulder and rose smoothly to her feet.

Natalie stood. "I'll show you where her room is."

Myles merely nodded, allowing his sister to call the shots.

"Like I said, give him a little time to get used to…things," Natalie whispered as they climbed the stairs to the second floor. "He's the only boy in the family, so he's not used to sharing."

"Uh-oh. I'm an only child, so what does that make me?" Whitney said lightly.

Natalie motioned to the first door past the loft. "It makes you the only mother Haylee's ever had."

Five minutes later—one for a diaper check and four to watch her daughter as she slept—they returned downstairs to find Myles standing in the hall, close enough to the front door that she couldn't miss his obvious hint. He'd done his good deed for the day. Now it was *au revoir. Adios. Goodbye. Vamoose.*

"She's all tuckered out, so I guess my work here is done." Whitney directed the teasing comment at Myles, hoping to coax a smile from the stern line of his mouth.

"You're so good with her," Natalie said. "If you ever feel like taking on another two, remember she has cousins nearby."

Whitney laughed at that. "I can't wait to meet them." She turned to Myles. "I need to call Cedrick to pick me up, and then I'll be out of your hair."

"I can give you a lift home if you want," Natalie volunteered.

"That's okay. I'll be fine. But this is one of those times I wish I could drive," she admitted with a self-conscious laugh.

Natalie let out an audible gasp. "You can't drive?"

Seriously, Whitney was sure she'd get the same reaction if she admitted to being a serial killer. Not knowing how to drive wasn't a crime, but it appeared to some it came pretty damn close.

A glimmer of amusement lit Myles's eyes, but he remained silent.

"No, but as I assured your brother, I plan to get my license by the end of the year."

"I didn't get my license until I was eighteen, and Myles was the one who taught me to drive. And for someone who only had his license for two years, he was a pretty good teacher."

"Hold on," Whitney said, confused because the math wasn't mathing. "I thought he was older than you." By a couple years at least.

"He is by ten minutes."

Now it was Whitney's turn to gasp. "Oh my god, you're

twins?" she exclaimed, her gaze bouncing between the two, trying to see if there was more resemblance that she'd overlooked.

"Myles didn't tell you?" Natalie regarded him accusingly.

"What?" he said, shrugging as if he couldn't understand what the big deal was. "The subject never came up."

"When does the question *are you a twin* ever come up in conversation?" his sister asked tartly, sending Whitney the *see what I have to put up with* look. "You have to tell people, Myles. They won't be able to tell by just looking at us. You're six inches taller."

Whitney snorted a laugh. She loved Natalie's sense of humor.

But that explained how close they were, why she had a key to his house and walked in as if she lived there, and why she was so close to Haylee. They had that twin bond thing going on. *We shared a womb together* and all that.

"Anyhoo," Natalie said, sighing and rolling her eyes. "You should have Myles teach you, although I'm not sure he deserves to now."

"No, that's okay." Then, realizing the hair-trigger quickness of her response, Whitney attempted to soften her refusal. "I mean, I'm sure he's a great teacher, but I couldn't put him out like that. Cedrick would be more than willing to teach me."

"I'd be happy to teach you," Myles said, and she couldn't tell if he was doing it to save his sister for offering up his services without checking with him first. He had a quietness about him that made him difficult to read.

Whitney didn't know what to say. Then she did what any mother wanting more contact with her child would do. Try to get on his good side. "That's nice of you."

He gave a curt nod. "Just let me know when you're ready."

"Thank you, I will."

If he thought she'd forget and wouldn't take him up on his

offer, he was going to be in for a surprise. *Operation: Win Over Haylee's Daddy* had just kicked into full gear.

If she didn't succeed at her mission, it wouldn't be because she hadn't given it her all—and then some.

13

"You're late." Myles's greeting was terse, and not a greeting at all. "And Haylee's sleeping."

Whitney grimaced as she strode beside him down the hall. "I know. I'm sorry." Her breaths came in soft pants, as if she'd sprinted from the car to the house. "I had to Uber it, and of course, today of all days, traffic was worse than usual."

In the past twenty-four hours, Myles had seen no less than three articles covering the highs and lows of Sahara's love life. One said she was seeing three different men, and the pictures provided suggested she was. Another claimed a source close to her said she'd gotten back with the tennis player. Suffice it to say, he was in no mood to listen to any excuses from her.

If she couldn't handle her careers, "motherhood," *and* juggling all her men, then it was best she acknowledge that now so they could cut their losses and go their separate ways. Children deserved a parent who, at a minimum, showed up.

Once they crossed the threshold to the family room, he turned to her. "In the future, if you're going to be late, I just ask that you do me the courtesy of letting me know." Out of consideration for his time, if for no other reason. Haylee wasn't old enough to know when her mother shirked her duties, but that day would inevitably come.

Watching her expression transform was like witnessing the gathering of storm clouds. Her eyes narrowed, and her mouth compressed into a line of displeasure. "You're right. I should have let you know I was running late. But after spending three hours at the ER this morning after my driver fell down the stairs at *my* home, I wasn't even sure I'd be able to make it today. I would have had to call and cancel if Cedrick's mother and girl-friend hadn't shown up."

Oh fuck!

Myles bit back a groan. He'd screwed up.

Chastened, he lowered his head and muttered, "I'm sorry about your driver. I hope he's going to be okay."

"It's a hairline fracture, and he has to wear a cast for six to eight weeks, but the doctor said he'll be fine." She sounded as stiff as her posture, which was rigid.

"Well, I'm glad it's nothing more serious."

What followed was a silence that lasted long enough to be categorized as uncomfortable.

Whitney finally broke it with, "Do you want to know why I didn't contact you when I knew for sure I was going to be late?" She paused, her chest rising and falling on a dramatic inhalation of breath.

Myles did his best not to follow the movement but failed to prevent his gaze from darting down to her breasts before returning to her face.

"Because I knew that if I did, you would've told me not to come."

He opened his mouth to refute the claim even though he knew what she said was true.

"Don't you dare try to deny it," she continued, cutting him off. "You know damn well you would have."

Myles blinked. That was the closest she'd ever come to cursing at him. Although according to his niece, *damn* was a bad word, and Sophie should know as keeper of the family curse jar.

"You've been waiting for me to screw up. Waiting for a reason to criticize me. Any reason. Today, I get here and you're all Mr. Sourpuss Face because I was twenty freaking minutes late. Yet a few weeks ago, when your sister was late and I was the one who had to wait, you didn't see me pitching a fit."

Myles instinctively became defensive. "I wasn't pitching a fit. I simply asked for some consideration for my time."

A part of him thought—maybe even hoped, if he were being honest with himself—that her interest in Haylee would have begun to wane by now. That her multiple careers would have retaken center stage in her life, and she'd be too busy to keep up with the visitation schedule they'd agreed to. Then he'd made the mistake of reading stories about her harem of men. So when one o'clock had arrived with no word from a woman who'd always been punctual, he'd been angry. And when she finally showed up, he'd been itching for a fight.

But the truth was that Whitney Richardson was everything he could've hoped for, never missing a visit and showering Haylee with all the love Holly never did. If one of them had a right to be mad, it was her at him.

A wave of guilt accompanied that realization. What the fuck was wrong with him? Why was he being so hard on her?

It didn't happen often, but sometimes he had to eat crow and swallow it down dry. Now was one of them. "You're right, and I'm sorry for being an ass."

Her head jerked slightly back. She looked more surprised by his apology than his unwarranted attack. "You should be," came her sharp reprimand.

Sighing, Myles thrust his hands in his pockets. He had to get a grip, and in order to do that, he had to figure out what it was about her that had him acting so out of character.

"I'm going now." She spoke quietly as she transferred her handbag to the other shoulder. Despite his apology, she looked anything but vindicated or appeased, and he hated being the cause of the defeated look on her face.

Ignoring the voice in his head telling him to leave well enough alone and let her go, he found himself saying, "You don't have to leave."

She glanced at the staircase to the second floor. "I thought you said Haylee's sleeping."

"She went down almost two hours ago, so she should be up any minute now." He could only pray.

Turning back to him, her gaze met his. "Are you telling me she was already asleep when I was supposed to arrive?"

Myles understood what she was getting at, and his face warmed in embarrassment. "I was going to call and warn you."

"But you didn't, did you?" she said, the entire incident now coming full circle in three hundred and sixty degrees of irony.

"I thought by the time you got here, she'd be up."

It must have pained her not to call him out on his hypocrisy, but she didn't. At least, not with words.

"What did I tell you? I was being an ass," he said, this time attempting to elicit a smile from her.

"That's one thing we can agree on." She sniffed. And then, seconds later, a whisper of a smile crossed her face, causing his chest to constrict.

"Stay," he insisted. "Unless you have somewhere else to go." For all he knew, she'd made plans for after the visit. According to the tabloids, she did have three men to juggle.

Cocking her head to the side, Whitney studied him for several long beats. "You know, I do have a lot of places to go,

Myles, but I'm going to stay because there's nowhere I'd rather be than here visiting my daughter."

"Come on, then. She should be up soon. In the meantime, let me grab the baby monitor, and you and I can talk. Get to know each other a little better."

It was time to find out if what was written in all those articles was true. Did she or did she not have a man in her life?

Why he cared was a question for another day.

So much for her charm offensive. After weeks of success, *Operation: Win Over Haylee's Daddy* was on life support. The question now was, could it be saved?

Certainly, his suggestion that they get to know each other better was preferable to him jumping down her throat for every minor infraction she committed. She also recognized a peace offering when she saw it and she didn't have the heart to refuse.

They sat opposite each other at the patio table in the back by the pool, a huge umbrella shading them from the sun. Myles was nursing a cold beer, and she was enjoying an iced glass of lemonade. The baby monitor sat in the middle of the table, sounds of rustling emanating from the speaker.

"So, Whitney, what do you like to do for fun?" he asked out of the gate, with no warning.

"Um. I like to read, watch movies—good ones—hang out with friends, and go for walks in the park." Whitney grimaced inwardly. The last one sounded like a corny line from a dating app. She hoped he didn't get the wrong idea.

"That doesn't sound very Hollywood. You don't like going to the parties?"

Whitney shook her head. "For the most part, I only go to the ones I have to because they're a part of my job. And sometimes even that can be too much. Most of my friends aren't in the business, so when we get together, it's pretty low-key and private."

"What about relationships? Are you seeing anyone?"

Whitney's eyes widened. Well, that escalated quickly.

His tone was nonchalant, but his eyes told a different story, expressing a keen interest in her response.

"You know that I'm getting a divorce…"

"So it's only fair that you know if I'm seeing anyone? Is that how this works?" she asked, smirking.

"If you're seeing someone, you'll want to tell them about Haylee. For instance, Cam Mitchell knows about Haylee, and as far as I know, the two of you aren't related," he said in a deceptively conversational tone.

"He told you?" She was going to kill him. Kennedy told him not to say a word to anyone. But that explained how chummy the men had looked at the party. She'd equated it to them being the same age, not them getting *that* personal.

"He didn't have to," Myles drawled. "He was the only one at the party who asked about Haylee more than once. It was clear he knew something."

Damn you, Cam. "I didn't tell him. I told his sister and our friend Aurora, who accidentally said something about it when Kennedy was on the phone with him. He promised he wouldn't tell anyone."

Myles continued to watch her.

Whitney let out a nervous laugh. "There's nothing going on between me and Cam. We're just friends."

"That's what he said too."

"And you didn't believe him?"

"I believe him now that I know you didn't tell him about you and Haylee," he said, appearing more at ease. "Which is good, because I liked the guy. He offered to manage my money, and I may just let him."

Cam was in wealth management and had made the same offer to her. He currently managed ten percent of her portfolio, and so far, so good.

"Well, I'm not seeing him or anyone, so you don't have to worry about that. And I wouldn't introduce anyone to Haylee unless we were serious. By that time, my relationship to her should already be public." As it was, she didn't have time to date, much less be in a committed relationship.

Myles nodded sagely before taking a long swallow of his beer.

"What about you? What do you do when you're not working or taking care of Haylee?"

"These days? Not much except go to the gym."

The gym. That explained the superb condition he was in. The man could definitely rock a pair of jeans, and his chest and shoulders sure knew how to fill out the T-shirt he was wearing.

"Really? Which gym? I've been meaning to join one." Five years ago, when she was young and stupid.

"Rally Fitness on Wiltshire Boulevard. It's close to my office." He took another drink of his beer. "You should give it a try."

Whitney smiled. "I just might. Thanks for the rec." A beat of silence elapsed. "I take it you're not seeing anyone either."

Her question was met with an arched brow. "Didn't I just say I'm currently going through a divorce?"

"That doesn't mean you're not casually seeing someone." To some married couples, filing the papers meant they were as good as free.

He chuckled. "Then to answer your question, no, I'm not seeing anyone, casually or otherwise."

"Okay, how about this? Why did you pick a fight with me today? And I want the truth." She'd been warming up for this, and by the look on his face, it was clear he hadn't seen the question coming.

Quick to recover, he came back with, "I don't pick fights."

Whitney wasn't surprised that his initial response would be an unequivocal denial.

"Maybe not generally, but you have with me. Twice," she said, holding up two fingers.

Myles opened his mouth as if to issue another denial but then closed it abruptly. He stared at her as he toyed with his glass.

Whitney gave a start when she felt something brush her bare leg under the table. It took a moment to realize it was his leg. She recognized the rough feel of the denim against her calf.

"Sorry about that," he muttered, quickly moving his leg away. "I was just stretching."

They were like two long-tailed cats in a room full of rocking chairs.

"I'm still waiting." She refused to allow him to dodge the question.

"If I do, I don't mean to pick fights with you."

Whitney shook her head. "Nope, that's not an answer. Try again."

"I said I was sorry. I thought we put it behind us."

Maybe he had, but she hadn't put it behind her. At least not fully.

"Because I don't want this to keep happening. I don't want to have to walk on eggshells when I'm around you. I'm human. I'm going to make mistakes, and I don't want to worry about which ones will turn you into judgmental Mr. Sourpuss. Do you realize that you're holding me to a standard that you wouldn't hold yourself to? That I wouldn't hold you to if our positions were reversed?"

Myles didn't respond for what felt like an inordinate amount of time. His eyes shifted between her and the sweaty glass at his fingertips, an almost brooding quality to his gaze.

If nothing else, she'd gotten him thinking. Hopefully, he

was reflecting on the specific incidents and how he was going to make it up to her.

"I'm not going to say *put yourself in my place*, because I don't think your place is any easier." He paused. "It's probably worse in some ways. I hate to say this, but when I look at you, I see a celebrity. Your face is recognized all over the world, and you're a household name. I think because of that, sometimes it's hard for me to see you as Haylee's mother."

"Are you calling me a diva?" Translation: stuck-up. It wasn't as if it hadn't been said about her before. At her ten-year high school reunion, a few girls had said it to her face when she'd ignored their overtures of friendship. As if she couldn't spot a clout chaser when she saw one—much less three—especially when they were the same girls who'd made fun of her back in high school.

"Because I'm as down-to-earth as they come," she continued in her defense. Okay, so she didn't know how to drive, or cook, and owned a company that had recently been valued at $1.4 billion. That didn't mean she wasn't down-to-earth.

"I didn't call you that."

He didn't have to say it. She could read above, below, and in between all the lines.

"Okay, then, what do you mean when you say it's hard for you to see me as Haylee's mother?" she asked. "Is it because we didn't have sex?"

It happened rarely—like a total solar eclipse. But sometimes Whitney gave voice to thoughts that shouldn't see the light of day. This was one of them.

Myles stared at her in shocked silence while she wallowed in the mortified version of it.

"What did you say?" He sounded as if his throat needed clearing and maybe his ears too, because he asked her to repeat it, something she wouldn't do if he paid her.

Whitney knew she could handle this in one of two ways. She could grimace in embarrassment and tell him she was sorry if what she said offended him or made him uncomfortable. Or she could try to bullshit her way out of it.

After the scantest bit of introspection, she decided bullshitting was the only way to go.

"I mean, because we didn't have her the old-fashioned way."

"If I'm not mistaken, sex is the old-fashioned way." He said it with a straight face while his eyes bored into her.

In seconds flat, her face felt feverish enough to have her admitted to the ICU. But far from a hospital bed, what she needed was a sinkhole to disappear into.

"What I mean is that as her biological father, you expected to have an intimate connection to her mother, whom you naturally assumed would be your wife. So I think you'd be saying the same thing about anyone who isn't her," she said on her third attempt to save face.

Myles continued to stare at her, his expression giving away not one iota of his thoughts. Then he slowly nodded. "Yes, that's probably what it is."

It wasn't, and they both knew it. But sometimes it was better to let sleeping dogs lie...through their teeth.

14

Whitney could count on one hand the number of her friends who would pick her up at cock-a-doodle-doo o'clock in the morning and accompany her to the gym. Actually, forget the entire hand. She only needed one finger, and that friend was Trinity.

A striking, lanky brunette, Trinity Rogers was Oasis's creative director in charge of brand management and marketing and Whitney's first hire. She was also one of the few friends she'd told about Haylee.

Trinity had arrived at her place five minutes earlier in a green one-piece bodysuit, looking ready to crush the competition in her next 10k marathon.

When Whitney wanted to relax, she read a book under an umbrella by the pool or flopped on the couch and watched TV. Trinity, strange creature that she was, ran. Or more accurately, she jogged for long periods and distances. Whitney had one rule when it came to running. She did it only when someone was chasing her.

"So you're really doing this, huh?" The skeptic in Trinity

found it difficult to believe that the same person who disdainfully used the term "organized workouts" to describe gyms had actually joined one. "I half expected you to still be in bed when I got here."

Trinity had recently returned from a two-month-long business trip to Europe, and this was the first time they'd seen each other in person in as many months.

Whitney stared at her reflection in the floor-length mirror of her walk-in closet. "Yep, ready to work up a sweat." Her heart would thank her, and her hair would get revenge by frizzing up.

"I thought the only sweating you like to do was between the sheets?"

"I never said that." She might have implied it, but those words had never come out of her mouth. Although one could argue that sweating it up between the sheets was better for the skin. Or so one of her exes once claimed.

"No, but it's true, isn't it?"

Whitney couldn't argue with her there. But it had to be sex with a man who knew what he was doing. Too many of them simply did not, and as much as she loved a man with an excellent foreplay game, he also needed to be able to end things with a bang of the big O variety.

"I told you, Myles goes to the gym, and I'm trying to show him that I'm a regular person. Like the typical mother next door. My life isn't all limousines, concerts, and red-carpet events." It would have shocked most people if they knew how small a part of her life those things were. As glamorous as being a celebrity appeared to those outside of the business, the day-to-day grind of movie-making and performing was anything but.

Trinity propped her hands on her hips and eyed her from head to toe. "You think that him seeing you working out in *that* is going to get him to see you as a regular person?" Her raised brow conveyed clear skepticism.

"What do you mean? What's wrong with what I'm wearing?" Whitney twisted around to get a closer look at a rear view of herself in the mirror. She was wearing standard workout gear, red-and-black yoga pants and a matching sports bra—one of the ones that crisscrossed in the back. Everything appeared to be tight, toned, and in working order. She attributed most of that to genetics and a tiny bit of her being fairly active during the day. Only in the past few years had she started watching what she ate. She watched the ice cream pass her lips, melt on her tongue, and slide easy-peasy down her throat.

"Nothing, and that's the problem."

Whitney rolled her eyes. Pretty was as pretty does. She wasn't everyone's taste.

The way Myles reacted when she'd suggested he couldn't picture her as Haylee's mother because they'd never been in a sexual relationship told her the man was *not* interested.

And she should have been happy about that. One less attraction she had to fight, because if there was one thing Whitney Richardson wasn't, it was a glutton for punishment. She wasn't attracted to men who weren't interested in her. Seriously, what was the point?

Trinity sighed. "Okay, first of all, you are a regular person—whatever that means. And honestly, if you want him to see you doing normal stuff, you should have him drop by your house when you're cleaning. That's as down-to-earth and real as most people get. Haven't you had a chance to change your kid's poopy diaper?"

"Yes, more than once." Whitney chuckled, remembering the poop explosion, and how Myles had handed Haylee to her with a facetious, *"Welcome to motherhood. Enjoy."*

"And that wasn't everyday people enough for you?"

"I want him to see me doing something that has nothing to

do with Haylee, and it's not as if I'm going to ask him to go grocery shopping with me."

"Don't you get your groceries delivered?" Trinity was quick to ask, therefore missing her point entirely.

"Which is why going to his gym is my only option. It isn't as if we hang out at the same places or I'm likely to bump into him while I'm out running errands. Except for Haylee, our lives don't overlap or intersect, and we don't have much in common. I also figured this would give us something to talk about when I visit."

"Yes, your mutual love of exercise," Trinity said dryly.

"At least he'll be able to see me outside of his office and his house." She could only imagine how hot he looked in his workout gear, sweaty from exerting all that energy. She bet he looked even hotter when he used that energy to pleasure a woman in bed, namely her.

Whitney didn't know if that was the angel or devil on her shoulder whispering, *Nope. Not him, babe. He's not for you.*

"Which gym are we going to? I'm afraid you're going to cause a mini riot."

Pushing inappropriate thoughts aside, Whitney replied, "Rally Fitness. And don't worry, it has celebrity members. No one is going to bother me there." She'd personally checked out the place before signing up for a trial membership. Taylor Swift and Zac Efron were members, so she was safe.

"Come on, then. You look gorgeous—"

Whitney rolled her eyes.

"—in a regular, mother-of-a-young-child, down-to-earth way, so let's go," Trinity said, executing the midsentence course correction with a guileless smile.

"Don't go overboard," Whitney muttered, feigning annoyance.

"Now, come the fuck on, woman," Trinity said, clapping

her hands together, part cheerleader, part drill sergeant. "Those weights aren't going to lift themselves. But then again, you probably aren't going to lift them either," she said, cackling.

"Ha ha ha. Very funny." Whitney gave her the finger. Then she grabbed a red satin hair band and wrangled her hair into a ponytail. Having thick hair had its drawbacks, especially when it was hot. To keep the sweat-to-frizz ratio at a minimum, she tossed a headband into her purse. Her hair was straight now, but it wouldn't be for long.

Grabbing her duffel bag off the closet island, she said, "Okay, I'm ready. Let's go."

At the gym, the guy at the front desk did a subtle double take when checking Whitney's identification. There was no whiplashing of the neck or anything like that, just two successive very intense stares. Her real name wasn't a secret, but for the most part, only her die-hard fans knew it. If he recognized her, he didn't let on.

"He's cute," Trinity whispered once they were out of earshot.

"He also looks like he's barely out of college." Whitney snorted in amusement.

Trinity shot him a quick look over her shoulder. "There's no way he's younger than twenty-four, twenty-five."

"And you my dear, are thirty-five. Besides the obvious," Whitney said dryly, "what would you want with a man his age? Their frontal lobes aren't even fully developed."

"The obvious," Trinity deadpanned.

They both burst out laughing.

Since Whitney had declined the obligatory tour, they were on their own. They made a beeline to the area with all the weight training equipment, which was empty save a man on the other side of the room at one of the bench presses.

"Come on," Whitney said as she headed toward the free

weights. "My arms could use some toning." She needed to be doing something if and when Myles arrived. He told her he was usually at the gym by six-thirty, worked out for an hour, and was showered, dressed, and in the office before eight-thirty. Which meant he should be here in fifteen minutes, more than enough time to have her working up a sweat.

"You mean these little twigs?" Trinity playfully poked her arm.

"That's exactly why they could use some muscle." Whitney had been, if not painfully skinny as a child, close to it. She'd had the knobby knees and all that. Kids at school would tease her mercilessly. She spent the majority of her early teen years going to singing lessons and trying to gain weight. Ten pounds had been her goal. It had taken her years to get to the weight she was most comfortable.

Thank God for college and the freshman fifteen said almost no one ever, except her. While her suitemates bemoaned the weight gain, Whitney had been thrilled to finally have hips, boobs, and a bit of a butt. What a confidence builder that had been. However, the days when she could eat what she wanted and not gain weight were behind her.

Once they reached the free weight area, she grabbed two fifteen-pound weights off the rack. Not too heavy for a newbie like her. She immediately began doing curls.

Trinity watched with hands propped on her hips and a long-suffering look on her face. "You have no idea what you're doing, do you?"

"What?" Whitney looked at her askance. "I'm working my biceps. It's not exactly rocket science." Evidenced by the fact that ten reps in, she was already starting to feel the burn.

"It isn't when you're doing it wrong. Take it from someone who was actually trained by a professional. You're doing them too fast. You need to slow down to get the maximum benefit.

And you want to stand with your legs apart like this." Trinity demonstrated by widening her stance so that her feet were shoulder-width apart.

Whitney slowed the curls down and immediately felt the difference. The fifteen-pound weights now felt like thirty. Or she might be weaker than she thought.

"There, that's much better," her friend said, nodding approvingly.

Now she was really starting to feel the burn. Or it could just be fatigue. The effort must have shown on her face because Trinity clucked her tongue and said, "I can't wait to meet the guy who has you coming to the gym at six in the morning."

As timings went, it couldn't have been more perfect, because the guy in question walked in carrying a black duffel bag. Whitney swore her heart fluttered as her gaze leisurely, swept his tall, muscled form. The man looked good in everything, and workout clothes ranked high on the list.

As she and Trinity were the only ones in his immediate vicinity, Myles spotted them right away, his surprise giving way to...pleasure? At least, she thought he looked happy to see her. It had been weeks since their talk by the pool, and so far so good. Plus, he was the one who'd suggested she give his gym a try.

"Don't look now, but that's him coming towards us. Act natural," Whitney whispered, speaking out of the side of her mouth as her eyes tracked his approach.

And naturally, Trinity turned and looked at him. She then directed her attention back at Whitney, giving her a sly side-eye. "Okay, now I get it. You want him to see you as the kind of regular woman he'd want to have sex with."

Whitney prayed to God he couldn't read lips. "Would. You. Shut. Up," she muttered, her face on fire. "And don't you dare say anything like that to him or I will kill you where you stand, do you understand?" She used her talent as a ventriloquist to threaten Trinity while keeping her smile in place and her gaze trained on Myles.

"He—" Trinity paused to clear her throat "—looks nice."

For Trinity, the pause and the "looks nice" translated to, *Holy hell, he's hot!*

"He's Haylee's father," Whitney reminded her.

"Tell your daughter her daddy is very nice," was the last thing Trinity whispered before clamping her mouth shut seconds short of Myles's arrival.

"What are you doing here? I thought you didn't get up before eight unless you had to." Myles was all easy smiles as he nodded a greeting at Trinity.

"I told you I was looking for a gym, and since this one came highly recommended—" Whitney flashed him a grin "—I thought I'd give it a try."

She then hastily introduced the two, and both were at their charming best, all smiles and amusing quips.

"You arrived just in time to give Sahara here some pointers. She could really use them." This was Trinity's subtle way of matchmaking by pointing out some of her inadequacies. What a gem.

"I'd be more than happy to."

"Are you sure? I don't want to interrupt your workout." Whitney didn't want him to feel obligated.

"No, it's my pleasure," Myles said, waving her protestations aside.

That was more than enough for Trinity, who swiped her hands together, effectively washing her hands of her. "Great. Now that you're in capable hands, I'm going to hit the treadmill and then the elliptical. Give me a shout when you're done."

After Trinity strode off, Whitney became more acutely aware of him and how his leanly muscled thighs were something to behold. His arms were great too. "How's Haylee?"

"I think she was asking for you last night. She kept looking toward the door. I eventually pulled a picture of you up on the computer, and she got excited and started pointing."

Whitney placed her hand on her chest as a wave of emotion caught her square in the heart. "You're going to make me cry." She sniffed, once again struck by the reality of her plight. How much of her daughter's life she was missing. She would give anything to be there when Haylee woke up in the mornings and went to sleep at night. Instead, she'd agreed to an hour-and-a-half visit three times a week, which had seemed reasonable at the time. But soon it would be time to reconsider the schedule in their informal agreement.

Then Myles gently touched her arm, which only heightened her awareness of him and made her miss her daughter even more.

"Please don't do that. I just wanted you to know that she misses you."

Whitney liked to attribute it to the mother-and-daughter bond that was as old as the earth itself. Haylee was beginning to feel the connection.

"Now all I want to do is see her." The next visit wasn't until the day after tomorrow.

"Why don't you come by after work today?"

Her gaze flew to his. "Really? Are you sure? I wouldn't want to upset her schedule." Whitney knew how important it was to keep babies on their schedules, and she'd seen what happened when Haylee went off hers. Bedtime mayhem. Myles ended up getting four hours of sleep—if he was lucky.

"I wouldn't say it if I didn't mean it. You should know that by now."

You should know that by now.

Her heart gave a loud thump at the intimacy of those words and the flash of one of his crooked smiles that made him look five years younger and twice as approachable. Did he have any idea what that smile did to her? It would explain why he was so frugal with them. He was the type of man who wouldn't want to give a woman hope where there was none, so he doled them out sparingly.

"Then I'd love to. Thank you." Whitney accepted before he changed his mind.

Or she changed hers.

15

Myles wasn't sure what just happened, but the result was that he'd be seeing Whitney tonight. This would be the first time they'd deviated from the schedule.

Yes, it was great they'd been getting along as well as they had, but maybe he'd been looking forward to her visits a little too much lately. Because when he'd walked into the gym and spotted her, the way his body reacted had dashed cold water on the lies he'd been telling himself.

In three short weeks, he'd gone from telling himself he wasn't attracted to her to admitting he was attracted to her but not interested in anything happening with her. Today, like all good negotiators, he'd moved the goalpost again, now resolving that nothing could happen with her no matter how much he wanted something to.

He couldn't even say it was what she was wearing. He'd seen her in a bikini, so it wasn't as if he didn't know that her body was as beautiful as her face. It was just the more he got to know her, the more he liked her, and the more he liked her, the harder it became for him to think of her strictly as Haylee's mother.

"I'm ready when you are," she said, yanking him back to the present.

For a moment he thought she'd been reading his mind until he realized she was talking about the workout.

"Then let's get started," Myles said, smoothly transitioning into personal trainer mode. "Did you stretch?"

Letting out a self-conscious laugh, she said, "I guess I should've started with that."

He turned, grabbed two exercise mats, and arranged them on the floor in front of them. "Just follow my lead."

Myles took her through his regular routine. They started with the quads. Whitney was lithe and limber and could contort her body like a gymnast, which made it even more surprising that she'd taken him up on his suggestion to join the gym. She seemed more suited to Pilates or yoga.

Bent at the waist, she shot him a glance over her shoulder. "Am I doing it right?"

Swallowing hard, he hastily tore his eyes from her ass and tried to answer as if he hadn't been checking her out. "Yeah, your form looks good."

"Myles."

Instantly recognizing the voice, Myles pushed to his feet. Striding toward him was his friend and workout partner.

Sam, who was stocky and muscular with thighs the size of tree trunks, owned an HVAC company and worked in the building across the street from the law firm. They'd struck up a friendship five years ago when Myles joined the gym. They usually worked out together two to three times a week.

"You're late," Myles said with an easy smile.

"Yeah, I'm ten minutes late, and you go and get a workout partner better-looking than me," he joked, winking at Whitney. "I'm not sure I can compete."

He couldn't compete. Whitney won hands down.

Suddenly, Sam narrowed his eyes at her. "Have we met before? You look familiar." Then his eyes widened in recognition. "You're the singer!"

"Guilty as charged," Whitney replied, amusement lighting her eyes.

The only thing he'd told Sam about the current situation was that he and Holly were getting divorced and he'd gotten custody of Haylee. All Sam had to say about that was, *"Parenthood isn't for everyone,"* and *"Make sure she forks over child support. You shouldn't be the one shouldering it alone."* Myles had merely grunted in response. Explaining why he hadn't asked Holly for a dime required telling him the truth or a version close to it.

Sam shot him a look, eyebrows raised. *A celebrity? You keeping secrets?*

"Ms. Richardson is one of the firm's new clients." It was the first thing that popped into his head. If he didn't explain why he was exercising with one of the biggest stars on the planet, Sam was going to come up with something fit for the tabloids.

"New client?" Sam turned back to Whitney. "You're in good hands with this one. And I'm not saying that because he's my friend and spotting partner. The guy's a veritable encyclopedia when it comes to business law."

"That's why I hired him. I was told he's the best," she said without missing a beat.

"Ms. Richardson was just telling me that she's in the market for a new gym. I offered to show her around and give her some pointers." At least that wasn't a lie.

"If you're also in the market for a personal trainer, a buddy of mine is open to new clients. I'm sure he'd be more than happy to take you on."

Whitney snorted a laugh. "Yeah, that'll be a big no. A personal trainer is way too much of a commitment for me, but thanks for the offer."

"Can't blame a guy for trying to help out a friend," Sam said with a good-natured shrug. He glanced around the room. "It looks like I'll be going solo today."

"One day isn't going to kill you," Myles mocked.

"Why can't we all work out together?" Whitney asked, looking at Myles.

"Because—"

"Don't mind me," Sam said, cutting him off. "I was just pulling your leg. I'm good. It was nice meeting you." Then, with a casual wave and a smile, he headed toward the long row of stationary bikes at the other side of the room.

"He seems nice," Whitney commented.

"He's a good friend."

She resumed stretching, this time working on her hamstrings. "So, I'm a new client, huh?"

"Yeah, I'm sorry about that. I didn't want him to get the wrong idea."

With her right leg extended in front of her, she peered up at him as she pulled her toes toward her. "And what idea would that be?"

Why was she playing coy? She knew what he meant. If he didn't know better, he might think she was flirting with him. But her deadpan expression made her impossible to read.

"That something's going on between us."

"Something other than us sharing a child?" she asked mischievously, her voice a near whisper.

Myles stifled a groan. This woman. The gym was bringing out a side of her he hadn't seen before.

"You know damn well what he'd be thinking."

Whitney let out a husky laugh, her eyes sparkling with humor. "Seriously, Myles, you need to relax. And so what if he thinks something's going on between us?"

Myles stared at her, not shocked but slightly taken aback.

If she were anyone other than the mother of his child, he'd swear to God she was coming on to him. "Are you saying you wouldn't mind?"

She switched legs to stretch her other hamstring, drawing attention to her perfectly rounded ass and the long, slim length of her thigh. "I'm used to being gossiped about. According to an article a friend sent me last week, my ex is going to propose to me on my birthday."

Her ex? Did she mean the tennis pro whom she was supposed to have split with months ago? As she'd opened the door to prior relationships, it seemed an appropriate time to ask, "Is there any truth to that?"

"That he's going to propose?" Whitney snorted in amusement. "Not a chance in a million. I barely had time for a relationship when he and I were seeing each other, and I have even less time now. He was always traveling, and when he was stateside, we were rarely on the same coast. Needless to say, it didn't work out."

"Does he know that?"

"Know what, that we broke up?" she asked, chuckling, mistakenly thinking he was kidding.

Myles gave a careless shrug. "Since he's supposed to propose to you."

"I asked him about it yesterday, and I can confirm that he will not be proposing to me in this lifetime. But who knows about the next one."

"You keep in touch?"

Done with her leg stretches, Whitney stood up straight and clasped her hands behind her back, pushing her chest out. He willed himself not to look. He looked, but it was cursory at best. He was simply checking her form. More importantly, he didn't stare.

"Sure. I mean, why not? It's not as if we parted on bad terms.

It was exactly the opposite, in fact. Daniel's a great guy and a good friend."

She keeps in touch with her last boyfriend.

He couldn't imagine going from being in a sexual relationship with her to just being her friend. He'd never voluntarily kept in contact with an ex after they broke up, so in his not insignificant experience, men couldn't be friends with women they wanted or used to fuck. Only women could pull off something like that.

"Yeah, Daniel sounds like a great guy." The guy was full of shit.

"He is. On the other hand, there's always going to be people in your life willing to sell tabloids a bunch of lies to make a quick buck, which is what happened with the whole proposal story." She paused in the middle of an arm stretch and looked him directly in the eye. "In my business, you get used to hearing and reading lies about yourself all the time. A lot of people will believe it, and some won't." She shrugged. *"C'est la vie."*

"That might be your life, but it's not mine."

She flinched as if stung, and he immediately wanted to take his words back. He hadn't meant it as a slight or a criticism. It wasn't her fault that people made a living trafficking in lies and that others ate it up like starving pups. But just because an entire cottage industry was dedicated to it didn't mean she had to accept it.

Her lips parted as if she was about to say something. Then she seemed to think better of it and instead said, "You know how you told your friend that I'm a client? Would you be interested in making that a reality? I'm thinking of taking the company public, and I could use a reputable IPO attorney. Word has it that you're one of the best."

Myles was both stunned and flattered. "Are you sure?" he

asked. As if their lives weren't entwined enough. Did she really want to hire him too, and did he want her as a client?

Whitney nodded. "Yes. I trust you. And more importantly, I need your expertise if we're going to do this right."

I trust you.

Even if he wanted to, he couldn't say no to her. "Okay then, you've got yourself a lawyer."

"Great. I'll have Ellen Sato contact you to get things going. She's the CFO."

"Sounds good."

They smiled at each other. After several seconds of silence, she said, "So are you going to join me or what? For the last ten minutes, all you've done is watch."

Myles stifled a laugh. If only she knew. He hadn't watched her as much as he'd wanted to.

"I was taking it easy on you since it's your first time. But if you're ready for a real workout, let's go."

"It is not my first time working out," she said with an exaggerated roll of her eyes.

Myles took her eye roll as a challenge, replying with just enough heat to give her pause, "It's your first time working out *with me*."

Satisfaction was watching her lips part ever so slightly and her pretty eyes flare in awareness.

"She likes you," Sam told Myles an hour later as they watched Whitney and her friend exit the gym and step out onto the sidewalk.

"Of course she does. I'm a nice guy," he replied lightly, ignoring his friend's transparent-as-glass inference. "Everyone likes me."

Okay, maybe not everyone. The opposing counsel might re-

spect his command of the law, but that was as far as any positive feelings went.

Laughing wryly, Sam gave him a knowing look. "I mean,
she wants to fuck you, likes you."

Myles briefly met his friend's gaze before returning his attention to Whitney. He watched as she gracefully ducked into
the waiting car. "Nah, man, it's not like that."

"Yeah, man, it's exactly like that."

"The ink isn't dry on my divorce papers," Myles reminded
him, even though it felt much longer than that. His life with
Holly felt as if it occurred in another lifetime. She rarely crossed
his mind these days. Except for her call last week, which he'd
ignored. If it was important, she'd have left a message.

"Are you saying you still have feelings for Holly?"

Sam thought Holly did Haylee and him a favor when she
bailed. There was no love lost there.

"You mean other than regret?" It had taken him months to
come to terms with the fact that he didn't know Holly as well
as he thought he did when he proposed. Although his crappy
judgment wasn't solely to blame. She'd deliberately hidden the
parts of herself she hadn't wanted him to know, and the inevi-
table happened. He'd learned the hard way.

"Then what's this garbage about the ink not being dry on
your divorce papers?"

"I'm saying it's been two weeks since the divorce was finalized." A little over six months from the day Holly packed up
and went to her mother's house. Theirs was quick for a California divorce. Processing the paperwork alone could take six
months. Fortunately for him, being president of the California
Bar had its perks. Speedy paperwork processing turned out to
be one of them.

"And?" Sam shrugged. "So what?"

"For God's sake, Sam, she's a client." That was their story, and he was sticking to it. Sam was a good friend, but he wasn't ready to let him in on the secret. He would eventually, but not yet.

"Okay. So you wait until you're not her lawyer anymore. Then you make a move. How long is that going to be? A few months?"

Myles rolled his eyes. "For the last time, nothing is going to happen between us."

"So if she were to make a move on you, you'd turn her down?"

"She's not going to." Although given the way she was acting today, he didn't know if she would kick him out of her bed if he somehow ended up there, but he couldn't see her making the first move. She was a woman accustomed to being the pursued, not the one doing the pursuing, and he wouldn't be the one to cross that line.

"But if she did, you'd tell her to take a hike?" Sam looked understandably skeptical because few single, straight, red-blooded men would. The woman was a smoke show that came with flames hot enough to burn.

"What the hell is it with you? Do you want to fuck her? Is that it?" Myles did his best to laugh it off.

His friend's eyes lit up. "If she was interested, fuck yeah," he said, grinning like an idiot.

Myles's eyes narrowed at him.

"I'm kidding," Sam said, chuckling. "Actually, no I'm not, but see how you're reacting? You don't like me being interested in your new client, do you? Which proves my point. You're interested in her no matter what you say."

Sam's stubbornness was both his strength and his weakness. "What are you even talking about? You're acting as if something happened. Whit—Sahara has done nothing, and I repeat, nothing to make me think she wants anything from me other than legal advice. Whatever you thought you saw today was a figment of your imagination."

Sam released an exaggerated sigh. "Fine, if you want to bury your head in the sand, have at it. Just don't come crying to me when she moves on and hooks up with someone better." The latter was a knife in the ribs, meant to wound.

"Are you done?" Myles asked in a bored voice. He'd never cried over a woman, and he wasn't about to start now, even if she was the mother of his child.

"Knowing you, I give it until after she's no longer your client. And when it happens, I expect an apology...and a pair of tickets to next year's Super Bowl."

His friend's challenge elicited a full-on smirk from him. "What makes you believe I'd tell you if something happened?"

"I assume you're speaking in hypotheticals unless that ship's already sailed?"

They wouldn't be having this discussion if it had.

"*If* is innately hypothetical."

"You wouldn't need to tell me. I'd know just by looking at you." Sam looked as if he'd just won a battle in their war of insinuations and hypotheticals.

"You're full of shit."

"Maybe, but at least I'm not blind. I can see when a beautiful woman has the hots for me. It's clear you can't."

Myles smiled. "Here's what I'm going to do for you, Sam. I'm going to give some free legal advice."

"As long as it's free," Sam drawled, smirking.

"Stick to your day job. You're a horrible matchmaker and an even worse psychic."

16

"I mean, she wants to fuck you, likes you."

Myles couldn't get Sam's words out of his head, and it was worse now that he and Whitney were alone, waiting for his sister to bring Haylee home. Natalie had taken the kids to the children's zoo and the park and asked that he allow Haylee to stay another hour because the kids were in the middle of a game.

"Can I get you something to drink?" he asked once Whitney was comfortably ensconced on the sofa in the family room.

"Water would be great," she said, flashing him a smile.

The sight of her dimples made him forget that only six years separated them. She was thirty, soon to be thirty-one, therefore not considered too young for someone in their midthirties.

Stop thinking about her dimples, her sweet peach of an ass, her perfect tits, and those beautiful legs wrapped around your hips. Just get her some goddamn water.

"She wants to fuck you, likes you."

No she does not, he argued with the devil on his shoulder doing its best to steer him down the road that led to court and a custody battle. If he listened to it, that was where they'd inevitably end up.

"Water coming up," he said, and quickly escaped to the kitchen.

Myles had always commended himself for not being one of *those* men. The kind who took the slightest overture of friendliness by an attractive woman and turned it into something sexual. Yet Sam's words kept playing over and over in his mind. If Whitney had been extra friendly at the gym, it was because he was Haylee's father. Kaput. The end. Her motives were that simple, and her methods were working like the charm she possessed in spades.

The ping of an incoming message sounded, and a look at his phone revealed a message from his sister. A cacophony of noise accosted his ears when he clicked on the video in the message. Haylee, Jonah, and Sophie were on swings in the backyard, shrieking at the top of their little lungs, having what appeared to be the time of their lives, while Natalie took turns pushing each one.

Moments later, the phone rang. When his sister's face appeared on the screen, he knew what was coming. In typical Natalie fashion, she liked to soften the ground before the ask, like the strategist she was. The video of the kids served as the preemptive strike.

He took out a bottle of water and a can of soda from the refrigerator. "Don't tell me, the kids want Haylee to spend the night."

"How'd you guess?" she said, a smile in her voice.

Sighing, he retrieved a glass from the cupboard. And here he had Whitney waiting for Haylee to come home. He lifted his gaze to her to find her staring back at him. She quickly looked away.

"And I thought you could use a night to yourself. Get yourself a full night's sleep. Doesn't that sound good?"

Did it sound good? It sounded like heaven.

Yet Myles was torn. What he should do and what he wanted to do were at odds. He should tell Natalie that Whitney was here waiting for Haylee. He should tell her not to worry about dropping Haylee off, because he'd come pick her up. If only life were that easy and the prospect of an uninterrupted night's sleep didn't sound so enticing.

"Hold on a sec." Muting the call, he grabbed the glass of water and returned to the family room and Whitney.

"You didn't need to bother with a glass," she said, accepting the drink.

"Hey, listen. My sister's on the phone. Her kids are begging for Haylee to stay the night…" He left the sentence hanging.

Her eyes widened as she realized what that meant for her visit. "Oh. Right. No, that's fine," she said, smiling. "As an only child, I completely understand. I'd much rather be around kids closer to my age than a bunch of adults."

Myles couldn't tell if her smile was forced or not, but she appeared genuinely understanding of the situation.

"I didn't tell my sister that you're waiting for—"

"Please don't. It was an impromptu visit anyway," she cut in. "Honestly, I don't mind. I'll see her on Saturday as planned. It's no big deal."

Unmuting the call, Myles told his sister Haylee could stay and that he'd pick her up tomorrow after work. Whitney was already on her feet by the time he hung up.

"I guess I better get going."

"I'll take you home," he offered, ignoring the voice in his head telling him to leave well enough alone. But he reasoned that since he was responsible for her wasted trip, it was the least he could do.

"Oh, you don't have to. It's just as easy for me to call the car service."

"I know I don't have to. I want to," he insisted.

Whitney's eyes searched his face. "Are you sure? I wouldn't want to—"

"—be a bother. Believe me, you're not," he assured her.

"Since you've made it impossible for me to refuse, I guess the answer is yes, and thank you very much," she said with a light laugh.

"Good. Just give me a couple of minutes to change and I'll be right back."

This time when she smiled at him, he felt it in his gut—and a few inches lower. He had to caution himself not to read too much into her smiles or what he'd earlier perceived as flirtatious behavior. To some people, flirting came as naturally as breathing. Whitney appeared to be one of them.

He needed to get laid. That was his problem. It had been over six months, and his hand wasn't doing it for him anymore. He missed a woman's touch, the feel of a soft body against his and being snug inside of her.

Now, for God's sake, man, go change and then take the woman home before you say something stupid. Or worse yet, do something stupider.

Then he'd come back home and jerk off to the mental image of her peering at him over her shoulder with her gorgeous ass in the air.

The drive to her house was exactly seven songs long. None of them were hers, thank God! But they had done their job, which was to fill the silence of the ride.

Whitney didn't know if it was because it was dark and Myles needed to pay close attention to the roads, or if he simply didn't like to talk while he drove, but after two attempts to engage him in conversation and his distracted single-word responses, she'd lapsed into silence and turned up the music on the radio.

Then she'd spent the rest of the drive counting songs and berating herself for accepting his offer to drive her home, no matter how much he'd insisted. The last time she'd felt this awkward in a car with a man, she'd been seventeen and on a date with a guy she knew she wouldn't be seeing again, even if he begged her. She'd practically bolted from the car when they'd reached her house to avoid the super uncomfortable *will he or won't he try to kiss me* moment of the date.

She almost did the same when Myles pulled into her driveway and stopped the car, but she forced herself to remain seated. She wasn't the same seventeen-year-old girl, and she wasn't about to make things awkward between them. Silent car ride aside, they'd established a good rapport, and she couldn't allow her attraction to him to interfere with that.

He cut off the engine and the interior light came on. After a moment of absolute silence, he said, "I played baseball in high school and college."

"Oh, so now you want to elaborate?" Whitney tsked, but was buoyed by it. It also didn't escape her attention that he turned off the car, clearly not in a rush to get back home.

Myles shrugged. "When we're talking, I want to give you my full attention. I can't do that when I'm driving."

He said it as if his admission didn't have the power to send delicious shivers through her, from the tips of her breasts down to her center. Heat flooded her face, but she did her best to feign lightheartedness, teasingly asking, "Were you any good?" knowing full well he had to have been to play at the college level.

"Not good enough for the minors, but it didn't matter, because I wanted to become a lawyer more than I wanted to go pro."

"Follow in your father's footsteps, huh?" she said, repeating what she'd said to him during their first meeting.

The interior light went out, signaling they'd been sitting there too long. The security light at the front entrance only partially illuminated his face, leaving a portion of it in shadow.

"Something like that." His tone was as flat as his response was evasive.

Whitney couldn't stop herself from probing further. "Did your father have a specialty? Was he a business lawyer too?"

"My dad was a medical malpractice lawyer. Never lost a case in twenty-two years."

Color her impressed. "Wow, he must have been a great lawyer."

"The best in his field," Myles stated with more than a hint of pride in his voice.

"I guess like father, like son, then."

Whitney intended it to come out light. A compliment she would give to a friend. But going by the way he was looking at her, the intensity of his hooded gaze, it hadn't landed that way.

"Remember when I said I had a hard time seeing you as Haylee's mother?" he asked, his voice quiet and low and the question coming from out of nowhere.

Whitney made a sound between a huff and a harrumph. "How could I forget?" She had no idea where he was going with this line of questioning.

"Now I have a hard time seeing you as anyone but Haylee's mother."

Her breath hitched, and it felt as if something was caught in her throat. She didn't know how to respond or what to say, or if she should say anything at all.

This was what she'd wanted, yet now it didn't feel like enough. She wanted him to see her as more than Haylee's mother. She wanted him to see her the same way she saw him. As a desirable member of the opposite sex, who just happened to be a wonderful, loving parent and was extremely talented at what they did for a living. But if this was the best she could get from him, she'd gladly take it.

"Thank you," she said. "That's one of the nicest things you've ever said to me."

"She's the most important person in the world to me. I don't want to screw this up."

Whitney reached across the console and gave his hand a comforting squeeze. "We won't," she said, making it clear she saw them as a team where their daughter was concerned.

When Myles's gaze lowered to where she was lightly palming the back of his hand, she self-consciously pulled hers away.

His eyes met and held hers. "We wouldn't mean to."

"As long as we always put Haylee's well-being first, everything will be fine."

Myles inclined his head in a slow, pensive nod before breaking his stare and looking around. While she was trying to get her heart under control, he began to laugh, a deep, rumbling sound that seemed to emanate from his chest.

"What's so fun—" Whitney broke off the second she realized all the windows in the car had fogged up. She burst out laughing, saying in between gasps, "Tell me you've been sitting in the car too long without telling me."

"The last time I was in a car with fogged windows with a girl, I was sixteen."

"That must have been fun," she teased. She'd never had sex in a car because the risk of being caught in the act wasn't her kink. Plus, she appreciated her comfort too much.

"Hey, I was sixteen. I was getting laid, and that was all that mattered," he said, still chuckling.

Whitney could only imagine what a sixteen-year-old Myles had been like. If he looked anything like he did now, he must have had his pick of girls.

"Would you like to come in? We can talk inside. Give the

windows a chance to clear," she said as if the offer was no big deal. Stay or go, it was up to him. She was fine with whatever he decided.

Myles glanced toward the house and then back at her. "No, I really should be getting home."

Whitney was surprised by the depth of the disappointment that came over her. After all, this wasn't a date. He'd only offered to drive her home, nothing more. And with Haylee gone for the night, he probably had other things he preferred to do with his free time and other people he'd prefer to do it with.

"Right. Of course. Well, thanks again for the ride. Kiss Haylee for me, and I'll see you Saturday." She quickly got out of the car to Myles's quiet, "See you then."

She didn't hear his car start until she was safely inside.

17

He did the right thing.

Going into her house with her alone would have been like playing Russian roulette with the promise he'd made himself not to get physically involved with her.

Would you get over yourself? the pragmatist in him exclaimed. *The two of you were in the car so long, you were fogging up the fucking windows. That's the only reason she invited you inside. To talk, not to have sex.*

By the time Myles went to bed that night, he was able to convince himself it had all been in his mind. Whitney hadn't been coming on to him. There had been nothing remotely sexual or romantic in the way she'd touched him when she'd given his hand a comforting squeeze—*comforting* being the operative word. But apparently that didn't matter, because it hadn't stopped him from salivating like Pavlov's dog when she'd invited him in.

The next time he saw her, his doubts were put to rest. Whitney's visit went off without a hitch or a moment of awkwardness. She was the same as she always was, beautiful, cheerful, and happy to see Haylee. She chatted nonstop, telling him about some of the scripts she'd been sent and the songwriters she was dying to work with, and that she planned to take her learner's permit test on Thursday.

Before she left, he reminded her that his invitation to teach her to drive was still open. She'd thanked him without saying whether she intended to take him up on it or not. No big deal. What mattered was that they were still on good terms.

So it came as a surprise when she called Thursday night. Before he could get a word out, she exclaimed, "I got my learner's permit! Now you can teach me to drive."

Myles couldn't help but smile. "Congratulations. How many times did you have to take it to pass?"

"Ha ha ha. Very funny. I aced it the first time. Didn't get one question wrong, which clearly makes me a genius."

"Aced your learner's permit the first time, did you?" He was all tongue-in-cheek humor. "Don't be surprised when NAS-CAR comes knocking, ready to sign you up."

Whitney giggled. "Yeah, for the celebrity NASCAR reality show. Do something like *Dancing with the Stars*, but on wheels, where they match us up with a professional driver. What do you think?"

"Forget I said anything. It's a horrible idea." The thought of her behind the wheel of a race car scared the shit out of him.

"What, not confident of your teaching skills?" she teased.

Myles huffed. "What I'm not confident of is *your* driving skills. Frankly, I'm terrified you'd kill yourself."

"Ha! You're not getting rid of me that easily."

"I don't want to get rid of you at all." It was only when the words were out that he realized how quickly she'd become integral to his and Haylee's lives.

"Well, that's good, because I'm not going anywhere," she said, her voice taking on a warmer tone.

"No, you're not," he agreed somewhat fatalistically. For him, it was a double-edged sword. She'd always be there for Haylee but out of reach to him, because that was a line he was determined not to cross no matter what.

"Anyway, getting back to my driving lessons. I don't want to be pushy or anything, but when do you think we can start? How about the next weekend Haylee stays overnight at your sister's?"

Myles would never characterize her as pushy—not now that he'd really gotten to know her—but she certainly wasn't a pushover. "Actually, Nat's friend's daughter is turning one this weekend, and the mother invited Haylee to the party. Nat said she'd be happy to keep her for the night and bring her home in time for your visit."

"She's not even a year old and is already being invited to birthday parties. That's wonderful," Whitney enthused. "I'm so glad her cousins live nearby, and she's getting to socialize with other kids her age."

"The plan wasn't for her to be an only child. Holly and I planned to have one more if everything went well the first time." Only after the words were out did Myles wonder why he'd decided to share that with her. He'd already told her he had no intention of getting married again, meaning no more children.

"I guess that means it's up to me to make sure she isn't an only child," she said, her tone light and upbeat as if her getting pregnant and having a baby with someone else was something she was looking forward to.

Unsurprisingly, he wasn't looking forward to it.

Selfish? Yes.

Understandable given the way he felt about her? Yes.

Did he ever intend to act on his feelings? His attraction? Absolutely not. Although they shared a child, he had no claim on Whitney and never would.

"How about we start your lessons on Saturday?" he said, steering the conversation back on course. No need to talk about something that might never happen.

"Is the afternoon, say about two, okay with you?" she asked. "I'm going car shopping in the morning. Figured I might as well get one, and we can use it for the lessons instead of yours."

"You're buying a car? Now?"

"I'm going to need one eventually, so why not now? And that way, if I accidentally run over a mailbox or sideswipe another car, it won't be on your insurance."

Okay, that made sense. "And you're buying this car off the lot?"

"Yep. I have an appointment at the dealership. I know exactly what I want, so I'm going to check it out."

"Alone?"

"What, you don't think little old me is capable of buying a car on my own?" she asked, no doubt rolling her eyes.

"Why don't I come with you? It's always good to get a second opinion," he added.

"You'd do that?" She sounded surprised, and he didn't know whether to be offended or flattered.

"Of course." It was nothing, really. Just a father making sure that the mother of his child bought the safest car for their child. It wasn't him wanting to spend more time with her because he was attracted to her and recently hadn't been able to stop thinking about her. Nope, that wasn't it.

"Okay, then I'll see you Saturday."

When Myles got to her place Saturday morning at eight-thirty, Whitney had been watching for his arrival. She was out the front door by the time he pulled into the driveway.

Opening the passenger door, she climbed in, her greeting a slightly breathless, "You're right on time."

Myles simply stared at her as she buckled in and then plopped her purse on her lap.

"Who are you, and what have you done with Whitney?"

Whitney laughed at the mixture of amusement and surprise on his face. It was exactly the reaction she'd been expecting after taking one last look at herself in the hall mirror.

"You're wearing a wig." His eyes had yet to budge from her face.

"Yep. It's my disguise. What do you think?" Smiling mischievously, she turned her head from side to side to showcase her new look. "Think anyone will recognize me?" Today, she'd decided on a sleeveless print top, a pair of white slim jeans, and strappy beaded sandals. The only thing different about her was the black chin-length wig on her head.

At her question, he did a slow sweep of her body, once again sending her mind into a tailspin. Her body tingled with awareness every place his blue eyes touched. The man was driving her crazy. After he'd turned down her invitation to come in and talk, she'd taken it as a sign not to ever do shit like that again. Rejection sucked.

She'd spent that evening licking her wounds and then made a conscious decision to treat him as if it never happened. And it worked. She was fine, he was fine, and everything between them was fine. Then he had to go and look at her as if he was wondering what she looked like without any clothes.

His gaze returned to hers. "Only if they come within ten feet of you."

Retrieving a pair of oversized tortoiseshell sunglasses from her purse, she put them on. "What about now?"

After studying her for a few moments, Myles replied, "If

your goal is not to attract attention, I suggest you wear a bur-
lap bag next time."

There he goes again, making me think there's something there.

What was going on with him today? She wondered if this
was some kind of test that had to do with Haylee.

Whatever it was, Whitney wisely chose to ignore it, laughing off his compliment of sorts. "I don't mind a bit of attention
as long as they look but don't touch."

So of course, what did he do? He kept looking at her as if
he wanted to touch.

His gaze narrowed. "Does that happen a lot?"

"The looking or the touching?"

Myles let out a gruff laugh as he turned the car around and
drove the length of the winding driveway. "Oh, I know they
look."

Whitney arched her brow at him. "Oh, you do, do you?"
Honestly, she was going to start calling him Mr. Mixed Messages because today, those were the ones he was sending her.

He shot a quick look at her before driving through the gates
and turning onto the main road. "Are you telling me they
don't?"

"Some do." Men were visual creatures. They looked. But
then, women looked too, although most not for the same reasons.

"You didn't answer my question."

The man was a dog with a bone. "A few of them get touchy
sometimes, but it's never been anything security can't handle."

"Security as in bodyguards?" he asked.

"Security at award shows and events like that. I only need
personal bodyguards when I go on tour." Whitney couldn't
think of anything more intrusive than having someone all up
under her every time she set foot in public.

"What about when you go out with friends? Or on dates?"

"I told you, I really don't go out all that much, and when I do, it's usually to places I trust to be discreet about my comings and goings. For everywhere else, I have my disguises."

Myles glanced at her out of the side of his eye. "That disguise wouldn't fool me."

Whitney didn't know if it was the way he looked at her or what he said, but suddenly she was all kinds of turned on. Humming commenced between her thighs, and her nipples turned into stiff peaks. It was a good thing he was concentrating on the road.

"It wasn't meant to," she said softly.

"So this is it, huh?" Myles ran a critical but admiring eye over the silver-blue SUV. He hadn't known what to expect, but a hybrid Volvo hadn't been it.

"Yeah, what do you think?" Whitney asked, peering up at him.

They'd been at the car dealer for the past forty minutes, negotiating the price with the salesman she'd been communicating with. They'd settled on a price three grand less than the one she'd been quoted over the phone. After handing Myles the key fob, Pete had gone back inside without demanding that he ride along on their test drive.

"I figured I'd need something safe and suitable for kids." Opening the rear door, she smoothed her palm over the dark gray leather back seat. "It has a built-in booster seat that will be perfect for when Haylee is older. And look," she said, pointing to the dual touchscreens behind the front headrests, "entertainment to keep her occupied for long drives."

Myles shot her an arched look. Where the hell did she think she'd be taking his daughter?

Whitney rolled her eyes and closed the door. "Don't worry, I won't be taking her anywhere without your permission."

"I thought you'd want to start with something smaller." He opened the driver's side door, slid behind the wheel, and began adjusting the seat to fit his height.

Circling the car, Whitney climbed in beside him, reverently smoothing her hands over the soft leather. "I'll probably get another one after I get my license. Maybe a convertible. I've always loved the thought of driving down a country road with the top down."

"I can see you in a convertible." And the thought of her driving with her top down was an image for his spank bank.

"Haylee will be able to ride with me in it when she's older."

His chest tightened at not being included in that future scenario. But then, why would he be? Inevitably there would come a time when he wouldn't be needed to supervise the visits. Whitney would come and pick Haylee up and bring her back when it was over. And when Haylee was old enough to ride in the front seat of a convertible, Whitney was likely to be married and the mother of siblings for his daughter, as she herself had said.

Eyes closed, Whitney inhaled deeply, a big smile on her beautiful face. "Don't you just love new car smell?"

"Clearly not as much as you," he replied, fighting back a smile of his own. For a woman who had so much, it seemed to be the little things that brought her joy.

"Come on," she said, "let's go for that drive. Pete's going to think we're up to no good if we aren't back with the car in fifteen minutes."

Myles guffawed. "Whitney, he knows who you are, so if we don't come back with the car, he'll know where to find you. Believe me, us having the car out too long is the last thing he's thinking about. It's a cash sale. For a salesperson, they don't come easier than that."

"Okay, then take your time since, according to you, we have all the time in the world," she said with a cheeky grin.

Myles rolled his eyes and started the car. No one spoke until a few minutes into the test drive.

"Nice, smooth ride. Easy to handle," he remarked while Whitney, after connecting her phone to CarPlay, was busy testing all the features.

"Are you saying even a newbie like me will be able to handle it?"

Newbie was a quaint way of putting it. "I'm saying I should sell mine and get one myself." Not that getting another car hadn't crossed his mind, but with his Lexus and Holly's BMW, they'd decided to wait for another kid.

"You don't need to do that. Just use this one. I'll only be using it for my driving lessons anyway, which will be with you."

Myles shot a quick look at her. "Did you just offer me unfettered use of your brand-new car?"

Whitney shrugged. "Like I said, I won't be able to drive it until I get my license, and who knows how long that's going to take?"

"Is that how you are with all your expensive possessions, or am I special?"

What are you, a teenage girl? Why don't you go ahead and ask her to be your date to the junior prom?

"Myles, you're my daughter's father. Of course you're special." She spoke softly, and in a way, that made it difficult for him to tell if she was teasing or not. But one thing he knew for sure. He didn't want to be special to her just because he was Haylee's father.

The subject of him using her car dropped after that. Fifteen minutes later, they were back at the dealership. Because she insisted they use her car for the lessons, Whitney coerced him into using the dealership's delivery service to drop his car off at her house.

Myles then drove to an office park thirty minutes away to practice in the empty parking lot, and she did much better than he thought she would, given she had no driving experience at all.

As far as Myles was concerned, the hour-long lesson ended too soon. But no matter how much he wanted to prolong his time with her, he was going to take her home, where she'd be out of his reach but not his thoughts.

18

"There's your car, safe and sound," Whitney announced as Myles parked hers beside it in front of the three-car garage. The guys at the dealership said they'd leave the key in the glove box.

"I'm shocked since you live in such a rough neighborhood," he quipped.

Myles didn't exactly live in Pottersville. There wasn't a house in his neighborhood worth less than two million.

Whitney had bought her house for the privacy. It sat on a three-acre plot of land, with camphors and big-leaf maples strategically placed to shield it from the ever-maligned, intrusive, and persistent paparazzi. No one would be snapping pictures of her through any of the windows unless they employed a drone equipped with a telephoto lens.

"This place does have its perks. I miss the quiet when I'm staying at my apartment in New York. Although the view of Central Park makes up for it a little."

When Myles cut the engine and turned to her, Whitney experienced a sense of déjà vu. "How often do you go back?"

"Not as often as I used to, so maybe three or four times a

year. After I got into acting and realized I'd be spending the majority of my time in LA, it made sense to buy a place and locate the company's headquarters here."

This was how it started last week. The two of them sitting inside a car talking.

"All things considered, it worked out for the best," Myles said. With Haylee being raised here, Whitney had been destined to live in California.

"As major mix-ups go, I'd say so. Now I couldn't imagine my life without her in it." Several beats of silence elapsed. "Anyway, I'd better let you get on with your evening." She quickly opened the passenger door and stepped down onto the granite-paved driveway.

"Hold on."

Whitney's eyes snapped to his.

"Don't you want me to park this in there?" he asked, tipping his chin at the garage.

"Um, yeah. I guess so." It made sense. She wouldn't be using it until their next lesson, which would be the following weekend. And yes, she realized she could easily hire someone and get her license a lot faster, but his sister was right. Myles was a good teacher, and she enjoyed spending that time with him— God help her.

"Let me go and get the opener. I think it's in one of the kitchen drawers." She rarely used it as Cedrick always dropped her off at the front.

Myles pointed at the keypad mounted on the side of the garage door. "You don't know the code?"

"I've never had to use it," Whitney explained, feeling simultaneously defensive and self-consciously gauche.

He must think I'm an absolute dolt.

An amused smile tipped the corners of his mouth. "Understood."

"I'll be right back."

Five minutes later, Whitney wasn't right back. She was breathlessly scampering around the kitchen a second time, re-opening and reclosing every drawer. Hearing a sound in the hall, she paused and looked up to find Myles making his way towards her, brows lifted and his expression conveying the age-old question, *what is taking you so long?*

Exasperated, she said, "I'm sorry to keep you waiting, but I can't find it," before resuming an even more frantic search.

"That's what I thought." He appeared to be fighting back a smile.

It had to be here somewhere. She opened the junk drawer and began riffling through it again. And that was where she found it, under an empty envelope in the back corner.

"Here it is," Whitney said, holding it up triumphantly. He was going to think she couldn't find it on purpose to lure him into the house. She made a move toward the door to the garage.

"Hey, what's the rush? The car isn't going anywhere."

Myles's words stopped her dead in her tracks. Flustered her.

"I—I've taken up enough of your time today. I'm sure you want to get home."

He responded with a negligent shrug of his broad shoulders, but his gaze was intent on her when he said, "Not really."

At a momentary loss for words, Whitney could only blink. Another beat passed before she regained the use of her tongue. "Um, does that mean you want to—"

"Stay?" He nodded. "That is, if you don't have other plans for the night."

Still somewhat bemused at the turn of events, Whitney re-plied, "You're more than welcome to stay for a drink." Or two.

He stood, arms folded across his chest, and continued to watch her. "Only if you're sure," he said, effectively lobbing the ball back into her court.

She moved from the door back to the counter. They stood an arm's length apart. "I'll do you one better. What if I also feed you? That way, you won't have to go home and order takeout."

A smile slowly crept across his face. At the sight, her breath hitched. He held out his hand for the opener. "Then I'll go put the car in the garage."

When Whitney handed it to him, their fingers brushed, and her body tingled with awareness. She felt the contact into next week and beyond.

"I'll be right back." There was a rough sexiness to his voice, causing more tingling.

True to his word, he was back in less than a minute.

After she put the key fob away, Whitney waved a hand in the direction of the grand room. "Make yourself comfortable while I go and change. I shouldn't be long."

With that, she hurried upstairs and made a beeline for her bathroom, where she was certain her shower set a Guinness World Record for speed and thoroughness. Then she spent the next ten minutes picking out something to wear. It needed to be feminine, casual, and classy, but she also couldn't look as if she was dressing for him, even though the short wraparound dress she selected was with him in mind.

Whitney had no idea if anything was going to happen tonight between them, but she was prepared if something did. If Chey were advising her, she'd tell her to go down there and shoot her shot. Last week, she'd been rebuffed before she got the opportunity, so tonight she'd be more than happy to follow his lead.

Downstairs, she found Myles reclining on the sofa in the sunroom, a glass of bourbon in his hand, the open bottle on the side table beside him.

He held up his glass, his gaze never wavering from her as she passed through the French doors. "You didn't tell me *I shouldn't be long* translates to thirty minutes," he said with an engaging grin. "I hope you don't mind me helping myself to some of your bourbon."

Whitney's face warmed as she shifted on her bare feet. "Sorry about that. I didn't mean to be gone that long."

His lids lowered to half-mast as his gaze slowly toured her body. Finally he said, "You changed."

"I just freshened up a bit." She certainly wasn't going to confess to the showering and lotioning part of her prolonged absence. Then he'd correctly believe she had prepared for the *in case of sudden nakedness, grab a condom* part of the evening, should it come to pass.

"Because you weren't fresh before."

Whitney wasn't imagining the sexual undertone in his voice.

"Are you hungry?" she asked, needing to change the subject and tamp down the growing tension between them.

Myles's lips twitched, and his eyes darkened. "You did promise to feed me."

Whitney wasn't sure they were talking about food anymore. "And I don't go back on my promises. What do you want?"

His gaze briefly dropped to her bare legs. "What's on the menu?" He took a large swallow of his drink.

Everything he said sounded so damn sexual, reminding her how long it'd been since she'd had some. And even longer since she'd had *good* sex.

"There's an excellent Thai restaurant not too far from here. But if you prefer Italian, I use Julia's a lot."

"Hold on a second," Myles said in mock affront. "When you said you'd feed me, I was expecting a home-cooked meal."

"What gave you that idea?" Whitney laughed, her hand landing on her hip. "I'm pretty sure I already told you that I don't cook."

"You also said you'd have to learn for Haylee's sake."

"I can only multitask so much. I'm already learning how to drive. I have to pace myself. Plus, I have some time since Haylee isn't on that type of solid food yet."

"Are you saying that you lured me here under false premises?"

"Lured?" Whitney chortled. "You're the one who said you didn't want to go home. And I can't believe you think I'm the kind of woman who has to lure unsuspecting men to spend time with me with promises of home-cooked meals," she said, feigning offense.

The amusement in Myles's eyes dimmed and began to smolder as he regarded her. Placing his drink on the side table, he pushed to his feet until he was looking down at her. "I think you're the kind of woman who has to beat men off with titanium baseball bats."

Whitney's breath caught in her throat, noting the stark heat in his eyes. "I don't condone violence." Her words came out in a whisper.

Everything after that seemed to happen in slow motion, as he was giving her time to get away, walk away from the fire that erupted and now threatened to engulf them. She shivered when she felt the light press of his hands on her hips, and then he was pulling her until her body was flush against his. She could feel him hardening against her. Her hands instinctively went up, her palms flat against his chest.

She stifled a moan. *Oh, that feels nice.*

"Is this what you wanted to happen when you invited me in?"

The rough huskiness in his voice, combined with the substantialness of his erection, set off sparks between her thighs and had her nipples standing at stiff attention.

"I don't know. Maybe. All I know is that I didn't want you to leave." She was telling the truth, but confessing it to him put her in a situation she didn't frequently find herself in. Feeling vulnerable to a man.

Myles let out a groan, the sound rumbling in his chest as his arms encircled her waist, and his hands smoothed over her ass before cupping each cheek. A bolt of desire shot straight to her core, quickening her breathing.

"I'm not talking about today."

Whitney stilled as she stared into his cobalt-blue eyes. "You mean last week when you didn't want to come in and talk?"

"That was the problem. I wanted to come in and do a hell of a lot more than talk. I was trying to be good."

Whitney couldn't have been happier it appeared he'd abandoned that effort.

"These past few weeks have been torture," he said on a low groan.

She gulped. "Torture?" His heart beat strong and steady beneath her palms.

His gaze dropped to her mouth. "From having to restrain myself from doing this." And then his mouth covered hers.

19

Whitney's mouth instantly opened under his. She'd been waiting for this. Had imagined it too many times to count. And Lord, the man could kiss. It made her feel drugged, sapping her of the ability to think of anything but him.

"Your bedroom?" he asked in a husky voice, his mouth leaving hers and trailing kisses down her neck.

Whitney couldn't do anything but nod. The next minute passed in a blur of movement. Hurried footsteps down the hall, up the stairs, and into her bedroom. His hands and mouth were on her the entire time, driving rational thoughts out of her mind.

"Nice," Myles remarked after a cursory look around the room. His lust-filled gaze returned to her and was followed by a reverent, "Beautiful."

Turned on and impatient, Whitney reached for the loose hem of her skirt, only to have Myles brush her hands aside and take control. "No, let me," he said, his gaze hooded as he dragged the tip of his tongue along his full bottom lip. "I've wanted to do this since I saw you in it. You were thinking about me when you changed, weren't you? You wanted to make it easier for me to strip you naked."

To prove his point, he sank to his knees, reached under her dress, and deftly removed the thong she'd put on twenty minutes earlier. Whitney's breath quickened as she absently kicked it aside.

"I don't know whether to explore you now, sight unseen, or lay you down on the bed and pull this up—" peering up at her through hooded eyes, he slid his hand between her thighs "—so I can see every inch of you. Which do you prefer?" As he came slowly to his feet, his fingers grazed her center, tempting and torturing her.

Whitney let out a soft gasp and began to pant.

He wanted her to choose? Now she was turned on *and* speechless.

"On the bed it is, but how about we take the dress off altogether?" he murmured, walking her backward until the backs of her thighs hit the edge of the mattress. Soon he stripped off her dress, and then she was on her back, looking up at a ravenous Myles.

"Goddamn, you're beautiful."

Whitney found her voice, even if it was slightly breathless. "So are you. Now it's your turn to take off your clothes, unless you want me to do it for you," she purred.

For a second, she thought he was going to ignore her and pleasure her within an inch of her life while fully dressed. But with a devilish grin, he backed away from the bed and made quick work of removing every stitch of clothing.

Whitney pushed up on her elbows to enjoy the show and found herself licking her lips when his shirt came off. Broad shoulders, muscled arms, and six-pack abs, she was there for it. When he dropped trou, her panting began anew. His navy boxer briefs came next, causing Whitney to damn near swallow her tongue.

No wonder he looked so confident. The man was packing a lot of heat, and she'd soon be the recipient of all that firepower.

"Condom?" he asked in all his beautiful, naked glory. Whitney wanted to lick him from head to toe but had to be content to map him with her eyes.

She nodded toward the night table. "Top drawer," she said, her voice little more than a squeak.

After he retrieved one and set it on top for future use, he made a place between her legs. Whitney sucked in a breath and tried to prepare herself, but nothing could have prepared her for the intensity of the pleasure that coursed through her when he parted her with his fingers.

"Perfect," he growled, the tip of his tongue making another appearance between his lips as if he was in deep concentration. He ran his finger down the slippery seam of her sex.

Whitney let out a whimper, bucking her hips against his hand. If he didn't get inside her right now, she feared she was going to explode. Usually it took more than a kiss, a hasty strip tease, and the slow drag of a finger down her sex to get her off. Orgasms for her tended to be hit-or-miss. Currently, Myles was firing on all cylinders, and he'd yet to venture near her breasts.

She was convinced that one of his talents included mind reading because seconds later, he wrapped his lips around her nipple, laving the tip with his tongue.

Whitney's back came off the mattress, and the hands that had been clenching the sheets sought purchase on his shoulders. Then she mindlessly ran her fingers through his hair.

"Enough, Myles," she said, short of breath, her senses swimming. "I can't take any more. I need you."

In response to her plea, he switched his attention to her other breast. He started with a gentle bite and followed it with a lick around the areola. Whitney bit down on her lip, stifling a scream when he took her nipple gently between his teeth before sucking it into his mouth.

The man was a monster.

"Myles, please."

He pushed inside her with his finger, which was quickly joined by another, stretching her and making her writhe. "See, that's what I'm looking for," he whispered, the easy glide of his fingers in and out of her demonstrating how slick and ready she was for him.

Running her palm down the hair-roughened ridges of his chest, Whitney wrapped her hand around his erection.

A tortured sound emerged from the back of his throat.

"This is what I want," she said, pumping his cock for emphasis.

Myles let out a hiss and grabbed the condom. Whitney loosened her grip and watched, mesmerized, as he rolled it on his impressive length. Once it was in place, he stared down at her, devouring her with his eyes.

"Come here." His voice was roughened by desire and want. Holding one slim leg in each hand, he hooked her knees over his shoulders, opening her up to him even more. "It's time for me to give you what you want." His blue eyes blazed with lust as he lined himself up at her opening. In the next breath, he was inside her.

Whitney savored the inexorable feel of him filling her. The firm, slow glide until he was lodged as deep as he could go. Then he stilled, dropped his head, and closed his eyes, his face the picture of tortured ecstasy. "Christ Almighty, you feel so fucking good."

In response, she flexed her inner muscles, clamping down tight around him and encouraging him to move.

Myles's eyes snapped open, desire blazing in them. From

that moment on, his gaze never left hers as he slowly pulled out and then slammed back in, wringing cries of pleasure from her with every thrust.

The ending came too soon as an orgasm took control of her body, and she rode the wave to its peak. As her sex convulsed around him, Myles quickened his pace, his hips like pistons as he raced toward his release.

His hoarse cry of satisfaction reverberated throughout the room. And then there was only the sound of their breathing, labored and choppy...and music to her ears.

Whitney let out a hum of sexual satiation. "Do you realize we've come full circle?"

Myles turned his head and raised an eyebrow at her. "I have no idea what you're talking about." Whitney shivered at the sexy, low growl of his voice.

"I just mean that we had a baby together, and now we've had sex. Full circle."

His shoulders shook in silent laughter. "No, I think what you mean is ass-backward." Then that devilish smile was back on his face. "And speaking of asses, have I told you how much I love yours?" he said, grabbing a handful to emphasize his point.

Whitney giggled—she couldn't remember the last time she'd done that with a man in bed—and scooted closer to him, essentially molding herself to him, her breasts flush against his chest.

"I'm kinda fond of yours too." If she'd thought his ass looked spectacular in jeans, the view had only gotten better when he stripped down to his birthday suit. Her baby daddy's body was a work of art.

For a minute, neither of them spoke, Whitney content to revel in the aftermath of the toe-curling orgasm while running her palm across his chest and over the defined ridges of his abs. His time at the gym was paying off in spades.

When the silence grew protracted, Whitney tipped her head back and peered at him. His sudden solemnity made her nervous. Was he already regretting it?

"What's wrong?" After the question was out, she wasn't sure she actually wanted to know.

"What are we doing here?"

A nervous laugh escaped. "Your parents never told you about the birds and the bees, or didn't you take sex ed in school? Don't tell me you attended a Catholic school."

His mouth twitched. "You know what I mean. We're going to be in each other's life in some capacity for the rest of our lives. Did we just fuck it all up?"

"Well, we did fuck, and I enjoyed it very much," she replied glibly.

"Oh yeah?" he said, staring into her eyes, searching. For what, she wasn't sure. "And do you see us doing it again?"

"Since I'm not into one-night stands, and you're so very good at it, I sure hope so. Unless you don't want to."

"Oh, I want to, alright. I just don't want us to—"

"I know, I know," she said, cutting him off. "Fuck this up. And we won't. Let's promise not to interfere in the other's love life when it's over. Let's be adults about it, okay?"

Right now, he didn't know her well enough to know that she wasn't possessive or clingy. When whatever this was between them ended, she'd simply move on as she always did, and they'd co-parent Haylee like the well-adjusted ex-lovers they would be. It was as simple as that. And in the meantime, she intended to enjoy every bump of the ride.

A look flashed across his face. One she couldn't discern.

"What is it? Tell me," she coaxed softly. She hoped to God he didn't think she was incapable of that, acting like an adult when it was over.

"I'm thinking about how much you're talked about. Written about. This week alone, I saw four articles about your love life, and I don't want to be the subject of every sleazy rag in the country," he said gruffly.

Whitney pushed up on her elbow until she was peering down at him. "If you don't want to do this, I would completely understand."

Sometimes she forgot who she was dealing with and that among other things, she came with baggage. Big, heavy baggage in the form of ravenous paparazzi with telescopic lenses, invasive questions being shouted at her while having mics shoved in her face when she was out in public minding her business, and whoever she was seeing getting the equivalent of a media colonoscopy, every part of his life scrutinized and dissected. All the things Myles hated about…her life.

Gazing at her, he slowly lifted his hand and slid his fingers through her hair, which had begun to go wavy in spots. "No, count me in."

Until he said the words aloud, Whitney hadn't realized she'd been holding her breath—figuratively. The pressure in her chest eased.

"Don't worry, I know how to be discreet," she quietly reassured him, and began planting kisses along his bristled jaw.

Shifting his weight until he lay flat on his back, Myles pulled her on top of him, his body signaling that he was ready for round two. "As long as you're never discreet when we're alone."

Lowering her mouth to his, she murmured throatily before their lips touched, "Oh, that's something you'll never have to worry about."

20

"You look happy and rested," Shannon commented, handing him the financials he'd asked her to print out. She said it as if he usually dragged himself into the office with bags under his eyes.

Myles leaned back in his chair and regarded her, eyebrows raised. "What exactly are you insinuating? That I usually look sleep-deprived and act like a boor?"

To that, his paralegal threw her head back and laughed. "Only you can take a compliment and turn it into an insult. You were humming a song. What else am I supposed to think?" she asked with an innocent, wide-eyed blink.

"No I wasn't," he instinctively denied. Then he remembered falling asleep last night to Whitney's latest album. He'd purchased it purely for research purposes but hadn't been able to get one song in particular out of his mind: "When It's Right, Make It Good."

Okay, so maybe Shannon was right.

Shit. Is that what it had come to? One night with Whitney had him acting out of character enough to elicit a comment from the person who worked most closely with him. He had to fix that, and fast.

"My sister took Haylee for the weekend again, so for the second time this month, I got a full night's sleep." Not a lie, but the multiple rounds of sex with Whitney had certainly contributed to him waking well-rested and hard as a hammer and ready for the morning round.

"Ah. Well, that makes sense," she said. "I hope you were able to do something fun and relaxing."

She'd never know the half of it. "I had dinner with friends," he replied before quickly changing the subject. "How was your weekend?"

After a few minutes of idle chitchat, Shannon returned to her desk, closing his office door behind her. Myles picked up the folder with the information Oasis had sent in preparation for their potential IPO.

The numbers for the company were solid, and their financial forecast was strong. The only thing that worried him was the steep drop in operating costs. That wasn't something that typically occurred from one quarter to the next, especially in a significant amount. He'd have to follow up with Ellen Sato and give Whitney a heads-up.

Call her now, the voice in his head urged him. And it had nothing to do with the fact that her visit with Haylee wasn't until tomorrow and they hadn't made plans to see each other before then. This was business, and she'd specifically asked that he keep her in the loop.

Whitney picked up on the second ring. "Missing me already?"

Myles's body instantly reacted to the playful intimacy of her greeting as he pictured her beautiful face in his mind. His senses stirred, and something warm bloomed in his chest.

"From the moment you left." They'd had to be home by

noon the following day, when Natalie brought Haylee back for Whitney's visit.

"Whew!" she said with a giddy laugh. "I'm glad I'm not the only one." She paused before saying, "But seriously, I was hoping you'd call."

Myles took that as an invitation. "Does that mean I'll be seeing you tonight? I know Haylee would be thrilled." This wasn't about sex. Well, it wasn't *just* about sex. He wanted to see her. Spend time with her. She was the first woman in a long time whose company he simply enjoyed.

"How about I come over and send Eunice home a few hours early? That way, when you get home, I'll be there with another one of my home-cooked meals, courtesy of Julia's."

"Or I can leave work early, pick up some groceries on the way, and teach you to cook," he countered. "How does that sound?"

"What're we making?" She didn't sound convinced his was the better plan.

"Shrimp and steak."

"Oh, sounds yummy." She made smacking sounds with her lips that had him remembering their pillowy soft perfection as they had parted under his. He hadn't been able to get enough of them. Of her.

"Okay then, I'll see you when I get home."

"Wait, was that why you called? To invite me to cook dinner for you?" she asked in mock affront.

No, but he wasn't about to tell her that. His concerns about her company's financials could wait. He could tell her about them later tonight.

A wicked grin took over his face. "No, I called to see if you were sore."

"You're lucky I can walk, considering the girth of that hammer you've got between your legs," she said, cackling.

"Then I did what I set out to do, which was to give you multiple orgasms and leave an impression."

One would think that after three months, Whitney wouldn't get choked up and be filled with such a sense of awe every time she laid eyes on Haylee. It was like she was seeing her for the first time.

"Hi, my sweet little girl," she cooed as she lifted her out of Eunice's arms. A gummy smile wreathed her daughter's face, showcasing a pair of dimples and two little teeth. Her arms stretched out and wrapped around Whitney's neck.

"She's happy to see you," Eunice stated with a fond smile at Haylee while patting her gently on the back.

"And I missed her so much." Whitney showered kisses all over her flushed cheeks.

When they'd agreed on the visitation terms, Myles promised to revisit them once Haylee was comfortable with her. She didn't want to overstep just because they were now sleeping together, but she hoped he'd agree that it was time to revisit the terms.

Whitney took advantage of the two hours before Myles came home to enjoy some alone time with her daughter. They spent a solid thirty minutes of it playing peekaboo before moving on to watch Haylee's favorite yellow bird in action on *Sesame Street*. She was also crazy about Elmo, pointing excitedly at the TV whenever he appeared on screen.

But her father's arrival elicited a whole other level of excitement. Something Whitney completely understood when he entered the family room.

Good Lord, the man revved her engines like no other man ever had. Tailored suits had never been this much of a turn-on for her until she got a look at what he had going on under

his, and the blue-gray striped one he had on now only exem-
plified why.

His gaze briefly met hers before alighting on their daughter
as she lunged toward him.

"Someone's excited that Daddy's home."

"I hope she isn't the only one." Myles plucked a squirming
Haylee from her arms.

Smiling, Whitney watched their daughter wrap her arms
around his neck, hanging onto him like a climbing ivy.

The adoration in his eyes reflected the love he had for her,
and the entire scene damn near brought tears to Whitney's
eyes even while a part of her envied their bond. Would Haylee
ever feel that way about her? Would their connection ever be
that strong? The logical answer was no, not as long as things
remained the way they were. Haylee had yet to see the room
she'd readied for her over two months ago.

Pushing to her feet, she smoothed her palms over her jean-
clad thighs. "I'm excited in a different way."

Myles peered at her from above their daughter's head. "I
would hope so." The sexual heat in his eyes promised something he couldn't deliver, at least not tonight.

What she and Myles had wasn't like any of her other relationships. There was a list of things she didn't know. For instance,
were they allowed to be affectionate in front of their daughter?

Myles soon answered that question by leaning down and
pressing a firm kiss on her mouth that included a too-brief
parrying of tongues. The taste proved more than enough to
whet her appetite.

"Hi," he murmured in a gravelly voice. "How was she?"

Whitney pulled her head down from out of the clouds. "She
was an angel."

"How was your day?"

"I got an audition for *Kaleidoscope*. The director thinks I'd be perfect for the lead female role."

"That's wonderful." Myles looked genuinely happy for her.

"Nothing is guaranteed, but I'm crossing my fingers and hoping for the best." She couldn't get too excited about it. From what her agent, Avery, had told her, several very talented actresses were up for the coveted role that had Oscar contender written all over it.

"I'm not worried. You're a shoo-in," he stated with all the confidence of the man giving her orgasms. "They'd be fools not to cast you."

Whitney's face warmed under the glow of his praise even though she was certain he'd never seen any of her movies.

"And I'm not saying that because I've seen you naked," he said as if reading her mind. "I saw *Land of Riches*, and you were brilliant in it."

Whitney's gaze immediately flew to Haylee, whose head ping-ponged between them from the secure perch of her father's arms.

Myles chuckled. "Don't worry, she doesn't understand what we're talking about."

"I'm sure a lot of parents think that until the day their kid screams *Daddy saw Mommy naked* in the grocery store."

"So you've met my niece," he said wryly. "That's something she would do. But the thing is, Daddy is allowed to see Mommy naked."

"Not if they're not together," she said in a tone of mock reproach.

Myles threw his head back and laughed. "We've still got a few years until she'll be able to embarrass us like that."

He said it forgetting that they wouldn't be an "us" by the time Haylee's vocabulary was that advanced. The knowledge caused a pinch in her chest.

"Come on, let's get the cooking lesson over with," she said. "I got some salmon just in case I make a mess of the shrimp."

They spent the next hour cooking. Myles taught Whitney the proper way to cut an onion (who knew?) and how to use a potato peeler while Haylee wheeled drunkenly around the kitchen in her new walker. Myles had bought it for her last week, and it had been slow going at first, but as she'd gotten used to it, she'd picked up speed and now treated the thing like a bumper car and the kitchen, her personal racetrack.

In the end, they decided against steak and shrimp, opting instead for honey-glazed salmon—since it was delicious and one of the easiest fish to cook—crispy mashed potatoes, roasted Brussels sprouts, and a spinach salad. Since Myles was just starting Haylee out on solid food, he ordered her food from a specialty baby food service that offered organic fruit and vegetables and a variety of choices. Tonight, Whitney fed her creamed sweet potatoes and broccoli in between bites of her meal.

She couldn't believe how normal this felt, the three of them sitting around the table, eating a meal they'd prepared together. It felt so…family-ish.

"How are things at the office?" Myles asked, having already demolished half the food on his plate.

"Good. Sales are up. The new dress April designed is on backorder." Although that wasn't uncommon. April's designs were always a hit. Reason number one Whitney snapped her up when she did.

She'd been introduced to her at the ESPYs, where April's friend was receiving an award. Whitney had fallen in love with April's dress and demanded the name of the designer. Her jaw had nearly hit the floor when she'd discovered she was looking at her. And that—as they say—had been the beginning of a beautiful friendship and lucrative business arrangement.

"Why's that? Poor forecasting?" He took a drink of his wine.

"Andre—he's in charge of purchasing—said he increased the order thirty percent over last year's numbers against a comparable dress, and it still wasn't enough," she said, shrugging as she wiped the food ringing Haylee's rosebud of a mouth. "The factory is sending us more, but it's touch and go if they'll be here in time for the official fall rush."

Myles nodded, his expression thoughtful. "On the topic of your company, I was going over the numbers today, and I noticed a drop in the operating costs in the last quarter. You didn't have a layoff, did you?"

"No, but you noticed that too? I asked Trinity about it. She said ECO Apparel switched factories, and everything checked out."

"It's an awfully steep drop. Do you mind if I have one of my lawyers look into the factory just to be safe?"

"You're the IPO expert here. You do what you think needs to be done. I'll tell Nick over at ECO to give you whatever you need."

"I love working with companies that paint within the lines. Makes my job a whole lot easier." He treated her to a smile that made her stomach dip and her heart skip a beat.

She sent him a coy smile. "I don't mind a bit of painting outside the lines when it comes to other parts of my life."

Myles speared a piece of crispy mashed potato with his fork and shoveled it into his mouth, but a different kind of hunger darkened his eyes as he watched her.

Haylee banged her hand on the top of her highchair in a demand for more food, interrupting the moment. Basically, calling her mother out for failing at her duties.

"Stop flirting with me and feed your daughter," Myles said, smirking.

"Then stop looking at me as if I'm the dessert on the menu," she shot back.

"But sweetheart, you are," he said with a husky laugh. Then he sent her a wink that scrambled her brain.

"That was quick," Myles said when Whitney returned downstairs after putting Haylee to bed.

"I'm not sure she had her afternoon nap. I forgot to ask Eunice before she left."

It was eight o'clock, only late by bedtime for small children standards, and he was ready for bed but not to sleep. How were they going to do this?

Stopping in the middle of the room, Whitney regarded him as he sat sprawled on the couch. "I don't think we have time for dessert tonight. You have work, and I'm shooting a commercial tomorrow. Plus, I'm not sure it's a good idea for us to—you know—do anything with Haylee here. What if she wakes up?"

Oh, hell no. Myles immediately sprang to his feet and started toward her as he tried not to laugh. She watched his approach with a mixture of regret and desire. Smiling, he silently slid an arm around her waist and pulled her close. "First of all, it's not even nine o'clock. I can have you home well before midnight, and the good thing is, you don't need beauty sleep, so anything more than six hours will suffice. Second of all, are you out of your mind? If parents didn't have sex with their children in the house, they'd never have it. And it isn't as if there's a risk of Haylee climbing out of her crib and coming into my room."

Sighing heavily, Whitney wrapped her arms around his neck. "You know what I like to do after sex?"

"Wait until I recover and do it again?" A suggestive waggle of his brows accompanied his question.

"I mean after that," she said, giggling. "The answer is sleep. But if we have sex here, I'm going to have to drag myself out of bed, wait for a car to pick me up, and then spend thirty minutes on the road just to go home to an empty house and bed."

She had a point. Myles wished he could at least drive her home. "Since you're already going home to an empty bed, wouldn't it be better if I gave you a few orgasms first?"

"You're too much." Whitney laughed and playfully hit him on the shoulder.

"Yeah, but I still fit."

Giggling, she slapped him again.

"Come on. You know I'm right. Admit it. And just think about it. In a month or two, you'll have your license and be able to drive yourself home."

"Let's hope I'll be coming more than going," Whitney said, her brown eyes twinkling with mischief. "But for tonight, I really should go home now. I didn't bring anything to change into, and there's nothing I hate more than not having a fresh pair of panties to put on. Next time, I'll come prepared."

Myles closed his eyes and let out a groan as his arms tightened around her. "You can't mean that."

"I'm sorry," she said, her fingers idly playing with the hair at the back of his head. "People have their quirks, and that's one of mine."

Lowering his head, he began nuzzling her neck. God, he loved the way she smelled. "Then how about you don't put them back on?"

She emitted a sound that was between a whimper and a laugh, but the way she angled her head to give him better access indicated that his argument was meeting with some success. "I can see why you're such a good lawyer," she said in a breathy voice. "Your persuasion game is strong."

Smiling, Myles gently nipped the tip of her chin and filled his hands with the cheeks of the most perfect ass he'd ever seen. "What do you say? Are you going to ditch your panties so we can have dessert?"

Whitney's response was a sharp intake of air. He relished the feel of her fingernails digging into his scalp.

"I'll take that as a yes," he growled before his mouth covered hers.

An hour and a half later, Whitney forced herself away from the seductive heat of his body, bringing his fondling of her breast to a halt. "Myles," she moaned, "when you touch me like that, it only makes it harder for me to get out of this bed."

"It can't be harder than I am right now." He caught her hand and placed it on his erection. The man's recovery time rivaled that of an eighteen-year-old. Her hand instinctively closed around him before she caught herself and scrambled off his bed.

"Stop tempting me," she said, laughing. If she gave in, she'd be there until after midnight, and come morning, when she had to wake up at six and be in the makeup chair by seven, she'd be cursing herself to hell and back.

Myles let out a disappointed sigh, settling back on the bed, hands clasped behind his head, his navy blue sheet strewn across his naked form, but unable to hide his growing erection. "I guess I'll just lie here and watch you dress."

Whitney gave a huff of amusement as she bent down to retrieve her jeans from the rug where she'd hastily discarded them.

Myles let out a low groan of despair at the sight of her ass. "You're not playing fair."

"Says the guy who just put my hand on his dick when he knows I have to get up early tomorrow," she countered. To torture him some more, she made sure she put extra shimmy in her hips while pulling on her jeans.

Another masculine groan reverberated throughout the room.

Plucking her bra from the foot of the bed, she turned to face him and took her time adjusting the cups over her breasts. Myles watched her perform the opposite of a strip tease, nostrils flaring and hunger in his eyes, his cock now fully erect. She ignored the sharp stab of lust and the rush of moisture between her thighs.

"You're going to pay for that," he mock-threatened, flinging the sheet aside and climbing buck naked off the bed.

Whitney hastily scooted backward when his hand extended toward her. Myles reached past her, picked his sweatpants off the floor, and quickly yanked them on. "What did you think I was going to do?" he asked, feigning innocence. "I'm being a gentleman and walking you to the door."

But the moment she relaxed her guard, his hand snaked out and grasped her wrist, tugging her into his arms. She surfaced from his kiss minutes later, lips swollen, a little dazed, and a lot turned on.

"Okay, time to go," he announced as if he hadn't just kissed her senseless. "I wouldn't want to be accused of making you late for your shoot tomorrow."

"If I'm late tomorrow, it's going to be all your fault," she groused as she ran her fingers through her hair in an attempt to tame the errant curls.

She snuck a peek in at a sleeping Haylee before they returned downstairs to wait for her ride. Thankfully, Myles had put on a T-shirt, so she wasn't distracted by the scrumptiousness of his chest.

"Are you doing anything this weekend?"

Whitney stood in the loose circle of his arms, her back against his chest, his mouth pressed lightly against the shell of her ear.

"You mean besides my visit with Haylee on Sunday?" she asked, staring out the living room window into the dark summer night.

"I mean Saturday night. My sister is—"

The buzzing of his phone interrupted the rest of whatever he was about to say. She turned as he retrieved it from his pocket.

A scowl formed on his face when he glanced at the screen. He pressed a button and put it back in his pocket.

His eyes met her quizzical stare. "Please tell me that wasn't work."

At first, he appeared reluctant to tell her, but then he blew out a breath and ran a hand through his hair. "No, it was Holly. My ex."

Whitney stilled and swallowed hard. Something that closely resembled jealousy caused her thoughts to jump to conclusions.

"You did say you're officially divorced, right?"

Myles's eyes narrowed, and his scowl became more pronounced. "Would you like me to show you the divorce papers?"

Whitney held her hand up in surrender. "I was just checking," she said with a humorless laugh. "I've gone thirty years without sleeping with a married man, and I'd like to keep it that way."

Myles's expression instantly cleared. He gently caught her hand in his. "I didn't mean it to come out that way."

Weaving their fingers together, she pulled him closer. "What's going on? Why is she calling, and why don't you want to speak to her?"

His response was to briefly avert his gaze from hers. He gave his head a weary shake. "She's just being a pain in the ass."

A feeling of dread unfurled in her gut. "Don't tell me she's asking for alimony." That was one of the more preferred options.

"She's been asking about Haylee, pretending she cares." His tone was dismissive.

"She wants you back." Whitney tried and failed to tamp down the sense of panic his words caused.

"I'm not getting back together with her," Myles stated firmly. That he didn't deny her claim spoke volumes.

"And she thinks she can get to you through our daughter?"

Haylee could have been hers, but she hadn't wanted her. How dare she think she could abandon her and then try to use her to get Myles back?

Absolutely not. Haylee was hers.

"She's not getting to me. Our marriage is over." The finality in his voice was unequivocal, and Whitney believed him. He loved Haylee more than anyone, and he would never jeopardize her well-being.

21

"What are you doing here?" In all the time they'd been married, Holly had never been to his office, and he couldn't believe her first time would be after they divorced.

The only reason he'd told the receptionist that he was available to see her was to put an end to the ever-increasing phone calls once and for all. He intended the meeting to be short and to the point.

"What else am I supposed to do, Myles? You refuse to answer my calls," she said as if she still had a claim on him.

"Listen, I'm not having this conversation with you again," Myles snapped. "We have nothing more to talk about." How many times did he have to tell her that? Honestly, in all the time he'd known her, she'd never acted anything close to this clingy.

"I don't understand why you're getting so mad. There was a time not long ago that you wanted me to show interest in our daughter."

Myles's jaw clenched as he tried to keep his temper in check. "Not anymore, I don't. And Haylee is *not* your daughter. You voluntarily terminated your parental rights and had your name removed from her birth certificate. She's mine, and I'd appreciate it if you stopped calling me. We are done."

"You seem to forget I'm the only mother she's ever known."

Myles made a derisive sound in his throat. "You've got to be kidding. You haven't seen her in months, and you barely saw her before that."

Holly had the grace not to deny the truth, but it wasn't enough to deter her. "I've been doing a lot of thinking, and I admit that I could have handled the entire situation better."

Better than high-tailing it out of town and staying gone for months, weeks after they'd brought Haylee home from the hospital? Better than that?

"Look, Holly, whatever epiphany you've come to, it's too late. Haylee doesn't need you in her life, and I've moved on. I wish you would too." And he didn't want her in their lives. Haylee had Whitney, and so did he…for the time being.

Her brows shot up in surprise. "Are you already seeing someone?"

The accusatory tone in her voice set his teeth on edge. "That's none of your business, just as what you do and who you see is none of mine. That's how divorces work."

For a moment, his ex-wife appeared incapable of speech. They hadn't slept together in months before she'd filed for divorce. How long did she expect him to go without sex?

"Now, if that's all, I have a lot of work to do," Myles said, effectively drawing their meeting to a close.

"You yourself said that Haylee needs a mother."

Myles treated her to a level stare. "My daughter has everything she needs."

"Does her biological mother know you're raising her alone?"

If she wasn't being such a calculating bitch, he'd find the entire conversation amusing. "The biological mother knows everything about this situation. She certainly knows the kind of mother you turned out to be," he said in a tone that could cause frostbite.

"Then I seem to be the only one who's thinking about what's best for Haylee."

Eyeing her, Myles had to give her high marks for audacity. Without saying a word, he strode past her and opened his office door, motioning her to leave.

She stared at him with eyebrows raised, and then her mouth compressed into a line of displeasure. She sailed past him without uttering another word.

Shannon watched the scene from her desk. When her gaze returned to him, Myles tersely instructed her, "If she ever shows up here again, tell her I'm not in."

"Understood," Shannon replied with a brusque nod.

After closing his office door, Myles returned to his desk. He dropped into his chair, tipped his head back, and scrubbed a hand over his face. "Fuck!"

Whitney didn't function well on three hours of sleep, but that's what she had to contend with the day after she concluded Myles's ex wanted him back. The thought of them getting back together, though distressing, wasn't what had kept her awake at night. Okay, maybe that had factored into it just a bit.

No, what scared the crap out of her was the realization that without some document—besides the DNA results—she had no legal claim to her daughter. Her name wasn't on the birth certificate, and she'd done nothing to establish her parental rights. All she had was what amounted to a promissory note outlining visitation rights. Who even knew if the thing would hold up in court?

Whitney needed to talk to Chey. She would know what to do.

"How do I establish my parental rights...in the eyes of the law?" she asked the second Chey picked up her call.

"Well, hello to you, too," her cousin said in an amused voice. "Nice of you to call."

"Sorry. Hi. Now, can you answer my question?"

"I have to be in court in twenty minutes, so I don't have much time."

"In a situation like mine, what do I need to do to establish maternity? Would presenting the DNA results to the courts be enough?"

"DNA establishing maternity would be a good start, and there's also the matter of the birth certificate. Having you listed as the mother would boost your case. It would also be good if you could get something in writing from the custodial parent. Something detailing your current visitation arrangement. It'll also be good if you're contributing financially to her upbringing. It would prove to the judge that you've already taken on the responsibility of the role."

"Getting my name added to the birth certificate may be a bit of a problem," Whitney fretted. "Stacy doesn't want this going public until after the movie is out at the end of the year. And frankly, neither does Myles. He'd be happy to keep that a secret forever," she said with a mirthless laugh. "Or until Haylee's a little older. Of course, financial support won't be a problem." She'd work that out with Myles. All they had to do was agree on a monthly child support amount. While she was at it, she'd set up a trust and college fund for her too.

"Honest to God, your manager is a tyrant. What does she think's going to happen if people find out you have a child? Stop going to your movies and listening to your music?" The eye roll was insinuated in her cousin's tone.

"You know it's not about me having a kid but the circumstances around her birth," Whitney said, defending her manager, who'd been with her since the beginning. She owed a good portion of her success to Stacy. At the very least, she had more than earned her fifteen percent as well as Whitney's loyalty.

"Personally, I think something like this would boost sales for the movie. When it eventually comes out, the story is going to be all over the news. Someone is going to turn this into a movie."

That was exactly what Whitney was afraid of. Myles would have a fit. It was the last thing he wanted, and she understood why.

"Anyway, Whit, I gotta run. I hope that helped. Let me know if you need me to draw up the papers," Chey said, and by the sound of her voice, she could tell her cousin was on the move.

After thanking her, Whitney slowly placed her phone on the kitchen counter and debated how best to broach the subject with Myles. She didn't think he'd have an issue with the money—she had a lot of it, and what was hers was Haylee's. It was the birth certificate part that might give him pause.

Suddenly, a thought struck her. Whose name was on the birth certificate now? Probably his ex-wife's. They'd all assumed she was the mother when Haylee was born. Unless her name had been removed since then. No use stressing out about it when she could just ask Myles.

Whitney grabbed her phone, her heart racing, and quickly shot a message off to him.

Are you busy?

When her message remained in the delivered status after a minute went by, she slid off the stool and opened the fridge in an effort to distract herself.

Whitney sighed. Her mother would have a fit if she saw the sad, empty state the fridge was in. She'd tried to browbeat her into hiring a cook if Whitney wasn't going to learn to cook for herself. Whitney couldn't think of a bigger waste of money. The chef would have been cooking for one picky eater who didn't eat all that much. Instead, she'd subscribed to a food delivery service.

Her phone buzzed, the screen lighting up briefly.

Whitney looked down and snorted in laughter when she saw Myles's response.

I don't text. I'm calling...

The phone had barely begun to ring when she answered it.

"In the future, just call. My fingers are too big to be messing around with these miniature keyboards," he said in greeting.

"And that's what the lovely little microphone on the keyboard is for. It's called voice dictation. You should give it a try." She wasn't a fan of digital keyboards, big or small.

"If I'm going to talk, why not just pick up the phone and call? It's easier and faster," came his reasonable retort.

"Okay, fine. I won't text," she said, ready to let the subject drop. This was trivial, and they had important things to discuss. "I've been thinking, and I'm going to set up a trust for Haylee."

Not that she'd expected him to hoot and holler or jump for joy, but she hadn't expected the dead silence that followed, either.

"I wanted to let you know," she added in her need to fill it.

Because he was the custodial parent, and that's the kind of thing he should know.

"And I'm putting aside money for her education," she continued.

"I've already put money aside for her college fund," he said, finally breaking his silence.

"Okay, but that doesn't mean I can't, right?"

More silence. This time she resisted the urge to fill it and won.

"Look, I don't want to discuss this over the phone. We can talk about it when you come over tomorrow."

Well, that answered the other question she'd been about to ask. If she could come over tonight. "Good, then we can also talk about child support." She might as well put it out there and let him get accustomed to the idea.

"Child support?"

"Yes, Myles, child support," she said in a calm voice. "Haylee is my child too, and I want to contribute equally to her upbringing."

Most custodial parents would be thrilled at the offer of financial help. Yes, she knew that Myles was wealthy in his own right, but he shouldn't have to bear the entire financial responsibility of raising Haylee alone, regardless of the circumstances, especially as she was able and willing to help.

"We'll talk about it," was all he said, and then told her he had to get back to work.

"Gee, that went well," she muttered after they ended the call.

22

Myles tried not to read too much into Whitney's sudden offer of child support, but the prospect dogged him for the rest of the day. When he put Haylee to bed that night, he sat by her crib and watched her sleep.

He loved his daughter more than anything and couldn't imagine his life without her. Apart from the nuisance calls and the visit from Holly, everything was going better than it had in a long time. Haylee adored Whitney, and he was pretty fond of her too. He didn't want that to change, and he knew introducing money into the mix would do just that.

Child support arrangements were for divorced or unmarried couples who, by word or deed, had taken on the financial responsibility of their child. Whitney didn't fall into either category, and wealthy or not, that responsibility shouldn't fall to her, which was what he'd tell her when she came over tomorrow night.

After several minutes, he stood and lightly touched his daughter's smooth cheeks before going to his room. He'd deal with it in the morning. Right now, all he wanted was sleep.

The next day brought a fresh wave of problems. One of the lawyers working on an important case was in a motorcycle accident and would be out of commission for a couple weeks. He was lucky to have walked away from it with a broken ankle and a dislocated shoulder. Shannon was out sick with the flu, so unless he could share Elie's paralegal, Gerald, he'd be doing his own research.

To top it all off, he couldn't stop thinking about Whitney. Last night, he'd made the mistake of watching one of her music videos when he'd gone to his room. After watching her dance around the stage wearing a bustier top and black leather pants that looked painted on, he dreamed about her riding him wearing only that bustier. For his sin, he'd woken up with a raging hard-on, not his normal morning wood.

When his cell phone rang, Myles welcomed the distraction. Despite exchanging numbers at the party and promising to keep in touch, Myles was surprised to see it was Cameron Mitchell calling.

"Hey, Cam, to what do I owe this pleasure?" Myles stopped what he was doing and leaned back in his chair, stretching his legs out under the desk.

"I bet you didn't think you'd hear from me," Cam said, chuckling. "I meant to call you after my sister read me the riot act. She says you know that I know about Haylee and Sahara."

"Hey, it's not your fault I figured it out." Myles had been more relieved that there was nothing going on between him and Whitney. That he was in on the secret didn't bother him. Whitney and his sister were tight. Myles didn't think Cam would betray either woman.

"Yeah, well, I should have kept my big mouth shut. Those were my sister's exact words, by the way," he said, his tone dryly amused. "Anyway, I want to make it up to you, and since I'm going to be in your neck of the woods today, I called to see if you wanted to grab lunch. My treat, of course."

"There's nothing to make up," Myles protested. No harm, no foul was his motto.

But Cam was insistent, replying, "I'm not taking no for an answer."

Given the day he was having, it would be nice to get out of the office for a bit, something he rarely did.

"I'll go, but you're not paying for me." He could be stubborn too.

They agreed to meet at a restaurant that was within walking distance from Myles's office, and Cameron was already seated at a table when he arrived two hours later.

When he'd first seen Cam at the party, Myles thought he was an actor. He had the looks for it, that was for sure. He'd never seen a Black guy with blue eyes in real life. But as it turned out, Cam was the director at a private wealth management firm, nothing nearly as glamorous.

They shook hands and patted backs before taking seats across from one another. Their server arrived seconds later as if she'd been awaiting his arrival. Tara, who was pretty and looked to be in her early twenties, took their order but didn't appear in a hurry to leave, asking them how their days were going so far and if they had plans for the weekend.

When she finally left, Cam said, "I still can't figure out if she was flirting with me or you."

Myles chuckled. "I'm pretty sure it was both."

"These college girls." Cameron shook his head, looking faintly amused. "I know a lot of guys don't mind them that young. Not me. I prefer women who have a bit more mileage on their odometer. You know, done a few more laps around the track. They know the score."

"Hell, I'm starting to think that I'm the one in the dark," Myles said with a gruff laugh.

"That's the divorce talking. You just need to find the right woman," Cam assured him. "And you won't find it in a girl barely out of college who's never lived on her own and doesn't know the first thing about balancing a checkbook."

"Sounds like you're talking from experience." He couldn't balance a checkbook at that age either.

"Something like that," Cam admitted. "I was thirty, and she was twenty-two, right out of college. I should have known better. But you know how it is. Sometimes the dick wants what the dick wants."

"An eloquent way of putting it," Myles said wryly. "So what happened? Bad breakup?"

"You could say so. When I transferred out here with my job, she showed up on my doorstep a month later saying she wanted to 'surprise' me. She moved more than halfway across the country to be with me because I'd said I didn't do long-distance relationships."

"Oh shit."

"Yeah. Kennedy read me the riot act—she does that a lot—saying I should have just broken up with her instead of leading her to believe it was the distance that was the problem. Sue me for trying to let her down easy. How the fuck was I supposed to know she'd up and move out here without a job or a place to stay?"

Myles felt for the guy. "Did she go home?"

"Hell, yeah, she did. I made sure of it. I let her crash at my place for the night and bought her a one-way ticket back to Norfolk the next day. Never heard from her again."

"And you don't think if she'd been older, she'd have done that?" Myles was skeptical. He'd heard stories of women and men doing crazy shit for love.

Cameron gave a derisive snort. "Not if she had to sell her house or break a lease and quit her job. You only do shit like that when you don't have much to lose."

"Are you talking about youth or money? Because money changes that whole scenario. She wouldn't need you to buy her ticket and would be staying at the Waldorf until she got her own place."

While Cam contemplated his point, the server returned with their drinks. Myles picked up his Coke and took a healthy swallow.

"I really don't think money would have made a difference," Cam finally concluded, holding his whiskey sour.

Myles snorted. "Believe me, money makes a difference."

His eyes narrowed. "Are we talking about Sahara now?"

Sometimes Myles forgot some of her friends called her by her stage name. "Why, because she's rich?"

Cam lowered his voice. "And because you have a kid together." He stared at Myles, his silver-blue eyes unwavering. "What's going on? Things between you two not going well?"

"She wants to start giving me child support."

Cam's eyes widened, and then he smiled and held up his glass in a toast. "Congratulations, man. Lucky you."

"I don't need her damn money," Myles griped, and took another drink of his Coke. He wasn't in a hurry to get back to his office, and Cam informed him he'd be heading home after this.

"Right, but the money isn't for you. It's for your daughter, who is her kid too."

As if he didn't know that.

"I have more than enough to give Haylee everything she needs."

Cam sat back and watched him, his gaze quietly assessing as he idly tapped his finger on the side of his glass. "You're not one of those guys who feels emasculated if a woman makes more than him, are you?"

Shaking his head, Myles smiled ruefully. "No. That's not it at all." His situation was different. Yeah, maybe he felt insecure, but it wasn't about that.

"Well then, it's not a competition. Accept the money, and thank God she's not asking *you* to pay," his friend said with a harrumph before taking a sip of his drink.

"Yeah, but why offer if I didn't ask?" Had his two failed marriages jaded him so much that he couldn't accept a gift in the spirit in which it was given? Not everyone had an ulterior motive, and he didn't want to believe Whitney's offer came with strings attached.

The woman he'd come to know didn't operate like that. She'd been transparent and direct with him in their dealings with each other.

"Why shouldn't she offer? It's her kid, and it isn't as if she's going to miss the money." Cameron stared at Myles like he was daft.

"Right, but it isn't as if she—" Myles abruptly broke off once he realized he'd given this argument before.

But it seemed it didn't take a mind reader to figure out what he was going to say, because Cam came back with, "It doesn't matter how she came into her life. Sahara wants her. Kennedy says she's crazy about her. Talks about her all the time. So my advice to you is just to relax." Cam smiled. "Don't look a gift horse in the mouth. She's doing what any responsible parent would."

The tension he'd been carrying around in his shoulders eased. "I'm a lawyer. Our job is to look gift horses in the mouth," he said wryly.

That he'd instinctively called her motives into question must have been caused by lingering feelings he had when she'd changed her mind about terminating her parental rights, and he'd feared a custody battle. But Whitney was happy with their co-parent-with-benefits arrangement, and he'd been worrying for nothing.

Cam shuddered and made a face. "One of my friends is a lawyer, and I couldn't do what you guys do. Way too many years in school, and I've heard nightmares about the exam."

Myles laughed gruffly, thoughts of how much studying had gone into passing it on his first attempt. There had been days he'd fallen asleep fully dressed with the study guide in his hands.

Brutal.

"Believe me, it's not for everyone. After five years of doing criminal law, I reached my breaking point. Dealing with the penal system in this country burns you out fast. I admire and respect the lawyers who can go the distance, but I couldn't." Walking away from criminal law had been one of the easiest decisions he'd ever made.

Cam held up his drink again. "Kudos to the five years," he said with a tip of his glass. "And about the child support, stick the money in an ESA for your daughter. By the time she's an adult, she'll have enough saved up to put herself through college several times."

If he wasn't able to convince Whitney that he didn't need the monthly stipend, that's exactly what he intended to do.

"Give me a call if you want me to go over some options with you. I can have it set up within hours," he added.

"Sounds good." Myles had a feeling he'd be taking him up on his offer.

After lunch, the two men parted and promised to get together again before the end of the month. It had been a long time since Myles clicked with another guy, and it was nice to talk to someone outside of his profession.

He returned to the office to find Hunter George talking to Gerald, who was going through a folder on Shannon's desk. On his approach, their heads swung in his direction.

"There he is," Gerald said, appearing relieved.

"I didn't know I'd be gone that long." Normally, he didn't go out for lunch, preferring to order in and eat something at his desk. "Come on in," he said, preceding Hunter into his office.

Inside, Myles leaned against the edge of the desk, legs crossed at the ankles and arms crossed over his chest. Regarding his senior IPO attorney, he said, "Okay, what you got?"

Hunter handed him a thin stack of papers. "I checked into that anonymous LLC, and you're not going to believe what I found."

Myles looked at him, eyebrow cocked, before lowering his gaze to study the document in his hand. "What am I not going to believe?"

"The trail leads to a state contractor that received a no-bid contract last year with the state prisons."

Myles continued his perusal, noting the name of the contractor and the start date of the contract. But it was when his gaze landed on the line titled *Labor* that he realized what they were dealing with.

"Jesus H. Christ," Myles exclaimed in disbelief, tossing the papers down in disgust. "ECO Apparel is using prison labor?"

Hunter responded with a grim nod.

Myles sat stunned as a barrage of thoughts ran through his mind. There was no way Whitney knew about this, and he hated having to be the one to tell her. God only knew what would happen when he did.

"Okay," he said, coming to his full height and squaring his shoulders. "Let's put the brakes on things for now. There's no way Oasis will be able to IPO this year. I'll talk to Ms. Richardson and see what she wants to do."

"I'm pretty sure she's going to want to shut it down."

"Without a doubt." Whitney was going to freak out. She and her employees were keeping control of fifty-five percent of the stock. There was no way she wanted any part of this.

"Do you think she knows?"

"Hell no."

If Hunter was surprised by the vehemence of Myles's response, he didn't show it. But there was a clear note of warning in his voice when he said, "If the press ever gets a hold of this…"

"They won't," Myles shot back before conditioning his response with, "If they do, it won't be through us."

"Okay, I'll wrap up the analysis—hopefully, there won't be any other surprises—and wait for word from you on how Ms. Richardson wants to handle this."

23

Whitney could tell something was wrong. Not with Haylee, who met her visit with her usual exuberance, but with the man of the house. As had become the norm these days, she'd gotten there early and sent Eunice home before he came home from work.

She was at the stove heating up organic mashed potatoes when he entered the kitchen, and what was immediately noticeable was the strain around his mouth despite the smile he bestowed on their daughter.

At the sight of her father, Haylee started babbling in excitement as she squirmed in her high chair, her arms stretching out to him, demanding to be picked up.

Whitney's eyes drank in the sight of him, jacket off, tie loosened around his neck, and the beginnings of a five-o'clock shadow on his jaw. Desire fluttered in her belly and thrummed between her legs. She'd missed him last night. That was what happened when the sex was that good. She wanted it all the time.

"Hey, you're home early," she said as he pressed a quick kiss against her hair on his way to Haylee. Not the lip lock he normally greeted her with. She'd been looking forward to that, but the evening wasn't over, and she hoped that once they put the "talk" behind them, things would return to normal. Their new normal came with mind-blowing orgasms.

"I knew you were here." Once he had Haylee in his arms, Myles turned, his gaze moving hungrily over her. "Are those new?" he asked, tipping his chin at her jeans.

"Nope. You like?" she asked coyly. She'd worn them because she loved what they did to her ass, knowing he was a big fan of said ass.

His gaze lifted to hers, a wolfish glint in his eyes. "I do." Two words that said so much more.

Smiling, she spooned the mashed potatoes and apple sauce into Haylee's *Little Mermaid* bowl. "Then mission accomplished." She snuck a peek at him.

His eyes promised retribution—the good kind. And just like that, things between them swung back to normal. Because she hadn't spoken to him for over a day, she'd worried that the prospect of legalizing her role in Haylee's life had spooked him, turning him into the Myles of old.

The next two hours flew by. After dinner, Myles joined Whitney in bathing and putting Haylee to bed, something they hadn't done together in weeks, but other than that, things were fine.

"We hit a road bump during the analysis portion of the IPO evaluation process," Myles said as they returned to the family room.

Whitney's eyes widened. They were supposed to talk about child support and all that. "How big of a bump are we talking?" She took a seat on the couch, and he sat down next to her, his thigh pressed firmly against hers.

"We discovered the cause of the big drop in your operating expenses."

"Okay," she prompted, "what is it?"

"ECO is using prison labor to assemble your clothes."

For a moment, Whitney couldn't breathe. It was more than a gut punch. It was a knife to the heart. "No, that can't be." Her denial was instinctive. Things like that didn't happen—shouldn't happen. It wasn't that she hadn't heard about prisoners making license plates, but somehow, this was different. She knew for a fact the work they were doing cost ECO less than they'd been paying the factory overseas.

Myles sighed and took her hands in his. "Everything's on pause. I need to know how you want to handle it," he said, his voice calm, but the worry in his eyes let her know how serious the matter was for her and the company.

"I'm—we have to stop it. I refuse to have anything to do with something like that. I'm going to call Donald myself. Tonight." Donald Edwards was ECO's CEO.

Whitney had never experienced this kind of panic before. Her entire career flashed before her eyes as it went up in flames. This was the kind of controversy that could ruin everything she'd worked for. It would undermine everything she stood for.

"It's okay." Myles pulled her against him and wrapped his arm around her waist. "We'll take care of it. No one's going to find out."

They both knew that wasn't a promise he could make. So much of this was out of both their hands, but she had to pray he was right.

"I don't understand. Is this even legal? Why would they do this?" She should have broken her contract with ECO after the whole email hack went down last year. She would have, but her lawyers had advised against it. They said that since ECO had fired the culprits involved, they'd take her to court, and the case could go on for years. So she'd stayed the course, and now look what that had gotten her. Another reason to follow her gut, a lesson she'd yet to learn despite the number of times something like this had happened.

"Is it legal? Yes, technically it is, but clearly it's something most companies don't want advertised. Given the way ECO tried to hide its association through a series of anonymous LLCs, they know the company's reputation would take a hit if it became public."

"A reputational hit is an understatement. It could ruin them, and Oasis and me along with them." Extricating herself from Myles, she stood. "I have to go. I've got to call Trinity and Grace. I'm not sure I'll be able to get in touch with Donald since they're on the East Coast, but I have to try."

Myles pushed to his feet. "Are you sure you want to do that now?"

"No, I'd rather have done it months ago," she snapped, irritated with herself. "Now may be too late, but I don't have any other choice."

Cedrick arrived a short time later—the duration of which Myles spent trying to allay her fears that the worst was going to happen. The moment she got in the car, she called Donald, but the call went straight to voicemail. Her call to Nick produced the same result. It was almost midnight there, but she prayed one of them would call her back.

Whitney had her assistant put a call out to all the senior executives and Austin, who was the company's point person with ECO, to inform them that there would be an all-hands-on-deck meeting first thing tomorrow morning. Unsurprisingly, the decision to move the assembly lines from the factory in China to dirt-cheap American prison labor by ECO had come as a shock to everyone she'd spoken to.

Kennedy was her final call of the night.

"Sar, you okay?" she answered, worry lacing her voice. And with reason, as Whitney never called her this late.

"Hey, sweetie. I'm sorry to call you so late, but I need you to talk me down off this ledge." She heard the low murmur of a male voice in the background.

"No, baby, nothing's wrong. It's just Sar with a question. Go back to bed. I'll be there in a few."

"Tell Nate I'm sorry. You and Aurora are the only ones I could think of to call. I should've probably called her first."

"No, it's fine. I'm here for you night and day. Now tell me what's going on," Kennedy urged.

That prompted Whitney to unload the nightmare she was living through, and finally ask, "What should I do? I don't want to go with my regular PR people because they've never dealt with anything like this. And I trust you."

Whitney didn't want a Hollywood PR team to craft the "right" response should things go sideways and upside down. She wanted someone who knew her and shared her values.

"Okay, hon, I got you. Now tell me what you want to do. Are you sticking with ECO?"

Whitney could tell by the hardening of her friend's voice when she said the company's name that she wasn't crazy about that idea. Kennedy had once temped for them. That was how they'd met and where her friend had gotten the idea to start her PR firm, Token.

"Absolutely not. The first thing I'm going to do tomorrow is talk to my lawyers about getting out of the contract. It's going to be a nightmare finding another clothing manufacturer to part-ner with, but it has to be done." The company would probably take a hit. It could be months before they were up and running somewhere else, but no way was she going to continue with ECO. This was the last straw. She was done.

"Perfect. Then should news about this come out, you can say that the moment you learned about it, you cut ties with them. No one is going to fault you for not knowing about the change, especially since they deliberately tried to hide it from you and the public."

Whitney took a deep, less panicked breath. "See, that's why I called you. You make everything sound logical. Can I retain your services and have you on deck, just in case?" She'd never used Token's services, but she felt good in the knowledge that her friend was waiting in the wings if she needed her.

"Like you even have to ask," Kennedy chided.

"Of course, I'll pay you," Whitney was quick to add.

"Oh hell no, you won't."

Knowing she'd encountered a brick wall in that response, Whitney decided to table the discussion and find another, less obvious way to pay her friend for her services. So instead of arguing, she simply said, "Thank you."

"I didn't do anything but speak the truth. Anyway, I'm sure it won't come to that. ECO has as much to lose if the truth comes out, and with your business gone, they'll be in a big hurry to make up the shortfall. Not that they'll be able to."

Oasis was sixty percent of ECO's annual profits, so they were about to take a massive hit, but Whitney didn't care. They'd brought this on themselves with their greed.

"Well, I'll let you get back to bed. I'm sure Nate is getting impatient."

"I'm not going anywhere," Kennedy huffed a laugh. "Twenty minutes without me won't kill him."

"I wouldn't be too sure about that," Whitney teased.

"Give me a call after your meetings. I'll prepare a statement about your split with ECO for when you need it."

"Thanks, sweets. Talk to you later. Say goodnight to Nate for me."

"Will do. Night, Sar. Sweet dreams."

After ending the call, Whitney inhaled a deep breath. The future didn't look as dim as it had an hour ago. She and the company would survive this. All wasn't lost. But what was sobering was how easy it could be. One wrong move, one bad association, one unfavorable headline, and she could lose it all, and where would she be then? It wasn't as if she spent her money as quickly as she made it, but this thing with ECO made it more imperative than ever to protect Haylee's financial future. She needed to put money aside right now to make sure it couldn't be touched.

And it was then she realized what had been forgotten with the news about ECO. She and Myles hadn't talked about child support. She'd already gotten the ball rolling on that. The only thing they needed to do was agree on the dollar amount, which she'd try to iron out tomorrow...on top of everything else.

24

As Whitney had expected, when Donald Edwards returned her call, he'd met her questions with weak excuses. First, he'd outright denied the allegations, but when confronted with indisputable evidence, claimed ignorance and promised to look into who okayed the change. But she wasn't having any of that and informed him that she was ending their contract, and her lawyers would be in touch.

She and her entire team were of one mind when it came to severing all ties with the company, and Trinity and Grace were currently reaching out to three of the other clothing manufacturers they'd passed over three years ago.

Whitney had only had two minutes to herself since she walked into her office when Myles called. She smiled at his impeccable timing.

"Hey, I was just about to call you. You must've read my mind," she said into the phone.

"Or you read mine."

There was an intimacy in his voice that had her thinking about how their evening would have ended if the issue with

ECO hadn't come up. The distinct ding of the elevator sounded in the background.

"I hope you have time to see me, because I'm on my way up."

Whitney instantly sat up straight in her chair, and her pulse quickened. "You're here?" She sounded like a girl with her first crush, all breathless and smitten.

"We need to talk, and this time, I thought it only fair I come to you." He sounded like a businessman on special terms with his client.

"Okay, I'll have Jasmine send you through." Whitney hung up and notified Jasmine at the reception desk while riffling through her purse for a compact mirror to fix her hair and make minor repairs to her makeup. Not that he hadn't seen her barefaced and her hair in a tangled mess. Her postcoital appearance didn't count, though. She wanted to look good for him.

She heard him—or the reaction to him—before he appeared at her door. "Is it safe to come in?" he asked, tongue-in-cheek.

Smiling ruefully, Whitney pulled him inside and closed and locked the door behind him. "Get in here before you cause a riot with my employees. How many women offered to escort you to my office? Given the time it took you to get here, I'm pretty sure there were at least two." Her money was on Anne, who was in her midforties and on the lookout for husband number three, and Lisa, whose head was easily turned by a good-looking, successful, well-dressed man. Myles fit the bill on all counts. Frankly, he exceeded them.

"Jealous?" he teased, kissing her soundly on the lips.

"No, but I was just wondering which one of my employees needs a refresher course on sexual harassment in the workplace," she joked. She'd learned the name of his cologne and had ordered a bottle for his Christmas stocking, which was less than five months away. It didn't matter if they were still sleeping together by then or not. She was giving it to him.

He dropped another kiss on her mouth, this time lingering a lot longer. "Let me know when I've crossed the line," he murmured, gently nipping her bottom lip.

"I thought you came here to talk business." She whispered the gentle reminder. "Don't worry, you can cross the line when we're alone."

"We're alone now," Myles said, his voice husky.

Pressing her hands against his shoulders, Whitney gently pushed him away and stepped out from the circle of his arms. "You know what I mean."

In a flash, he was all business. "Alright, what's the plan?"

Whitney told him how they intended to break the contract, and Myles agreed that charges ECO broke the morality clause was their best bet, concluding they'd revisit a public offering after her company partnered with a new clothing manufacturer.

With the immediate fire tended to, Whitney was eager to iron out the issue of their daughter.

"Now, about Haylee. We didn't get a chance to talk about it last night, but I'd like to get it out of the way. First, we need to agree on an amount. I spoke to Chey, and she suggested—"

"You already spoke to your cousin about this," he interrupted.

"Myles, family law is her specialty, so yes, I asked for her advice." She couldn't understand why he would have a problem with that. "I wanted to make sure the amount was fair, given our custodial arrangement."

"Whitney, I don't need your money." He sounded almost apologetic yet seemed to be under the mistaken belief it was in his power to refuse her. That wasn't how co-parenting worked.

"And once again, Myles, the money isn't about you. It's about Haylee, and I'm her mother. Of course I'm going to contribute equally to her upbringing." This wasn't a matter of if but of how much.

His eyes narrowed as he silently studied her, his gaze probing. "What brought this on? Why all of a sudden?"

"It's not sudden, Myles. It's always been my intention to pay child support and come up with some sort of agreement between us. Isn't this what divorced couples do? The custodial parent gets child support from the noncustodial parent?"

"Right, but we're not divorced. We're…" He appeared to struggle to find the right words. "Our situation is different."

Theirs was more appropriately deemed a *situationship*.

"Yes, but that doesn't make Haylee any less my daughter or me her mother." She sighed. "I don't understand why you're fighting me on this."

Myles's jaw firmed, and he got that flinty look in his eyes, indicating he was annoyed. "I'm not fighting you. But just because you have a lot of money, it doesn't mean you—"

"What does my wealth have to do with this? I'm being a responsible parent." Seriously, what the fuck? Now she was annoyed too.

"Whitney, you see her three, sometimes maybe four times a week. She's never even been to your house. I think you're jumping the gun a little when it comes to child support."

A gasp escaped her lips as an indescribable pain tore through her. "Please, Myles, tell me how you really feel." The words felt acrid in her throat, emerging bitter and hurt.

"Shit. I'm sorry. I didn't mean it that way," he said, immediately apologetic as he reached for her. Whitney jerked away from his touch, scuttling back behind her desk like a wounded kitten.

"No, you meant exactly what you said." She shook her head, still dazed and slightly numb. "All this time, I thought we were on the same page when it came to what was best for Haylee. I thought you accepted me as her mother. That I was a positive influence in her life."

"I do, Whitney. I swear to God, I do. It's just that—"

"No." She shook her head more forcefully, her tone brittle as her anger grew. "It's clear that this whole time, you were just humoring me. Waiting me out, thinking I'd get bored with playing mommy." How could she not have seen it?

You were too busy falling for him. Lusting after him. That's how.

She wanted to dismiss the chastising voice in her head, but it turned out to be a better judge of character than she was. She'd allowed her attraction to him to cloud her judgment and had ignored the warning signs. She couldn't ignore that after three months, Haylee had never been to her house. Hadn't seen the room she'd decorated for her.

"Whitney—"

"Don't Whitney me. The bottom line is that you don't trust me and never intended me to be anything but on the fringes of my daughter's life. You think because you were the one who hired the surrogate and it was your sperm, your claim on her is sacrosanct, and I'm just the egg donor who got caught up in the mess."

Apparently, he was at a loss for words, because he said nothing. He just stared at her, his expression one of torment and frustration. But he no longer tried to deny everything she'd rightfully accused him of because he knew she was right.

"Goodbye, Myles." She didn't tell him she'd be in touch, but of course she would. She had no choice. No matter how much he wished it wasn't true, they had a daughter together.

"What about Haylee?" He appeared taken aback by the finality in her tone.

Whitney let out a bitter laugh. No, contrary to what he must be thinking, she wasn't walking away from her child just because the father was being difficult. She'd dealt with worse in the course of her career, but not on a matter dearer to her heart.

"I'll see her on my next scheduled supervised visit. You know, the one we both agreed on." Until the courts put new rules in place—because it was clear that was what this would come down to—she had no choice but to play by his.

Sighing in frustration, he dragged his fingers through his hair. "Okay, I'll go. We'll talk about this later. Now isn't the right time."

Funny that. With Myles, the right time never came.

That night, it was difficult going home to a big, empty house. It was a stark reminder of how alone she was. With the majority of her family on the East Coast and Chey a three-hour drive away, Haylee was the only family she had close by, a child who didn't even live with her and never would if Myles had his way.

Whitney didn't know what to do. As things stood, she'd be lucky to get rights typically awarded to a noncustodial parent, but she'd push for it nonetheless. As much as she—and Myles—hadn't wanted to involve the courts, she wanted a legally binding agreement in all matters regarding Haylee. It was the only way forward.

Come hell or high water, she needed to get her name on the birth certificate. And if Myles continued to give her grief about the child support, she'd open an account in her daughter's name and deposit the money there. Haylee could do what she wanted with it when she turned eighteen.

Now all she had to do was get over her feelings for her daughter's father. This was what she got for giving in to her attraction to him.

Whitney wondered what other lies he'd told her. Would he have said anything about his ex-wife calling him and wanting to get back together if she hadn't been there when she called? Honestly, she wouldn't be surprised if they got back together. But she didn't know if she'd be able to stomach co-parenting with the woman who turned her back on her daughter.

God, how quickly things changed. Just a few days ago, everything in her life had been great, and now everything felt perilous. From her role as Haylee's mother and the state of her company to her relationship with Myles. It was like the gods were trying to tell her something. Which gods? She didn't have a clue.

Proceed with caution. Look both ways before you cross.

Whitney was in the kitchen when an ADT notification popped up on her phone. She clicked it to reveal a car pulling into her driveway. Alarm briefly had her body tensing up until she recognized the car and the man behind the wheel.

Myles.

What the hell was he doing here? Hadn't he done enough? She wasn't in the mood to talk to him and didn't care what he had to say. She could simply not answer the door and pretend she wasn't home. What else should he expect when he didn't even have the decency to call her beforehand? The man really did have a lot of nerve.

When the doorbell chimed a minute later, she was ready and waiting to give him a piece of her mind.

"What are—"

The sight of Haylee's beautiful brown eyes and dimpled cheeks cut her off at the beginning of her tirade. Before she could blink, her daughter was in her arms, having launched herself out of her father's. Instantly, the anger roiling inside Whitney began to melt away.

Her gaze flew to Myles, who was regarding her warily, unsure of his reception, as he damn well should be.

"What are you doing here?" she asked, unable to hide her surprise.

"I thought it was time I brought Haylee to see her other home."

It was then any remaining anger melted away, leaving her fighting back tears. But those tears didn't blind her to the man holding a pink diaper bag and the Black *Little Mermaid* doll she'd gotten Haylee a month ago.

"Oh," she said, sniffling.

"Can I come in?"

Clutching her daughter tightly, Whitney moved aside to allow him entry. He was clad in jeans and a blue button-down shirt, and she couldn't take her eyes off him.

Myles stepped inside, likewise without removing his gaze from her. At the click of the door closing, the corners of his mouth edged up, but not enough to be considered a smile. "I'm sorry."

Whitney continued to cuddle her daughter as she regarded him, wishing she knew what he was thinking. "I'm her mother. This isn't a part I'm playing."

"I know, and I'm sorry that I've ever made you feel less than an equal partner."

"Are we going to sit down like adults and agree to a child support amount?" she asked, feeling the time was right to push the issue.

"Yes. Absolutely."

With that, Whitney hoisted Haylee higher in her arms, turned, and trekked down the hall to the family room, Myles following closely on her heels. Once they were both seated, her daughter began squirming, eager to explore the new un-charted terrain. Whitney set her down on the rug, where Hay-lee promptly used the coffee table to pull herself up. Despite being unsteady on her feet, she turned and smiled at them as if to say, *look, Mommy and Daddy, I'm standing*.

Whitney clapped, beaming at her. "Mommy is so proud of you," she praised her, and in the next breath said, "I want to have my name on her birth certificate." Since she had him on the ropes, she might as well get as much as she could.

"Yeah, I was going to talk to you about that. Since Holly's

name has been removed from the birth certificate, all we need to do is complete some paperwork where we acknowledge your relationship with Haylee, and we can do that whenever you want."

Whitney's eyes widened as she swallowed hard, the relief almost too much for her beleaguered system to handle. "Your ex-wife isn't on it anymore?"

"Are you kidding?" Myles said with a mirthless laugh. "She made that a condition of her signature on the divorce papers. Said something about not wanting to risk being taken to court for child support years down the road."

"Then I'd think you'd be happy I want to do the opposite."

Head bowed and knees spread, he didn't say anything for several long beats. Then he looked up and pinned her with his blue gaze. "I can't lose her." His eyes shifted to Haylee, who was standing and happily banging her hands on the wooden table.

Whitney's breath hitched. "Is that what you *still* think, that I'm going to try to take her from you?"

"No, not like that—through the courts. Not deliberately." He paused. "But who knows what'll happen when she gets older? One day, she's going to realize that her mother is this big celebrity and lives in this huge house," he said, gesturing around the expansive room. "She may decide she'd rather live with you, and who would blame her?"

"Myles." His name was a soft exclamation. Gutted by his admission, she said, "No, that's not going to happen."

"You don't know that, Whit."

"Myles, Haylee's our child, not our parent. It's up to us to do what's best for her, and I hope we'll make those kinds of decisions together. You have primary custody, and that's not going to change unless we—" she motioned between them "—agree otherwise."

Had this been his fear all along? Not that she'd take their

daughter away from him, but that one day Haylee would choose her over him? The more she thought about it, though, the more his fears made sense. Myles had shown he had no problem saying no to Whitney, but Haylee would be a different matter.

"But what if it is?"

Her chest constricted at the vulnerability and uncertainty in his eyes.

"What? Do you mean it's best she lives with me?" she asked, gesturing to herself.

"Don't kids prefer to live with their mothers, especially girls?"

The question caught Whitney off guard. She'd always believed that a child needed a mother, but not above or exclusive of a father. A child deserved both, and with her in the picture, Haylee had that.

"Haylee will always have a home with me just as she's always going to have a home with you, but you will have primary custody, okay?"

He didn't say anything for several seconds, his gaze intent on her as if trying to gauge her sincerity. "Okay."

"And you have to promise that if you marry—"

Myles began shaking his head before she could finish and declared emphatically, "I told you, I'm done with marriage, so you don't have to worry about that. Haylee is never going to have a stepmother. You're the only mother she's ever going to have."

He said it with such conviction, Whitney was certain he'd convinced himself of it. But he didn't know what the future would bring. At thirty-six, he didn't know how'd he feel in a few years. Maybe even in ten years. But for now, she had to admit, his vow brought her nothing but relief for reasons that weren't entirely selfish. What if he married some odious woman who made Cruella de Vil or *Cinderella*'s Lady Tremaine look like Mother Teresa and cared nothing about her daughter?

But then again, she doubted Myles would marry a woman like that.

"You can't know that for sure, but if you do, I trust she'll love Haylee as much as we do. That she'll be good to her and treat her as her own."

She'd better, or she'll have me to deal with.

Myles huffed. "Haylee will have you and our families. She'll have all the female role models she can handle."

At that point, Whitney decided to let the subject drop. As Myles was so adamant, she'd cross that bridge if the time ever came. No use inventing problems when she had enough on her plate to deal with.

"So, are we good?" On the surface, his question was innocuous. But she knew he meant the part of their relationship that had nothing to do with their daughter.

"I'm not mad at you anymore, if that's what you mean," she replied, feigning ignorance. She wanted him to spell it out. If he wanted back in her bed, he'd have to do it the old-fashioned way. Romance the shit out of her.

His gaze dropped to her mouth, and his eyes became heated. "I took tomorrow off. I was hoping Haylee and I could stay the night."

Whitney tapped her finger against her chin, pretending to give it some thought. At least, that was the look she was going for. "I bet you were counting on me being so grateful to have Haylee for the night that I'd allow you to stay in one of the guest rooms," she deadpanned.

Myles swallowed, his Adam's apple bobbing against his throat. "Guest bedroom?"

Uncrossing her legs, Whitney rose to her feet, capturing her daughter's attention. "Where else would you sleep?" she asked, one brow arched.

"How about where I slept the last time." It wasn't a question but a strongly worded suggestion with sex written all over it.

If he thought she was going to let him into her bed again that easily, he had another think coming. "And where would I sleep?"

Her question brought him to her side, and now only inches separated them. Haylee stretched her arms up to him, and Myles quickly swept her into his before she could fall.

"The last time I checked, we were lovers. Are you telling me we aren't anymore? Are you calling it quits?" He spoke in a tone meant to seduce. Husky and low. "If so, I want it on the record that I object."

Whitney pursed her lips, trying not to smile. He was making it impossible for her to keep him at arm's length. "What is that, lawyer humor?"

Thumb in mouth, Haylee laid her head on his chest and began playing with his earlobe, her cue that she was ready to sleep.

"Is it working?" He gently palmed her cheek and stared into her eyes. Whitney couldn't find the strength to pull away or tell him to leave Haylee with her and go, but she didn't melt like a popsicle on a scorching hot day under his heated gaze.

The man was the devil. "You're lucky your daughter is so freaking adorable, or you'd be out on your ear."

A smile slowly spread across his face, hunger glinting in his eyes. "If that's your way of telling me I don't have to sleep in the guest room tonight, I'll take it."

"And if I let you sleep in my room, that doesn't mean you're getting anything from me other than a comfortable bed to sleep on, do you understand?" How committed was she to keeping him at penis length? That was yet to be determined. It was dependent on a variety of factors, like the strength of his persuasion game.

"Understood." He replied so readily, she was sure he'd have agreed to just about anything.

"C'mon, let's put Haylee to bed, and then we can discuss what we are and what we are not to each other."

Let him put that in his pipe and smoke it.

25

Thirty-five thousand dollars a month!

That was the number Whitney put on the table. To say that it was too much was an understatement. Nobody needed almost half a million dollars a year to raise one child. It more than covered what he paid Eunice—although he could certainly give her a generous raise with that amount.

But the way Whitney looked at it, it wasn't about what it cost to take care of her. It was about what she could afford to give.

He'd bitten his tongue and agreed because arguing would have gotten him nowhere. Certainly not three rounds of the best makeup sex he'd ever had. The woman he'd come to know possessed a rigid sense of duty, and nothing he said could change that. Myles knew when he was beaten.

"How did you find this place?" Myles glanced over at Whitney, who was pushing Haylee in a stroller next to him.

Sighing happily, Whitney looked around the park, which looked more like a garden. The walking path was lined with an overabundance of flowers and neatly trimmed hedges. "I used to rent a place a couple miles from here. That was before

I bought my house, of course," she added. "Anyway, I went for a walk, you know, to get the lay of the land, got lost, and ended up here."

"And you come here by yourself?" he asked. The place was a labyrinth of mostly tall arbors and oaks.

Whitney gave a one-shoulder shrug. "Once I dragged Trinity with me. And I've brought Chey, April, Kennedy, and Aurora here a few times. They all loved it. But yeah, I usually come by myself. I love it here because, as you can see, it's nice and quiet, and no one knows who I am."

Myles playfully tugged the ends of her dark–blonde–streaked wig. "It must be because of this amazing disguise."

She peered up at him, her dimples bracketing a brilliant white smile. Her eyes were hidden behind mirrored sunglasses, but he could tell they were brimming with amusement.

"Laugh all you want. They haven't failed me yet. And no one expects to see me here dressed like this." She glanced down at her oversized T-shirt and dark green mommy shorts.

In the two weeks since Haylee had first stayed overnight at Whitney's, the supervised visits had gone the way of the dinosaurs. Now she took Haylee for the entire day and kept her overnight one night on the weekends. Myles accompanied his daughter on most of the visits, but sometimes he bowed out, allowing them to enjoy some mother-daughter alone time together.

During those times, he played chauffeur. Her driving lessons were coming along, but she wasn't there yet. Her goal was to be a licensed driver by the end of the month, which gave her two more weeks.

"Well, no one will recognize you today, because this place is almost empty." They were alone in the shade-dappled park save two women who'd recently arrived with three young children. The women exchanged polite hellos with them and continued on to the playground, where the kids were currently playing on the swings.

"Which is the best part," she said. She peeked over the canopy of the stroller. "I knew the fresh air would knock her right out," she told him upon finding Haylee sleeping, her arm slackened around Twinkle Toes, Little Mermaid having lost her vaunted favorite toy status to the fluffy pink elephant.

"Yeah, that and the swings," Myles commented. Until she learned to walk, the swings were the only playground equipment made for children her age. Although Whitney had set her on her lap for rides down the slide. She'd had a blast with that too.

"Next week, I have to attend an award show, and I was wondering if—"

If he wanted to come with her. Myles knew that was what she was about to ask him.

"—I can take Haylee Sunday instead of Saturday, and keep her on Monday until you get home."

"Are you getting an award or something?"

She sent him a probing look. "Do I have to be getting an award to go?"

"No, but the entire time I've known you, I can't remember you—"

"Going out? Is that what you were going to say?" she said lightly. "What do you think I do when I'm not with you and Haylee? Sit at home twiddling my thumbs?"

"You do own a company," he reminded her. "I thought you were either at the office or doing movie or music stuff. Aren't you recording your next album?"

"I don't go to the office every day, and I finished recording that album last month."

Myles shrugged. "It just seemed you were spending most of

your downtime with Haylee." And him. "Plus, I thought you said you didn't attend a lot of Hollywood events."

"Yeah, but I can't avoid them altogether. I told you, some I'm contractually obligated to attend, and Saturday's award show is one of them. I'm a presenter."

Was she going alone? He was reluctant to ask. They hadn't specifically talked about being exclusive, but he'd assumed they wouldn't be seeing other people while they were sleeping together.

"Which award show?" If he wasn't mistaken, the Academy and Emmy Awards took place at the beginning of the year. The Grammys were somewhere in there too. What was going on in July?

"The ESPYs."

Myles stopped abruptly. Whitney halted and peered back at him over her shoulder.

"What's wrong?"

"You're presenting an award for sports?"

Whitney's amusement was obvious in the soft, lilting sound of her laughter. "Don't I fit the type?"

He resumed walking. "Why you?"

"Why else? They're trying to attract the young female demographics. Need to get more eyeballs on the screens and more asses in the seats. This won't be my first time presenting there either, but I agreed to do it this time when Daniel and I were dating. And because he's up for tennis player of the year, they asked me to present the award to the winner. It's all very Travis Kelce and Taylor Swift-ish, don't you think?"

Myles ignored the last part, because who the fuck cared? "You're not dating him anymore."

Whitney huffed. "Well, it's not like I can bow out now."

Sure she could. "So your ex-boyfriend is going to be there, and you'll be presenting him with an award."

This time, it was Whitney who halted their stroll and tilted her head to peer up at him. A pregnant pause followed, punctuated by the din of children playing in the distance. "Only if he wins."

Myles tried not to scowl but sensed he lost the battle when, after another pause, she said, "Please don't tell me you're jealous."

"No, I'm not jealous. It's just that—" Midsentence, he realized he didn't know what the fuck he was. He regrouped. "Aren't you worried that people are going to get the wrong idea?"

Whitney shrugged. "They're going to think what they want. There's nothing I can do about that now."

She could tell them she was seeing someone who wasn't her ex-boyfriend.

"Do you want to come with me? Be my date?" she asked, a trace of challenge in her voice.

"You know I can't." On the one hand, he'd hate it. On the other hand, he'd hate it and then some.

"Why not? And if you're going to say because of Haylee, it's been three months, Myles, and I'm not going anywhere. People are going to find out one day, and I'll have to explain the whole situation about the mix-up. We might as well rip off the Band-Aid and get it over with while she's too young to understand what's going on. And it's better the story come from us so we can control the narrative."

Myles was already shaking his head. "It will come from us, but it's too soon." He scrubbed a hand over his face on a harsh exhale. "I'm not ready to deal with the kind of media attention a story like this is going to garner." He'd rarely had to think about it before, but meeting Whitney made him realize how much he appreciated the anonymity of being who he was. Because he'd never had to think about it, he'd taken it for granted.

But one day, that anonymity would be gone, so he intended to savor every second of it while he could.

"Okay. I understand. But so that we're clear on this, I'd rather have you there with me. So when you see pictures of me with only God knows who, know that nothing is going on. To me, this is just a job, and my job is to smile, look pretty, and be my infinitely charming self." She scrunched her nose, making her sexy and adorable face at him.

Pictures of me with only God knows who. She damn well knew who. Her "just friends" ex-boyfriend, that was who. The guy everyone assumed would take home the best male tennis player of the year award. Daniel Woodson had cleaned up, winning three of the four grand slams the past year.

"But won't it be weird if you go alone?"

"It won't be the first time, and it certainly won't be the last. And even when I was in a relationship, it wasn't always possible for my partner to go."

Myles was torn. At this event, she'd be surrounded by professional male athletes, most at the peak of their careers and the best in their sport. As much as he disliked Hollywood, a part of him—admittedly a sizable part—wanted every one of them to know that one of the most famous bachelorettes in the country was taken. At least for now.

"Why don't you take your cousin—what's her name—Cheyenne?"

Whitney snorted a laugh. "I'd have to drag Chey kicking and screaming. No, my cousin doesn't do Hollywood. She lives vicariously through me and claims that's more than enough for her."

With a pause in her step, she gave him a reassuring shoulder nudge. "Don't worry about me. I'm sure I'll have plenty of people to talk to."

Myles shot her a look of disbelief. A laugh bubbled to the

surface. "Oh, I don't doubt that. I'm absolutely certain you'll have your pick of people to talk to." And a few dozen men more than happy to take her home and straight to bed.

"Are you saying you don't trust me?" she asked in mock affront. "I mean, I know you don't want the public to know about our relat—*situationship* and that I have to put on my disguise when we do go out, but that doesn't mean I'll act the man-eater the tabloids claim I am."

Myles caught her hand, bringing her to a stop in front of one of the many wooden benches that lined the walking path. "Come on, let's sit for a bit."

Whitney gave him a curious look before checking to see if Haylee was still asleep. She then locked the wheels of the stroller and gingerly lowered herself onto the bench. Myles sat close beside her, their hands still linked.

"Holly—my ex-wife—she doesn't know about you. She thinks that Haylee's mother isn't in the picture."

Whitney stiffened, and then slowly slipped her hand out of his. "Why does she think that?"

Myles cleared his throat. "Because when I told her I was going to raise Haylee alone, she assumed you weren't an option. And when things changed, I didn't tell her because at that point, it was none of her business."

"So she thinks I'm out of the picture?" Whitney reiterated slowly, enunciating every word with an air of foreboding.

Myles gave a curt nod and braced himself.

"And what do you think is going to happen when she finds out?"

"I'm not sure. She could decide to make a big deal about it. Blab it to the tabloids. Who knows," he said with a helpless shrug.

"Okay, since you're being *honest*," she said, stressing the final word. "What do you care what she does? Her name isn't on the birth certificate, she voluntarily terminated her parental rights, and you're divorced. Tell me what I'm missing here, because I don't get why you're treating her as if she comes with a *Fragile, Glass, Handle with Care* sign on her."

"It's not like that." His denial was swift and fierce.

"Then what is it?"

"My divorce lawyer said that if she asks to have her rights reinstated, we'd be back in court. I'm afraid that if she finds out you're Haylee's mother, she might do it just to make my life hell and drag you and Haylee down with me."

Whitney's eyes widened, her mouth forming an O before clamping shut. She gaped at him for a beat and then whispered, "How is that even legal?"

Myles wished he knew the answer.

"We're in uncharted territory. No specific law covers this situation. If something like this went to court, the case would be establishing precedent."

"Well then, of course we don't want her to know. And I wish you'd told me that from the beginning. Okay, maybe not the very beginning, because you didn't like me that much either, but—"

"Hey," Myles interrupted, catching her chin between his fingers and gazing into her eyes. "It wasn't you I didn't like. It was the situation we found ourselves in that I resented. It was never personal."

The corner of her mouth twitched. "Hmm. It sure felt personal."

Myles shifted his hand from her chin and cradled her face in his palms. "No, this is personal," he whispered before sealing her mouth with his. Her lips opened to his, deepening the kiss.

She was intoxicating. The feel and taste of her. Myles couldn't get enough, and for several moments, he forgot where he was. He couldn't think about anything but what his body wanted.

Whitney naked on his bed, her thighs around his hips and him buried inside of her.

The excited cry of a child reminded him that although the place was relatively secluded, they weren't entirely alone. And he could only do all the things he wanted to do with her when that was the case. The knowledge had him reluctantly breaking off the kiss. Pressing his forehead against hers, his breathing choppy and voice rough, he asked, "Your place or mine?"

She stared back at him, desire burning in her eyes. "Yours," was her throaty response.

"Then let's go."

26

Whitney wasn't surprised when Grace informed her that ECO threatened to sue her for breach of contract. She'd expected that. But she called Donald Edwards to tell him in no uncertain terms that she would countersue and that she was willing to fight it out in court no matter how long it took or how much it cost.

Donald was aware that she had the upper hand in this. ECO wouldn't be able to survive if news of their role in it became public, and he knew that. The conversation quickly went from suing her to haggling over which lines ECO would maintain the rights to, but Whitney was having none of that, and her position could not have been clearer. *Take your losses and call it a day. My relationship with your company is over.*

Whitney let him chew on that. In the meantime, she had to fly to New York to meet with the three clothing manufacturers on her list of prospective ECO replacements. That had meant four days away from her daughter and Myles, and with that came the realization of how integral they'd become to her life.

No, that wasn't exactly the truth. Haylee had captured her heart from the beginning. It was the realization about Myles that surprised her. Their relationship wasn't serious, but she couldn't say it was casual anymore. Actually, it hadn't been casual for a long time. If they didn't see each other, they spoke on the phone every day.

While she was in New York, he FaceTimed her so she could talk to Haylee and called back after he put her to bed. They spoke for hours. It was as if she'd been gone for weeks instead of days.

So it made perfect sense to her to have Cedrick drop her off at Myles's place after he picked her up from the airport. It had been a long day of meetings and travel, and the only thing she wanted was to see the two people who'd quickly become central to her world.

When Whitney landed, she'd called to tell him she'd arrived safely, and it had gone straight to voicemail. She left a message to let him know she was on her way and was surprised that he hadn't returned her call in the forty minutes it took to get to his house.

His car was in the driveway, so she knew he was home, but she had Cedrick wait just in case. She called Myles again, and this time he picked up.

"Hey, I'm back. Did you get my message? Are you home?" She fired the questions at him in quick succession, not giving him time to spit out a greeting.

"I'm home, and I just got your message."

"Is everything okay? You sound funny." As in distracted. So unlike the man who only last night had told her that he'd been suffering from a bad case of blue balls since she left, and the only cure for it was her pussy.

"Where are you? I need you to get to my place ASAP. We have a problem."

Whitney's heart began to race. She promptly rang the doorbell. "I'm here."

A moment later, the door flew open to reveal a bare-chested and barefoot Myles clad in light gray sweatpants, his hair a tousled, finger-combed mess. The stubble on his face had reached ten-o'clock proportions.

He practically yanked her inside and slammed the door shut.

"What's wrong? What happened?" Whitney's voice rose with every word, her stomach coiling into a knot. Why was he treating her like they were targets and the house was being watched?

"Someone saw us in the park last weekend," he said while grabbing a hold of her hand and leading her to his study, where the curtains were drawn over the double windows.

Once inside, he released her and ran a hand through his hair. "My sister just called. It's all over the internet."

Whitney shook her head, utterly confused and in the dark. She couldn't make heads or tails of what he was talking about. "What do you mean, someone saw us in the park?" First of all, she'd been in disguise, and there'd only been the two women and their children the entire time they'd been there.

"Just what I said." He was clearly agitated. "Someone saw us and took pictures. Now they're all over the fucking internet."

Shock froze Whitney in place, her eyes wide. Her brain scrambled, trying to remember what they'd been doing. Walking together, pushing Haylee in her stroller. And kissing.

"Okay, hold on a minute." Struggling to remain calm in the relative sense of the word, she tried to get a handle on the situation. "How do they know it was us? I was wearing a disguise."

"It's clear they must have seen through your disguise, because it's here in black and white." Grabbing his laptop off his desk, he brought it to her and thrust it in her face.

Sahara Has Baby With Married Lawyer

The famous beauty is said to be sharing co-parenting duties with Myles Redmond Jr., the president of the California Bar Association, of their nine-month-old daughter. No one knows how the two met, but rumor has it that the lawyer's affair with the Grammy Award winner and Oscar-nominated actress caused the breakup of his second marriage. We've reached out to Sahara for comment but haven't received a response as of the time of publication.

Whitney gaped at Myles, her jaw nearly on the floor, and the rest of her almost followed it there. "This has got to be a joke. I've never been pregnant, and I've never dated a married man, much less had an affair with one."

Myles snapped the laptop closed and returned it to his desk. "That's the first thing you think about? How about, who took the picture of us kissing at the park? How did they know we'd be there? How did they know it was you? Like you said, you were wearing a disguise. And how the hell do they know that Haylee is yours? Your name isn't on the birth certificate yet."

"What are you saying, that someone has been spying on us? Is that why you pulled me in the house like that?"

"I'm saying that someone would have had to tip off the person who sold this story to this garbage rag. Nothing else makes sense."

He stared at her, his gaze pointed and vaguely accusing.

"Oh my god, you think it was me?" If she sounded scandalized, that was because she was.

Myles gestured dismissively with his hand. "Not you, but maybe someone you know. Someone you told."

Whitney took offense to that. "No one I told would ever tell anyone, much less sell the story to a damn tabloid," she stated with one hundred percent certainty.

"I've only told members of my immediate family," he shot back.

Piqued, she put her hands on her hips, regarding him through narrowed eyes. "Why do I get the impression you think this is my fault?"

"That's not what I'm saying." He lowered his head and took a deep breath. "I'm just—just trying to figure this out."

"Myles, they think I had a baby with a married man. With you. I have to put out a statement and correct the record." Damn, when it rained, it poured. She'd just narrowly avoided one scandal to land face-first in another one.

"You did have a baby with a married man," he said without a hint of the tongue-in-cheek humor she would have expected to accompany such a remark.

"Right, but not like that, as you damn well know," she said, giving him a squinty-eyed glare. "The article makes it sound sordid." She compressed her mouth into a straight line. "We're going to have to come clean about Haylee sooner than we wanted."

"No, sooner than *I* wanted. You had no problem with letting the cat out of the bag a week ago. Lord, even three months ago."

Whitney could feel her defenses rising and tried to tamp down the irritation that accompanied it. "You say you don't blame me, but it's obvious you do."

Myles gave his head another mind-clearing shake. "I'm sorry. Ignore me. It's just that this couldn't have happened at a worse time."

No time was ever going to be the *right* time, Whitney thought, exasperated.

He was never going to not resent what public knowledge of this was going to do to his and Haylee's lives. She and fame and celebrity were a package deal. There was no getting around that.

"Would you rather people believe that the president of the California Bar Association cheated on his wife with a celebrity and had a baby with her? Never mind that I'm Black and you're white." She ended with a snort of derision.

"I'd rather they mind their own damn business, is what I'd

rather," he said, but now there was a note of resignation in his voice.

Life for him—for them—was about to change, and there was little either of them could do about it except try to control the narrative. And in their case, the truth was on their side.

Her expression softened. She reached out and rubbed her palm up and down his arm. "It'll be okay. I'll have Kennedy or Aurora put out a statement, which should put an end to the cheating allegations in the story."

Myles nodded, his jaw taut. "Holly probably already knows. What if she—"

"She won't win," Whitney said, shutting down whatever negative thing he was about to say. "I'm Haylee's mother. She voluntarily terminated her parental rights before I was even in the picture. And that's what people will know if she dare try anything."

Something in her voice must have made her sound ferocious, like a lioness defending her cub, because Myles's mouth tipped the slightest bit up at the corners. "You'll make sure they do, won't you?"

"You're damn right I will." Come after her daughter in any shape or form, and the woman was toast. Tarnish Myles's professional and personal reputation, she'd get more of the same.

They shared a smile, and a moment later, she was engulfed in his embrace.

"I'm sorry. None of this is your fault. I didn't mean to come across as if I thought it was." He punctuated his apology with a tender kiss on her lips.

"Don't worry. We'll get through this," Whitney replied, tightening her arms around his waist.

"We'll get through it together." He kissed her again.

They were two intimates not simply bound together by a child but by something more. Something almost as important.

★ ★ ★

If Myles thought he'd make it through the evening without getting a call from Holly, he was wrong. He and Whitney were going to bed—welcome home sex was just as good as make-up sex, and he intended to make up for the four days she'd been gone—when his phone rang.

Whitney had been the smart one. She'd turned hers off, declaring she'd deal with the fallout in the morning. She was exhausted.

"It's your ex, isn't it?" Whitney was sitting on the bed, wearing one of his T-shirts. At his grim nod, she said, "Go ahead and answer it. Get it over with. I'm not going anywhere."

He didn't want to answer it and certainly didn't want to have the conversation in front of her. Not that he had anything to hide. But he knew how difficult Holly could be. Seeing no viable avenues of escape, he bit the bullet and picked up.

"Holly, it's late," he said, his manner curt.

The first thing he heard on the other end was a sharp intake of breath and then, "You bastard! You told me Haylee's biological mother wasn't in her life, and all the time, you've been fucking her." Her voice held all the fury of a woman scorned.

"No, that's what you assumed, because I didn't tell you that." He looked at Whitney, whose gaze was glued to his.

"Were you fucking her when we were married?"

"Jesus Christ, Holly, I didn't meet her until Haylee was six months old. After you filed for divorce," he made sure to stress.

"Well, you're fucking her now."

"Look, Holly, I don't have time for this. We're divorced. What I do and who I do it with is none of your concern. Now, this is the last time I'm going to say this. Stop calling me. You're going to get your half of the settlement from the clinic. There's no need to call me, got it?"

"I should be getting all of it. You get to play happy family with Haylee and your famous billionaire girlfriend, and I'm left with nothing."

That was as close to bitter as Myles had ever heard in her. As if fate had deliberately targeted her.

"Goodbye, Holly." He hung up and released a weary sigh.

"I heard the word *fucking* very clearly," Whitney said, her tone arid.

A reluctant smile pulled at his lips as he slid into bed beside her. "She'd love to be able to say I cheated on her or some equally ridiculous shit, and she's pissed that she can't."

Whitney turned and cuddled up against him, her fingers playing with the hairs on his chest. "What was that about the settlement from the clinic? You said something about her getting half."

Myles let out a grunt of annoyance. "She said she should get it all."

"Maybe if you give it to her, she'll go away and never contact you again. And then we won't have to worry about her doing anything stupid like claiming she was emotionally traumatized when she terminated her rights to Haylee."

Myles put his arm around her as the other caressed her hip, enjoying the soft, smooth flesh. "She doesn't deserve it. But if I honestly thought that would do it, I'd let her have it all."

That she hadn't wanted to raise a biracial child was one thing, but then, to force him to choose between her and his own flesh and blood. He could never forgive her for that.

Tipping her head back, Whitney peered up at him. "Why not make that a stipulation of receiving your portion, too? Make her sign something that says she's never to have contact with you or Haylee again."

"A cool one and a half million to never contact me again? I'd take it."

Whitney brought his face down to hers and treated him to a slow burn of a kiss. "I wouldn't."

Myles smiled against her mouth, savoring the plush softness. "That's because that kind of money is pocket change to you."

"No, that's not why." She took a tiny bite of his bottom lip and then soothed it with her tongue.

Myles was hard as a pike. It had been almost a week since he'd seen her naked. Since he buried himself inside her. Since he'd made her come. He needed that tonight. Groaning, he rolled on top of her, his forearms bracketing her face.

"Then why?" he asked, his voice low and ragged.

She watched him, her eyes heavy-lidded and her voice sultry. "Because I like you too much."

Kneeing her legs apart, he settled between her slim thighs, his dick hot and hard against her center. A flex of his hips had her whimpering. She countered with a sensuous undulation of hers. "You only like me?" he teased.

Her eyes drifted closed as she bit her lip. "A lot. I like you a lot." Her words came out slurred, like she was drunk or high on something. Or someone. He loved that he could bring her to this state.

27

"I've been trying to get a hold of you since last night."

Whitney winced at the cheerfulness in her friend's greeting. Aurora's was the first phone call she'd picked up since she turned her phone off yesterday.

"I'm sorry, sweets. Things have been kind of nuts." She assumed the bombshell *cheating with a married man, secret baby* news was the reason her friend was calling.

"No kidding," Aurora said with a snort. "If I didn't know for a fact you've never been even a teensy bit pregnant, I'd think you're a home-wrecking jezebel and start collecting the stones."

"And if I didn't know that too, I'd get in on the stoning." After another snort of laughter, she growled in frustration. "Ror, what the hell am I supposed to do? We need this now like we need a hole in the head. Myles…isn't happy, and until the truth is out, I may as well be walking around with a scarlet A on my chest."

"Yes, and there's the matter of all the news vans congregating in front of your house."

Whitney closed her eyes. "Shit. Where are you seeing this? On the news?"

"That's what I was calling about. I'm here. At your house. In your living room, to be exact. I flew in last night."

Whitney blinked several times in quick succession. "What?"

"Surprise!" Aurora said. Her voice trailed off to nothing.

"What are you doing here? Why didn't you tell me you were coming when I saw you?" She, Kennedy, and Aurora had gone out to dinner the night before she flew back to LA. The night before that, she'd spent time with her folks, who promised to fly out before the end of the year to meet their granddaughter in person.

"Because this was a last-minute trip, and I haven't seen my folks in a while. I figured I could kill two birds with one stone while I'm here checking out future office space. Anyway, I didn't know I was going when I saw you, or we could have flown together. I got in a couple of hours after you. When I couldn't get you on the phone, I came here and waited, totally forgetting there was another bed you'd probably want to sleep in last night."

"Well, I should be home in a bit."

Her friend huffed. "First you'll have to get through the gauntlet of news vans and paparazzi parked in front of your house. This morning when I woke up, they were...just there. I have no idea what time they started arriving, but there seems to be a small army of them."

"Ugh. I don't really want to deal with that right now." This was one of the times that she hated being famous. Would sell her soul to be just another face in the crowd.

"Okay, listen to me, Sar. Do you trust me?"

"You know I do or you wouldn't have the security codes to my house," she said with a dry laugh.

"Good, then let me take care of this for you. As your friend, not as a client, okay?"

"Ror, I'm not taking your services for free."

"C'mon, Sar, just let me do this. And one day, I may ask you for a favor," she said, doing a laughable imitation of the Godfather.

"Okay, fine. What are you going to do?"

"What I do best, and what I suggest to all my clients who fall into these sorts of predicaments. Call a press conference. The truth needs to be clear and explicit, with no room for mis-interpretation. Normally, I would have you with me. In this case, I think it's better I insinuate you'll be there, but once everyone gets there, I tell them there's been a change of plans and you're a no-show. That will give you time to get out of town for a few days. Until the dust settles and everyone realizes that you're as much a victim of what happened as the ex-wife and that lawyer boyfriend of yours."

Get out of town for a few days. That sounded like heaven. But there was no way she could swing it.

"Seriously, getting out of town sounds great, but I can't leave Haylee and Myles right now. They're in this fiasco be-cause of me."

"Of course you can't. That's why they're going with you."

Whitney thought about Myles, who hadn't stirred when she'd gotten out of bed and tiptoed out into the hall to take Aurora's call. Unlike her, he was operating on West Coast time. Right now it was eight-thirty in New York, and her body had yet to readjust.

"Yeah, if I can convince Myles. The man does have a job," she said, as if Aurora needed a reminder.

"It's his firm. He can take some time off for his daughter's sake. You know the paps are going nuts trying to find out where he lives so they can get a picture of your poor baby."

As president of the California Bar, Myles's home address couldn't be found via the standard methods, making his harder to find than hers.

"And the only way to get the bounty off her head is to release a picture of her yourself. So, yes, my advice is to go underground for a few days, decide on the picture you want of her to put out there, and I'll take care of the rest. By the time you get back, your Q Score will be off the charts. I promise, Sar, you'll be more popular than Mickey Mouse and Snoopy at their height of popularity."

Whitney rolled her eyes. *As if.*

"But where would we go? We can't go to my apartment in New York or my folks' place." Those were the first places the press would look.

"You don't need to worry about that. I've got that covered too. My brother has a cabin in Vermont. It's out of the way. No one will ever look for you there."

"When you say cabin in Vermont, you mean…? Because you know I'm not a roughing-it kind of girl." She preferred her amenities decidedly modern and her toilets, indoors.

Aurora let out a gleeful laugh. "Don't worry. It's a rich tech's log cabin. Nate isn't the roughing-it kind, and as you know, Kennedy isn't either."

"But then, who really is, except for lumberjacks and the horse-and-buggy folks."

"You'd be surprised. Adam liked—" Her friend abruptly broke off, catching herself just in time. According to Kennedy, Aurora rarely talked about the New York lieutenant governor bastard who broke her heart, and if she did, she never said his name.

"What he likes doesn't matter," Whitney said with a *your enemy is my enemy* intonation in her voice. Which was too bad, because she'd liked his daughter when they met at her launch party last year.

"Anyway, I'll get in touch with my brother and make the arrangements, and I'll loop Kennedy in."

"Okay, but let me talk to Myles first." She wasn't going off to Vermont alone. It was going to be all or none.

After hanging up, Whitney took her time returning to the bedroom where Myles still slept, his features in repose. She gingerly slid under the sheets beside him. Without opening his eyes, he extended his arms and tugged her close.

"You're up early." His voice was a soft murmur in her hair, his hand splayed on her stomach.

"I'm still on East Coast time," she replied in a whisper.

"So what are the plans today?"

"Aurora called. She's at my place, and so is the press."

Myles responded with an irritated grunt.

"She thinks it would be a good idea if we got out of town for a bit. Or at least until the worst of this blows over." She felt him stiffen at her back but forged on. "She thinks a press conference is the best way to get the truth out—and I agree with her."

When Myles remained silent and relatively still, she turned and looked at him, taking in his shuttered expression. "What do you think?"

"Where would we go?"

Whitney noted his easy acceptance of "we" as it related to them. As if it were a given that they would all go together.

"To her brother's cabin in Vermont."

"What about work? I have clients and a firm to run." His gaze remained steady on her.

"Myles, you do realize that I'm not the only one the press will hound, right? You and Haylee are numbers two and three on that list. I say we stay gone until the truth gets out and the headlines change."

His mouth flattened into a grim line of displeasure.

Did he blame her? Was he going to regret getting romantically involved with her? Did he want to call it quits?

"Okay, when do we leave?" he asked.

She became dizzy with the relief that washed over her. She had her answer.

By the time Whitney, Myles, and Haylee touched down in Vermont, the news was everywhere. The headlines ran the gamut from comical to tawdry to ridiculous.

Sahara's Unconventional Road to Motherhood
A Mix-Up Made for Hollywood
She's Truly One in a Million
First Comes Baby
The Desert Queen Has Her Princess

Honestly, sometimes they tried too hard to be clever.

What typically followed the clickbait headlines dwelled on the statistical probability that such a mix-up would happen. Because the name of the clinic was yet unknown—Whitney knew they had to be digging for it—the articles were prone to a lot of speculation and posed many open-ended questions. Like why had she frozen her eggs? Was the mix-up the cause of Myles's divorce? When had she learned of her daughter's existence? When had the two unlikely parents become romantically involved? Would this unexpected motherhood change her life? Who would get the now coveted first interview with the star?

Aurora's bait-and-switch press conference had gone off without a hitch. Lured by the promise of getting the story from the horse's mouth, the media decamped from in front of her house to jockey for position on the steps of the Beverly Hills Waldorf Astoria.

Whitney had used that time to sneak into her own home, pack a week's worth of clothes at record speed, and meet Myles and Haylee at the airport, where they'd taken the private plane her manager had arranged for her to Vermont.

"At least they're not calling me a home-wrecker anymore or you a two-timing, social-climbing cheat," she muttered, directing her remark to Myles, who was scouring the SUV dashboard, searching for the high beams switch.

Myles snickered. "That's a new one. I've never been called a social climber before."

He kept his eyes firmly on the two-lane road leading to the cabin, the high beams now on, illuminating the surrounding woody terrain. They'd picked up a rental at the airport and were on their way to the cabin. The GPS indicated they were ten minutes away.

Whitney tore her attention from her phone and narrowed her eyes at him. "But you have been called a two-timer?" Her tone dared him to answer in the affirmative.

Myles's lips twitched. "Yes, but without cause. I couldn't talk to a girl without her accusing me of cheating."

"And who is *her* exactly, an ex-girlfriend?" Whitney asked with a single arched brow.

He paused before answering as if regretting he'd brought her up. "My first wife."

"Ah, you mean the wife you never talk about." Whitney wouldn't know her name—Amy—if not for the background check she'd had run on him.

He shrugged. "There isn't much to say. We married too young and for the wrong reasons, and it didn't work out."

"Is that why you divorced, because she thought you were always cheating on her?" Obviously, she hadn't known him that long, but he'd never given her the impression that he had a wandering eye. Or hands. Or dick. He went to work and came home to his daughter, and recently, all his spare time was spent with Whitney.

"We divorced because she was insecure, and I got tired of living like that. I got tired of being her entire world. Of her looking to me for everything. It took me five years to realize that we weren't compatible. We wanted different things, a different type of marriage."

Whitney hummed in understanding. "And then you married Holly."

He harrumphed at that. "The polar opposite of Amy. Or so I thought. But Amy would never have made me choose between her and my daughter. She didn't have it in her."

That's because Holly's a bitch.

But of course, she couldn't say that without sounding like a bitch herself, so Whitney simply nodded. "Well, you know what they say. Third time is the charm."

Myles shot her a side-eye look. "Not for me. I told you, I'm done with marriage."

Yes, he'd made that crystal clear. But then why did his response create a hollow emptiness in her stomach and prick her heart? Had it been a warning to her? As in, *don't go looking for something I can't give you.*

"That's right, you did. How could I have forgotten? And I'd probably feel the same way if I'd gone through two divorces too." She made sure to slap a smile on it at the end to lighten things up.

When Myles didn't respond—she thought he might say she wasn't the divorcing type or something to that effect—they lapsed into silence. She used that time to check on Haylee.

It had been a long day, and even given the convenience of a private jet, traveling with a child wasn't easy. She'd hoped her daughter would sleep a good portion of the seven-hour flight, but planes weren't like cars when it came to altitude, and Haylee's frets had turned into full-blown cries of misery an hour into the flight. Needless to say, it had been a bumpy ride, and not due to any turbulence.

Currently, Haylee was asleep in her car seat, her head at an awkward angle. Whitney had to resist the compulsion to crawl back there and straighten her up, but she didn't want to risk waking her, and the GPS indicated they were almost there.

"I think this is us," Myles said as he slowed the car. They had recently turned off the main road, and things had gotten darker due to the lack of streetlights.

Whitney turned and faced forward. Perched on the hill up ahead stood a log cabin, and the only thing rustic about it was its surroundings.

"Definitely not like any cabin I've ever stayed at," she said.

Myles sent her a quick look. "And how many is that?"

Good question. "Um, well, none, actually. I mean, that I've ever seen."

"Yeah, I thought so," he said, and she could tell by his voice that his mouth was set in a smirk.

"I'm not exactly a cabin in the woods kind of girl," she said in her defense. "But if I were, this is the kind of cabin I could get down with. I mean, if I'm going to be off the grid, I may as well do it in style." She shifted her attention to the two-story structure. The front was a gorgeous mix of logs and stone and a plethora of windows. The exterior lighting suggested a first-rate security system, which helped allay her fears of the nearest neighbor being half a mile away.

Myles pulled into the driveway and turned off the car. "Then it looks like you'll love this place."

And love the house she did. Whitney toured the three-bedroom, three-bath (all indoor) "cabin," a still-sleeping Haylee in her arms, while Myles unloaded the car. The goal was to change her daughter without waking her up and put her down in the portable crib they'd brought with them once Myles set it up.

The decor was stylish, tasteful, and suited all the lovely wood. She wasn't surprised at the electronics at play, given Nate was such a tech guy. The lights, door locks, and several kitchen appliances could be operated via an app. She noted two fireplaces, one in the owner's suite upstairs and the other in the grand room.

Whitney returned downstairs just in time to see Myles deposit the last two pieces of luggage in the entryway.

"Okay, that's everything." He locked and bolted the door and then turned around to appraise his surroundings. His whistle was low and appreciative. "Damn, this place is as big as mine."

"Ror said they also use it as some sort of camp for the school Nate's company sponsors. Classes come here for two weeks every semester during the school year and four weeks in the summer. Most of them have never been out of the city and don't get a chance to be 'one with nature.' So when they're here, they hike and do a bunch of one-with-nature stuff. And I think they do computer stuff, too."

"Yeah?" Myles appeared intrigued or impressed or both. "And they all sleep in here?"

"No, there are supposed to be four or five sleepaway cabins in the back, but I could only make out three."

Myles nodded. His expression softened when it shifted to their daughter, and then lifted to hers.

"Where should I put the crib?"

"I was thinking we should keep her with us—at least for tonight—until she gets used to the place. What do you think?" She didn't want Haylee waking up in a strange room all by herself.

"I think that means we won't be having sex tonight."

Whitney shook her head, chuckling. "Aren't you tired? Because I'm exhausted, and as much as I love my kid, I'm starting to feel like I'm lugging a bowling ball around." Funny how eighteen pounds of baby started to feel like thirty pounds after she'd been carrying her around long enough.

As soon as they put Haylee to bed, she planned on following her quickly to la-la land. Because of her recent trip to New York, she was suffering from a double case of jet lag.

Myles's brows shot up and he snorted a laugh. "Sweetheart, I'd have to be near death to not take advantage of every opportunity to have sex with you."

Haylee stirred in her arms, and Whitney placed her finger against her smiling lips. The man did have a way with words. "Shh. You're going to wake her up."

"Okay. Let me go set this up in our room," he said, following her example by keeping his voice low.

Whitney didn't miss his emphasis on the word *our*. He'd meant it as a gripe, but it gave her goose bumps. She loved the intimacy of it. How natural it sounded rolling off his tongue.

It took Myles less than five minutes to set up the crib. In the meantime, Whitney used their king-sized bed as a changing table. Haylee started to stir the second the diaper came off, only settling back down when Whitney began singing softly to her.

Getting her daughter into the crib without waking her up was a huge accomplishment considering the last twenty-four hours.

Myles encircled her from behind, pulling her back against his chest, his hand splayed on her stomach. "You look tired."

Whitney tipped back her head, resting it on his chest, and closed her eyes. "That's 'cause I am."

"Then go to bed. I'll bring up the rest of the luggage and set the alarm," he murmured in between light kisses to her neck.

A ribbon of desire began to unfurl where his fingers were stroking the flesh just above her panty line. "I'm going to take a quick shower first." She had a day's worth of sweat and travel to wash off.

His fingers slipped lower, hovering right above her pubic area. A ragged exhalation and his erection hardening on her back clearly signaled how he wanted to spend the early hours of the morning.

Suddenly, his questing fingers were gone, and he was easing away. The move was discombobulating.

The light tap on her ass was as surprising as it was arousing. "Go on, take your shower. I'll be back in a bit. I also have a couple of phone calls to make." And then he was gone.

In the shower, Whitney couldn't decide what she wanted more, sleep or sex. Myles had scratched her sexual itch, and like a mosquito bite, it wouldn't stop itching. So she did what any sleep-deprived woman would do. She covered the side of the crib facing the bed with a sheet and dressed for the occasion— T-shirt with no panties—and then climbed into bed.

Where she promptly fell asleep.

"So what'd you find?" Myles stood in the office—the only room he could find with a door—an AirPod in his ear and his cell phone in hand.

"Nothing yet," said Greg, the private investigator he'd hired to find out who leaked the story to the press. "James—the guy who wrote the article—won't give up his sources, but I have a lead on the last three people he called before he turned the story in to his editor. Just sit tight. I'll have an answer for you within the next forty-eight hours."

Myles wasn't about to ask him how he got the guy's tele-phone records. Save a few employees at the clinic, only a tight circle of family and friends had known Whitney was Haylee's mother. The list of suspects wasn't extensive.

"Okay. Let me know if my ex's name comes up. Going by her reaction, I don't think it was her, but I also wouldn't put it past her."

"You got it. I'll call as soon as I get something solid."

His sister was his next call. He'd promised to contact her when he arrived at the cabin. If not, she'd think he was dead in a ditch somewhere.

"Hey, you," she said, answering after the first ring. Knowing his twin, she'd kept her phone at hand, waiting for his call. "I was hoping you'd get in before eleven. Now I can go to sleep knowing you're not stuck in a ditch somewhere."

Myles chuckled to himself. That was Natalie, a worrywart by nature.

"I'm fine, Haylee's fine, and Whitney's fine. We're all fine, and I didn't see a single ditch on the drive here. How are things with you? I hope to God the press isn't bothering you."

"Eh, you know, I've gotten a few calls on the landline asking if I'm your sister, but no one has shown up at the house. They must not have my or Brad's cell phone number."

The last thing he wanted was to have his family dragged into this mess too.

"Let's hope it stays that way."

"Oh, I almost forgot. Holly called."

Myles tensed. "What the hell for?" His sister and ex-wife hadn't spoken since shortly after he and Holly brought Haylee home from the hospital.

"She said she's been trying to get in touch with you. Something about the settlement from the clinic."

"I told her my lawyer would be in contact," Myles groused.

"What's that all about?"

"I told her she could have all of it—every red cent—if she never contacted me again."

Natalie snorted. "Well, she tried to. Doesn't that make the contract null and void?"

Myles scrubbed his palm over his face and sighed. "Probably not."

She huffed in annoyance. "After what she did to you, she doesn't deserve a dime. Although I think she did you and Haylee a favor when she walked out."

"It'll be worth it to never have to see or talk to her again."

"I guess so," Natalie said begrudgingly. "Things definitely worked out better for Haylee, and from the picture in the tabloid, better for you too. Hint hint."

Myles rolled his eyes. His sister could always be counted on for her subtlety. "Would you stop."

Because his warning had little bite to it, she cheerfully ignored him. "When you said things between you had gotten better, I didn't realize how much."

He didn't have to see her to know she was grinning like a Cheshire cat.

"Nat, I don't want to talk to you about my love life."

"So it *is* love." Now she sounded like a Cheshire cat rubbing its paws together. "Well, that's encouraging. Whitney is a huge improvement on Holly."

Myles made a sound of frustration in his throat. "You know I didn't mean it that way."

He liked Whitney a lot. He lusted after her. He enjoyed spending time with her. And she was wonderful with Haylee. But he wasn't in love with her. If anything, he'd admit to an intense infatuation that would burn itself out...eventually.

"Never mind. Pretend I didn't say anything about your torrid love affair. And now I'll let you get back to the mother of your child. And take care of my darling niece. Tell her Aunt

Natalie misses her like crazy and can't wait until she gets back. I love ya. Bye."

With her laughter echoing in his ear, she hurried off the phone without giving him a chance to respond.

Classic Natalie always needed to have the last word.

28

Whitney's skin felt tight and hot when she slowly surfaced from sleep. Myles's morning wood was pressed against her butt, which explained the wetness between her thighs. Not yet fully conscious, she pushed back against him.

She heard and felt the groan that rumbled from his chest. The hand on her stomach instantly flattened, his finger lightly brushing the underside of her breast. She sucked in a breath.

"You're up," he said in a sleep-drugged voice.

Whitney smiled, and this time when she pushed back, she wiggled her ass. "So are you."

Myles emitted a sound, a cross between a chuckle and a groan. "That's because of you. If I'd known you were going to bed bare and completely accessible—"

He palmed her between her legs, his finger running the length of her slit. Whitney bit down on her bottom lip to stifle a moan, the ache in her core rising at a steady, rapid pace.

"—I would have come to bed earlier. But you said you were tired—" he paused to nuzzle her neck, and she panted in response "—so I did the gentlemanly thing and put your needs above mine and let you sleep."

At this point, she figured their needs were on par with each other.

She was so consumed by pleasure, it took a moment to surface from the sexual fog that had engulfed her to register Haylee's whimpers.

Myles stilled. Then he collapsed on his back, emitting a groan of frustration. She shivered at the sudden loss of his body heat and the orgasm-giving talent of his fingers.

"Mommy's coming, sweetie." Whitney shot into action, scrambling the width of the bed to tend to their daughter.

A dark laugh emanated from somewhere in her lover's twisted soul. "Mommy might be coming, but Daddy sure ain't."

Whitney had put it off as long as she could, but she had to face the music sometime, and it might as well be while Haylee was asleep.

She reluctantly unearthed her phone from her purse, where she'd buried it after messaging her mother, Kennedy, Trinity, Stacy, and Aurora to let them know she'd arrived safely. It was easier to resist the temptation of social media if her phone was out of sight.

"Here goes nothing," she muttered to herself before pressing the on button. The Apple logo instantly appeared, and then a series of notifications flashed in rapid succession on the screen.

"Are you sure you want to do that?" Myles asked as he entered the kitchen and spied the phone in her hand. He'd encouraged her to take a twenty-four-hour break from the outside world. She'd made it to hour sixteen.

He sat beside her on the chair at the island. She sent him a quick smile. "I just need to go through my messages. Avery insists I keep in regular contact. We're supposed to hear back from Alex Randolf. He's the director of the movie I auditioned for last week."

And yep, there it was. The first message was from her.

Call me back as soon as you can. I have a bunch of offers I need to go over with you. If you're following the headlines, you know all the news is good. Kiss the kid for me. And then CALL ME! 😜

P.S. And kiss that lawyer of yours for me too. You didn't tell me he was hot! 🔥 😂 😜

Whitney turned and looked at Myles, who was watching her, one eyebrow quirked. Holding out the phone to him, she let him read the message.

She worried her bottom lip with her teeth. "She didn't say anything specifically about the audition, and she would have if she'd gotten the call."

"What I want to know is why you didn't tell her I was hot."

His deadpan remark earned him a playful swat on his arm. "If I had known just how vain you were, I would—"

"You would have what?" he interrupted, a sensual challenge in his tone as he caught her hand in his and brought it to his lips. "Not had sex with me?"

Nope, not even a little bit, but she'd be damned if she'd ever admit that to him. His ego was big enough as it was, and so was his…

Focus, Whitney. You can't have sex with him now.

"Duh. It's because you're hot that I'm having sex with you, but I definitely would have skipped a day or two with that attitude." Not true either, but sometimes one had to compromise.

He chuckled, knowing she was full of shit. "So, are you going to call her?"

As she was mentally debating it, her gaze halted at a message from Grace, the VP at Oasis.

Donald called. ECO's dropping the lawsuit. There's nothing stopping us from signing with SunDay. I assume the news about the fertility clinic mix-up scared them off. Nobody wants to mess with America's Sweetheart. Now all that's needed is your signature. See you when you get back.

Whitney had been confident they'd inevitably prevail, but the threat of a prolonged court battle had been a weight on her shoulders. Just like that, it was gone, leaving her feeling light to the point of giddiness.

Tears pricked the backs of her eyes as she lifted her gaze to his. "ECO is dropping the lawsuit," she whispered, her smile tremulous. "It's over."

Myles stood, pleasure lighting his eyes as his arms closed around her, pulling her halfway off her seat. "Babe, that's wonderful."

The endearment slipped easily from his mouth as if this wasn't the first time he'd said it to her. However, her heart must have sensed it meant something more, the way it tried to jump out of her chest. The butterflies in her stomach also started a cacophony of fluttering. She didn't just return his embrace. She plastered herself to his front as if trying to make them one.

God, he felt wonderful, a combination of smooth skin, hard muscle, and an intoxicating scent now as familiar to her as her trademark perfume.

"You have no idea how—how—"

"Oh, I think I have some idea," he said when she couldn't find the words to convey the overwhelming sense of relief that had literally overtaken her body, leaving it boneless and malleable.

Myles dropped a brief but potent kiss on her lips. "Can you believe it's over without any of it leaking to the public?" she asked.

Whitney was still marveling at that. As she'd told Trinity, she believed, in the end, she and Oasis could have survived the prison labor scandal, but her brand might have been forever tainted by its association with the clothing manufacturer.

Myles harrumphed. "ECO is doing this to save themselves."

"I know. You just never know how far they intended to take it."

He leaned down and kissed the tip of her nose. "Are you done going through your messages? I'm thinking it's the perfect time for us to enjoy some more adult activities before Haylee wakes up."

As if to punctuate his point, he made certain she could feel the state of his package behind the fly of his jeans. Hard and growing harder and longer by the second.

But before she could do more than suck in a shaky breath, their daughter's cries sounded over the monitor.

Myles let out a groan and closed his eyes. His head dropped like an abandoned marionette. Whitney couldn't help but laugh at his pained expression.

"I'll get her."

"No, I'll get her. Clearly, I need a distraction." He gestured to his hard-on. "It'll be gone by the time I hit the stairs."

Aroused and flushed, she watched him go—a sight to behold—before returning her attention to her messages. Most of them could wait. There were two from Aurora. One she'd sent tonight at nine-thirty Eastern Time that said,

They're going crazy for your story. They can't get enough of it. TMZ has already posted a retraction on their website about all the home-wrecking and husband-stealing garbage they wrote in the initial article. People Magazine is now describing you as America's Sweetheart/Darling, and everyone wants to know if your first interview is going to Oprah. Sar, sweetie, right now you can do no wrong. Oh, and everyone is dying to meet your princess. I suggest you get that pic of her out there soon or the paps will descend on you and Myles like a pack of hyenas. TTYL. 😊 ♥

The last one came in at two a.m. Eastern.

Adam's here. I don't know what to do. Should I leave? OMG, why is this happening to me? I'm staying with my parents tonight. I can't be alone.

What the hell was he doing in California? Aurora had been doing so well, Whitney fretted to herself as she called her friend.

"Hi, Sar. You got my message, huh?" Aurora sounded drained.

"Hey, sweets. Are you doing okay? What happened?"

She let out a humorless laugh. "I'm sorry I even sent it now. In the cold light of day, I can see I had nothing to worry about. He barely said two words to me."

"Ror, you got to catch me up. What happened? Where did you see him?"

She then explained how she'd attended a political event hosted by her parents. The guest list was a who's who of political heavyweights in California and beyond. The governor of California had arrived with Aurora's ex, the lieutenant governor of New York.

"Did you two talk?" Whitney asked.

"He acted as if he'd never been anything but a client to me." She sounded gutted by that despite tagging on, "Which, of course, he should have. The last thing I want is for my parents— or anyone else, for that matter—to know that I risked my professional reputation for the man or the fool I made of myself."

"What was he doing there?" Through the baby monitor, Whitney could hear Myles talking baby talk and Haylee's responding babble. She moved to stand in front of the wood-framed patio doors.

"My mother says he and Governor Milton are friends. Apparently, they went to law school together."

Whitney hated to ask the next question, but the nosy Nelly in her couldn't help herself. "Did he bring a date?"

"He did, his daughter, Brittany."

"Ah, okay." Aurora and his daughter had grown close for a while there, but as far as she knew, they were no longer in contact.

"She invited me out to dinner next weekend before she heads back to school for a summer class, and I couldn't say no with everyone standing there. My parents would've known there was something wrong. So now I'm stuck."

"You can always cancel."

"No, you don't understand, I have to go. She—she has a lot of stuff going on in her life, and she trusts me."

"But if it's going to be too painful…"

"No, I can't do that to her. But don't worry, I'm sure it'll be a one-time deal. Plus, I'm over him. The freak-out last night was the shock of seeing him. I'm fine now. Good as gold, I promise."

Aurora didn't sound fine. She sounded like a woman putting on a brave front to hide the shaken and vulnerable parts of her. Despite what her friend proclaimed, she wasn't over him, but Whitney wasn't going to push it.

"Anyway, I have to go. My mom and I are going shopping. And don't worry, I've got all your stuff under control. I'm relaying everything to your manager."

After saying their goodbyes, Whitney hung up and stared sightlessly at the cabins that had been obscured by the dark last night. It had been six months, and her friend still wasn't over her ex, and she was going to have to face his daughter again in a week.

She imagined what it would be like if that were her and Myles. One day they would be over, but unlike Aurora, she'd have no choice but to see him, to talk to him, and to watch as he moved on with his life.

Whitney feared she would handle it just as well as Aurora was handling her breakup from the man she swore she didn't love anymore.

29

The last three days with Whitney and their daughter had been time off Myles hadn't known he needed. And it wasn't that they did anything different than during Whitney's visits. All of Haylee's waking hours they spent taking care of her, the majority of which focused on her entertainment. She loved the outdoors, so they spent a lot of time on the back patio with her toys. She was also fascinated by birds and butterflies.

When she'd had enough vitamin D for the day, they returned indoors to watch *Sesame Street*, her favorite show.

Right, so nothing super exciting, just normal activities, but he'd never experienced it to this extent before. In this space and time, they were a family in the simplest and easiest terms. He cooked, Whitney helped, and they both cared for their daughter. One of the unnerving things about it was how right it felt.

But even more so was how addicted he'd become to the sex. And it wasn't as if he hadn't had a lot of fantastic sex before. He definitely had, but with Whitney…he didn't know how to describe why he'd gone from praying to see the back of her—a beautiful sight to behold, for sure—to being unable to keep his hands off her in what seemed like the blink of an eye.

It was more than great sex, though. And it wasn't just that she was a knockout. Her beauty went so much deeper than that. He loved how much she loved their daughter, this child she'd never signed up for. He loved her intelligence, her talent, her business acumen, her ambition, and that she was ethical to a fault. And he loved how she made him feel: liked, desired, and respected.

"Hey, why are you so quiet? What are you thinking?" Whitney's voice was soft and sex-sated, her bare leg draped over his hair-roughened one.

"I never thought I'd enjoy the solitude of a place like this, but it's nice for when you want to get away from the noise for a while. What do you think?" He angled his head to meet her heavy-lidded gaze. God, he loved her eyes. Her smile. Her hair. Her dimples. Her beautiful face.

"I think you're right. Do you think Nate and Kennedy will let us stay here again? Or better yet, we—I should buy a house up here, and we could come whenever we wanted."

Her statement on its face—much less the telling slip—should have freaked him out. Her easy use of "we" gave off too many long-term relationship vibes. Surprisingly enough, though, he wasn't averse to the idea or the possible future it painted. He was only now getting a taste of what life would be like dating "Sahara," and he suspected getting away from hot spots like LA and New York would be critical to his peace of mind.

However, he'd noticed that since Aurora's press conference refuting the tabloid hit piece, there had been a one-hundred-eighty-degree shift in coverage. Whitney was now Tiana, Cinderella, Belle, the Little Mermaid, and Wonder Woman rolled into one. The country had taken her under its protective wing. Her ardent fans and supporters would have anointed her a saint had there not been a picture of them in the park enjoying every moment of their lip-lock.

He cocked an eyebrow at her. "You'd do that? Buy a house up here?"

One shoulder lifted and fell in an insouciant shrug. "Sure, why not? I don't want to bother Nate and Kennedy every time we need to get away, and this house isn't exactly child-friendly. Although at the rate the two of them are going, that won't be the case for long. I promise they'll be married within a year."

"And that's what you want, right? Marriage and more kids?" He didn't know why he asked as she'd already told him as much weeks ago.

Whitney tipped her head back and blinked up at him with wide eyes. "Yes—I mean not now, but eventually," she amended after an awkward pause. "And don't worry, you've made it crystal clear that you're done, which I completely understand. Two times is plenty. Once would be enough for me."

"My divorce isn't even four months old."

Myles didn't know why he offered that as his defense, as if he needed one. Whitney was fine with things as they were and had thought ahead enough to map out her future with another man. The man who would be her husband and the father of her future children. He hated that the mere thought of it bothered him.

"Hey, I understand," she said. "You don't have to explain yourself to me. At least, not when it comes to that. We said we'd enjoy it as long as it lasts, and that's what I intend to do. Are you with me?" By the end, her voice had dropped to a sultry murmur as her palm caressed his chest.

As long as it lasts.

How long would that be? Six more months? Another year or two? What if she called it quits before he was ready to let her go? Where would that leave him?

When they'd originally vowed that a physical relationship between them wouldn't negatively affect their co-parenting one, he hadn't had sex in months, and he'd been thinking with his dick. Had he now truly reached the point where the thought of her with another man after they were over felt like a punch in the gut?

Myles gave his head a mental shake. No point in thinking that far ahead. They were together in the here and now, and that's what he needed to focus on. And she made that incredibly easy, lying there in all her beautiful naked glory.

"Honey, I'm so with you. I'm wondering if men reach another sexual peak in their thirties and if that's why I want you again so soon." And he wasn't lying about that. His body should have been firmly in the recovery or replenishing stage, but the feel of her breast against his side and her hand caressing his chest had his dick swelling to life again mere minutes after he'd exploded like a rocket.

One orgasm down, at least another to go before the night was over. He hadn't had his fill of her yet.

"Hmm, then the same thing must be happening to me," she said with a throaty hum. Her hand started its march downward, briefly stopping to explore the first delineation of his abs.

Palming her right butt cheek, he gave it an approving squeeze, eliciting a sharp intake of breath from her. "I heard women reach their sexual peak in their thirties."

"I'm thirty, so I guess that explains the multiple rounds and my lack of control." Her hand continued its downward trajectory at a torturous snail's pace. His stomach clenched as his dick strived to reach flagpole status.

When she finally, *finally* reached her goal, she wrapped her hand around him. Myles let out a hiss, and his eyelids fluttered closed.

"Feels good?" she asked, her voice a seductive purr as she began to pump him.

Myles forced his eyes open. "Fuck yes," he groaned.

"What about this?" she whispered, and began kissing her way across his stomach. The closer she got to his dick, the harder it got and the more labored his breathing became. Then he was sure he'd died and gone to heaven as he watched her gorgeous lips close over the head.

Myles sucked in a ragged breath as sensation upon sensation overwhelmed him. And all too soon he was consumed by it.

This felt too good. She was too good. He wasn't going to be able to last long enough to get her off again.

"Condom," he rasped but made no move to get it as he watched his cock disappear inside her mouth over and over again. If she heard him, it didn't appear she was about to pause to let him grab one from the nightstand.

With a slash of her tongue along the tip, she took him deeper, ratcheting up the pleasure. Groaning, Myles pushed aside the long locks of her hair and grasped her hips, filling his hands with her delectable ass. Whitney hummed in pleasure as he squeezed and kneaded both cheeks, causing the ache in his balls to intensify. He knew he was reaching the point of no return, and he didn't want to get there alone.

"Babe," he said in a hoarse whisper, "I want to come inside you." Summoning up superhuman willpower—from where, he'd never know—he eased himself out of her mouth, reached over, and grabbed the condom.

Whitney blinked up at him, desire blazing in her eyes. "I wanted to—"

"Next time," he said, urging her up onto her hands and knees and positioning himself behind her while he made quick work of rolling on the condom. He paused to admire the tantalizing picture she made, only to lose it when she turned and sent him a sultry look over her shoulder.

What are you waiting for?

Myles's growl was feral as he plunged deep. Whitney let out a soft gasp that turned into a moan. Gripping her hips, he began thrusting in earnest, his growls and groans and her soft cries echoing throughout the room. The moment he felt her body stiffen and then begin to shudder from the force of her orgasm, Myles let his take control. With one final, desperate thrust, he reached his peak in an explosion of white-hot pleasure before floating back to earth, breathless and sated.

Whitney ended her call with Avery and turned to Myles. "That was my agent," she announced in a daze. "I got the part. I got the part!"

Myles's expression broke into a smile as she threw herself into his arms, tears of happiness welling up in her eyes.

"That's fabulous, babe. I'm so proud of you," he said, hugging her tight.

Haylee, who was playing on her activity mat, stared up at them, her big brown eyes dominating her sweet little face. Then she began babbling and stretching out her arms to them.

"You want to join in the celebration, don't you, Sweetie," Whitney crooned, bending to scoop her up and quickly returning to Myles to complete their circle. She kissed her daughter's flushed cheeks before tipping her head back to receive one from Myles. The kiss went on long enough for Haylee to wedge her fingers between their mouths. They broke apart, laughing.

"No kissing," Whitney mock scolded him.

"Not unless we're kissing her, apparently," Myles said, his tone dry but his expression loving as he gazed at their daughter.

Settling Haylee on her hip, Whitney said, "As much as I

would love to stay here for another month, I think it's time for us to get back."

A shadow passed over his face as if the prospect of getting back to their life in California wasn't high on his priority list.

She gently touched his forearm. "I know, it sucks, but we can go back on Sunday and start the week off fresh. That'll give us two more days to ourselves."

He treated her to a lopsided smile. "Don't worry about me. I'll be fine. And I do need to get back to the office. There's only so much I can do from here."

Myles had been working two to four hours every day, half the time on conference calls. She was in daily contact with her team at Oasis. They'd emailed her the contract with SunDay for her perusal and signature. Transitioning to them from ECO would take several months, but the process was already underway, starting with notifying their respective vendors.

She had also made it a point to check up on Aurora. Despite her friend's assurances that her two a.m. call had been a combination of fatigue, work stress, and loneliness (since Kennedy and Nate had gotten together, she confessed to feeling a touch of the third-wheel syndrome) and not because she was still hung up on her ex, Whitney remained skeptical.

She'd spoken with Kennedy, and the hope was that opening an office in Los Angeles would be just what the doctor ordered to put that damn man in Aurora's past. A change of scenery would also mean new faces and new relationship possibilities.

The call from Avery ended up being the highlight of the day, because an hour later, Haylee's incoming teeth became a source of distress for baby and parents alike. Her misery—aka nonstop crying—couldn't be alleviated by any of the countless methods they tried. Not the teething ring (refrigerated or not), or the gum massage (ouch, that kinda hurt), or the warm, soothing bath (apparently soothing it was not), or the clean, cold washcloth. None of it worked.

Exhaustion. That was what worked to the degree that Haylee finally succumbed to it, falling asleep late in the afternoon with a death grip on her teething ring and the other side clamped between her gums.

Myles had remained downstairs to take a call from someone at his office. Apparently, isolation mode wasn't equipped to filter out a screaming child ten feet away.

"Right. I'll be back tomorrow," Myles relayed to the person on the other end of the phone. As she approached the open study door, his gaze flicked to her, his expression inscrutable.

Whitney's brows shot up in question and concern. Tomorrow was Friday, and they weren't supposed to be going home until Sunday.

As soon as he lowered the phone from his ear, she entered the room. "What's going on? Who was that?"

"Justin from work. I got to get back right away. There's a problem with one of our biggest clients." Strain bracketed his mouth, and his jaw was locked tight.

As much as she wanted to whine and ask if there wasn't anyone else at the firm—his partner, for instance—who could deal with the emergency, she bit her tongue. The firm was his baby, much like Oasis was hers. She'd sound like a spoiled little brat if she whined about them having to leave early.

"How serious is it?"

"Nothing I can't fix."

After several moments of silence, it was clear he didn't intend to elaborate, so she let it drop.

"Okay, I'll call Stacy and have her arrange to have us flown home in the morning."

His expression softened as he enclosed her in his arms. "Thanks, babe."

30

"Myles, to what do I owe this pleasure?" Holly asked with more than a trace of smugness in her tone. It wouldn't be there for long.

"We need to talk." He felt like a ticking time bomb, minutes away from detonating.

She stood in front of the door, her body barring him entry to her new townhouse. "I signed a contract promising to have no contact with you. Are you trying to get me to break it and forfeit your half of the money?"

Of course, the first thing she thought about was the money. "When this is over, you won't see one red cent of it. Now, are you going to let me in so we can talk, or should I go ahead and call the police right now?" His tone was low and deadly earnest.

Alarm flashed in her eyes but was quickly replaced as her mouth twisted into a scowl. She cautiously took a step back and opened the door, allowing him in. "Call the police for what?"

Myles closed the door but didn't venture any further into her house. This was privacy enough for what he had to say to her.

"I'm going to make this quick, but it won't be painless. This is what I know. You paid Evan Campbell twenty-five thousand dollars to make sure the surrogate didn't get pregnant."

Holly blanched at the name of the fertility clinic's former lab technician. Color completely left her face at the end of his statement. Shell shocked would be an understatement to describe her expression.

"This is what else I know. Campbell knew you didn't want to be a mother, but he'd also gotten to know our surrogate and wanted her to get the full one hundred grand she'd get for carrying the pregnancy to term, so he decided to use my sperm and someone else's eggs during the fertilization process. But in order to give you a reason to question the paternity, he made sure the eggs came from someone of another race. Tell me how I'm doing. Did I get that right?"

Honest to God, he thought his head would fucking explode.

"Is that what Evan told you?" Her tone was as sharp as the look she gave him. But she couldn't hide the stark fear in her eyes.

She should be scared. Myles wanted nothing more than for her to pay for what she did. The depth of her deception was staggering, and her cunning ingenuity rivaled the kind he'd only ever seen on screen.

"It's what Campbell told the private detective I hired. All he had to do was follow the money once he zeroed in on the three lab technicians who'd left the clinic since they launched their investigation."

Campbell thought that since he quit two months after the other two were fired, he was in the clear, and he would've been had he not sold the trash story to the tabloids.

Holly stared at him, her expression a mixture of anger and fear. "What do you want me to say? That I'm sorry I don't want kids? That I felt you were pressuring me into doing something I didn't want to do?"

Myles's head snapped back as if struck. Struck by the breath-taking audacity of her accusation. He hadn't exactly expected remorse, but he had expected a healthy amount of embarrass-ment or shame. Pinning the blame on him took a lot of fuck-ing nerve.

"Jesus Christ, Holly, *you* said you wanted children. *You* said you wanted a family with me. What the fuck was I supposed to take from that?" He tried his level best not to raise his voice, but the last part came out a low roar.

"Because that's what you wanted me to say!" she screamed, abandoning any effort of self-restraint.

Silence fell then. Suffocating levels of it. Myles stared blankly at his ex-wife. It was at that moment he realized that he had no fucking idea who this woman was. Never did and had no desire to ever know.

"So you lied to me to get me to marry you, is that it?"

Pressing her lips together, Holly lifted her chin, refusing to answer.

Myles couldn't help but marvel that once upon a time, he'd loved this woman. He'd thought she was beautiful. He'd mar-ried her thinking they would have a family together. Looking at her now, he couldn't for the life of him understand what he ever saw in her. Beautiful was Whitney, inside and out.

"Was the part about you not being able to carry a pregnancy to term also a lie?"

Again, her silence spoke volumes and then some.

Myles's gaze flicked skyward, and he inhaled the longest breath of his life. His hands fisted at his sides as rage threatened to consume him whole. Eat him alive.

Everything had been a lie.

Everything.

And he'd fallen for all of it, hook, line, and sinker. Unbe-knownst to him, when they'd stood at the altar promising to love and cherish each other until death, their marriage had been doomed from its deceptive start.

The magnitude of this mistake was exponentially greater than any he'd ever made in his life.

"You are not getting one dime of that settlement," he informed her through gritted teeth.

Only then did her gaze dart back to him, her expression one of panic and alarm. "Half of it is mine," she protested.

His eyes narrowed in challenge. "Then take me to court. Let's see if the judge is going to allow you to benefit from your crime." Myles would have to check with a fertility lawyer, but he was sure she'd broken several laws. It had to be illegal to pay a medical professional to do what Campbell had done.

"I know you, Myles. You'd never do it because the publicity wouldn't be good for your *girlfriend's* career."

Myles saw red. He didn't know whether she was being serious or attempting to perform some reverse psychology bullshit on him, and he didn't care. "Leave her out of this," he bit out. "And like I said, you're not getting a dime."

She screwed up her face, resentment she had no right to feel blazing in her eyes. "You don't need it, and Haylee certainly doesn't because her mother is a freaking billionaire. And you can look down on me all you want, but don't think for a second it escaped my attention that between the two of us, you're the one who made out like a bandit. You got the child you wanted, and now you're fucking her celebrity mother. I'm the one who walked away with nothing. And don't you dare blame me for the shit Evan did. He did that on his own. He promised me Blake wouldn't get pregnant."

Genuinely stupefied, Myles could only stare at her. If he thought she couldn't sink lower, she simply grabbed another shovel and kept digging.

With nothing left to say, Myles turned and opened the door.

"Myles." The panic and stress in her voice were unmistakable.

He paused without turning around. He didn't have the stomach to look at her again.

"I'm not asking for the whole thing, just my half," she said with the barest hint of entreaty in her voice.

If he'd expected an apology to tumble out, he would have been disappointed.

But he hadn't, and he wasn't.

Whitney checked her phone for what had to be the fortieth time. And nope, no message and no missed call from Myles. (As if she hadn't turned the volume of her cell phone up to maximum and hadn't had it within arm's length the entire day, waiting for him to call.)

It had been over a day since they'd last spoken, which was on the car ride from the airport to his house. She offered to keep Haylee for the day since he didn't know how long he'd be at the office, but he'd said he'd arranged for his sister to take her for the night.

Boy, that had stung, but what could she say when he'd told her that his niece and nephew were looking forward to seeing her? She couldn't very well deprive her daughter of her cousins' company when she and Myles had just had her all to themselves the last five days.

But this—Myles going dark this long—she was having a problem dealing with. This wasn't like him. Since they'd started sleeping together, a day hadn't gone by when they hadn't at least exchanged a message or briefly talked on the phone.

Nada so far.

And it wasn't as if she could initiate contact. Before they'd kissed goodbye, she'd told him to call her when he came up for air because she knew how busy he'd be that day. Whitney wondered if he hadn't called because he was still busy. And if so, that meant she needed to wait.

But what if he'd been in a wreck and he was unconscious and trapped upside down in his car, waiting for someone to rescue him?

Ugh. She gave her head a vigorous shake, sending her hair flying around her face. She couldn't let her imagination get away from her. The most likely scenario was that Myles had worked all day, got home exhausted, and went straight to bed. The man did sleep like an Egyptian mummy left undisturbed in a crypt.

It was only 8:10 in the morning. When he woke up after sleeping in—something he could only do when someone else had Haylee overnight—he would call. If he didn't contact her by noon, she'd call him.

She gave a violent start at the sudden ringing of her phone.

Jumpy much?

Myles. Finally!

However, her euphoria was quickly followed by a sharp stab of disappointment when she looked down to see it was Aurora calling.

She didn't want to sound like one of those clingy girlfriends, but why hadn't he called yet?

"Hey, Ror." She tried to make her voice bright.

"Hey, Sar, are you back home?"

Whitney propped her hip against the counter. "Yeah, we flew in yesterday. How are things with you? Did you go to dinner with you-know-who's daughter?"

"I did. We went out last night."

"Okay, so how was it?" Talking about her friend's problems would help take her mind off her own.

"We had a great time." After a beat, her voice softened, becoming wistful. "Honestly, she's such a sweet kid. Adam may suck when it comes to romantic relationships, but he's a good dad."

Adam? Whitney's brows shot up.

That was the first warning sign. She then tried to approach the subject with as much consideration as possible. "I thought we weren't referring to him by his real name." Unless she was upset, which she had been during their morning call earlier in the week. Aurora wasn't rattled or upset now.

Since the breakup, she, Aurora, and Kennedy had gotten inventive in the numerous ways they referred to him. *You-know-who* had won out, with *Lieutenant Fitness*—he'd once been featured on the cover of *Sports & Fitness* magazine—coming in a close second.

At forty-one, Adam Faulkner was pure eye candy and a magnet for politician groupies (a group Whitney hadn't even known existed). His backstory of being widowed at thirty-two and raising his ten-year-old daughter alone made for great press. Women saw his single status as a challenge. But according to Aurora, one marriage was enough for him. In breaking things off, he'd told her he needed to concentrate on his political career, and she was a distraction.

The man was heartless.

Whitney said good riddance to him.

"It's okay, I'm fine."

In fact, her friend sounded downright chipper. But *I'm fine* didn't answer Whitney's question, which was a gigantic tell that everything was *not* fine.

"But she knows that's it, right? She's not expecting you guys to continue... I don't know, meeting up for dinners and stuff?"

"We agreed to keep in touch. But it won't be a problem," she hurried to explain. "Our relationship has nothing to do with her father. We don't talk about him, and it's not like she'll be bringing him along when we go out. I'm never going to see him—that is, unless I happen to attend one of my parents' political fundraisers and he happens to be there." The latter, she muttered under her breath.

"*Hmm.* Well, just be careful," Whitney cautioned. The breakup had hit Aurora hard, and despite a constant stream of successful, good-looking men her age asking her out, she'd yet to accept a single date and claimed her refusals had nothing to do with her ex.

She and Kennedy called bullshit on that, but they both understood that the heart required time to heal. Some longer than others.

"You and Ken worry too much," Aurora chided. "Anyway, I actually called for a reason. I think we should respond to Holly Redmond's interview. It'll look good if—"

"Wait, what?"

"Myles's ex-wife," Aurora said, her tone suddenly tentative.

"His ex-wife sat down for an interview?" Whitney found that hard to believe. She didn't exactly come out of the situation looking like a candidate for mother of the year.

"Not a formal sit-down interview, no. The reporter caught up with her in front of her house."

That meant they shoved a microphone in her face while firing questions at her. Whitney was intimately familiar with that "interview" tactic.

"What did she say?"

Aurora gave a breezy laugh. "Don't worry. It wasn't anything disparaging or defamatory. Just that the marriage was effectively over by the time Haylee was born and that Haylee wasn't the reason for the divorce."

Whitney liked to believe that even if Haylee had never been born, Myles would eventually have left her. She'd demanded he choose between her and his daughter. But that was Myles's story to tell, not hers.

"And you want Myles to confirm it?"

"It would be good to put out a statement saying there is no animosity between the three of you, and yes, confirm what she said. I mean, they recently saw each other, so I assume they're on decent terms."

Whitney hadn't seen the Mack truck barreling toward her until it was too late. The impact knocked the wind out of her, leaving her gasping.

"Did you say they recently saw each other?" According to Myles, he hadn't seen his ex-wife in months. Since she'd shown up at his house during Whitney's first visit.

"That's what she said." A beat elapsed. "Oh my god, Sar, is that a problem? Didn't you know?" Aurora asked in a hushed voice.

"No, no, it's not a problem. I—Myles mentioned that they'd spoken. Something to do with the fertility clinic."

"Well, thank God for that," she said with a nervous laugh. "For a second there, I thought I was letting the cat out of the bag. Anyway, I think that something from our side saying all is well between all parties involved would put a kibosh on any stories trying to turn what happened into some *Real Housewives* drama. She doesn't hate you, you don't hate her, the divorce was amicable, and everyone has moved on. It's obvious that you had nothing to do with the end of their marriage, but it's nice to have it confirmed by the ex-wife."

"Yes, absolutely."

When would the two have seen each other? They had only returned from Vermont yesterday. And there was no way the gaping hole that made up the number of hours she hadn't heard from him had anything to do with it. Myles had been at his office all day.

"Okay, great. I'll put something together and have you and Myles read it over. If you're both happy with it, I'll put it out."

"Perfect. I'll let Myles know."

"Okay, sweets. Talk to you soon. And kiss the little one for me. I can't wait to finally meet her."

"I will. And thanks again, Ror. I can't tell you how much I appreciate you taking care of this for me."

"Not to sound corny, but that's what friends are for."

Aurora didn't know the half of it.

31

Before Aurora's call, Whitney had been content to wait and give her lover time to sleep in. Fifteen minutes later, she was waking his ass up. She wanted answers.

"Hey, sweetheart." He sounded groggy with sleep, which was fine with her.

"Hi, you sound like you had a hectic day yesterday."

"You have no idea," he muttered.

"So hectic you couldn't call me?"

"Yeah. Look, I'm sorry about that. By the time I got home last night, it was late."

"By the time you got home from working in the office all day, taking care of the emergency, right?" she asked, throwing subtlety out of the window in favor of *I dare you to lie to me* passive aggression.

In the ensuing silence, she could literally hear the *woosh-woosh* of his mind racing. Questions like *what does she know* and *how much trouble am I in* clanking around in his brain.

"Did Holly contact you?" he asked, breaking the silence.

"No, but a reporter did get a hold of her, and you'd be

amazed at what she's saying about your divorce and current very cordial relationship." She'd spoon-fed him quite enough information. Now it was his turn to come clean with dates and times of his and his ex's recent encounters.

Instead of coming clean, he did that thing a person does when they've been caught: began making excuses.

"Okay, listen, whatever you're thinking, just stop, because it isn't close to the truth. I'm on my way over, and I'll explain everything as soon as I get there. Believe me, you'll understand."

Whitney put little faith in his assurances that she would. Because whether he'd straight-up, bald-faced lied to her or lied by omission didn't matter. They were lovers. They shared a child. And he'd kept her in the dark. Those things mattered. At least, they should.

Soon turned out to be twenty-five minutes. Twenty-five minutes of pacing, fuming, and racking her brain, trying to make sense of his cryptic statement. He couldn't fathom what she was thinking because she had no idea herself.

She threw open the door to him, her mouth set in a straight, unforgiving line. "What will I understand?" she asked, arms folded across her chest.

Myles eyed her warily as he entered and closed the door. "Can we at least sit down?" He gestured to the back of the house.

"Fine," she snapped. "And by the way, you look horrible." The latter she shot over her shoulder as she preceded Myles down the hall and into the family room in silence broken only by the sound of their footsteps.

"You know I saw Holly yesterday."

His admission almost caused her to pause and turn around, but she stifled the instinct and kept marching on, the bottoms of her feet beginning to sting from the force of her steps. Only when she stood in front of the couch did she turn and glare at him.

"I didn't know for sure, but I do now. Although I suspected as much when she said you'd seen each other recently."

For a moment, his eyes turned an icy blue. As if the mere mention of the encounter was enough to spark his anger. "Will you please sit so we can talk?"

Something in the way he looked at her had her lowering herself to the couch, where he quickly joined her. Then he took her clenched fists in his hands and gently ran his forefinger over her knuckles, coaxing her to relax.

"I hired a private investigator to find out who leaked the story to the press."

She didn't consider the tabloids "the press," but that was a discussion for another day. His revelation didn't surprise her, but it did make it easy to connect the dots.

"Oh my god, don't tell me she was the one who sold the story to them?" she asked in a strangled whisper. Why on earth would she do something like that when she'd soon be getting the entire settlement check? The story couldn't have gotten her more than fifty to one hundred grand.

Whitney was gobsmacked when he shook his head. "No."

Then the entire story came out. Every twisted, dystopian, *truth is stranger than fiction* bit of it. At the end, she could only stare at him wide-eyed and stunned to her very core.

"She did all of this so you would marry her?"

Myles slowly shook his head from side to side. "Yeah, I don't get it either."

Whitney snorted softly. He might not get it, but she did. As a woman, she was intimately aware of his appeal to the opposite sex. She experienced it every day. But never would she ever resort to the methods his ex-wife had to keep him.

The enormity of her lies was mind-blowing. And no doubt criminal.

"Why didn't you say anything when we were in Vermont? Why hide this from me?" His ex-wife was clearly in the wrong. She was Haylee's mother. They were in this together.

Releasing her hand, he let out a guttural sound of frustration and ran a hand through his hair. "Because we were married, and I had access to the account she paid him from. I had no idea what she was going to say when I confronted her. What she might say to you."

"What do you mean by that? What could she say?"

"That we were in this together to scam you or something like that," he muttered, his expression uneasy. As if putting the idea in her head was plenty discomfiting.

Whitney stilled. The thought had never occurred to her, but then, she wasn't a raving psychopath like his ex-wife.

"Were you? In this together?"

Myles's head jerked slightly back. "Of course not."

"Then why would you think I'd ever believe that?" she asked in a calm voice. "Myles, I know you, and I know that's something you're incapable of. Not for all the money in the world would you be involved in a scheme like that." She huffed a rueful laugh. "I mean, look how hard you fought me on giving you child support. Throughout this whole situation, you've only ever thought about Haylee. You—"

In that moment, realization dawned. "Oh my god, you thought I would try to get full custody of Haylee, didn't you? That even if I didn't believe it, it would give me leverage in court if I sought custody."

"No, not if you didn't believe," he said, vigorously shaking his head. "But what if you did? You'd have every right to demand full custody. Frankly, if I were in your shoes, I'd do the same thing."

Whitney looked into his eyes and saw his torment. She felt his uncertainty, and her heart wept. "Myles, I don't know if it's me you don't trust or yourself. But when I gave you all the reasons Haylee needed me in her life, I hope you didn't take that to mean that she'd be better off with me."

"Maybe she would be."

"Why, because I'm her mother, and she's a girl? Because I'm Black, and there's a high probability that's the way she'll present to the world? Or is it because you're not equipped to deal with any of it?"

His back went up at that. "I—"

"Myles, you will never have to do this alone, just like I won't. And as you've been doing this parenting thing longer than me, I need you. Haylee needs you."

She stroked from the backs of his hands to his fingertips. "No one is going to take her away from you. Not me. Not your ex-wife. Not the courts. I told you I'm fine with our arrangement. If one day you'd like to share physical custody, I'll be good with that too. You're her father, and you love her, and that is never going to change."

Myles swallowed visibly. "I trust you. I do."

"Good, then trust me when I say that there isn't an iota of doubt in my mind that you are the best thing that ever happened to her. You fought for her, and you wanted her even before you knew she was yours. I don't know if you realize what a gift that will be when she grows up. Knowing what you'd be facing having a biracial child, you made the conscious choice to raise her alone. A lot of men in your position would have walked away."

"I could never walk away from her."

Whitney smiled, tears pricking her eyes. "And that's only one of the reasons I love you."

As unplanned, first-time I-love-yous went, she had no expectation that the sentiment would be reciprocated. She suffered zero regrets when he responded by cradling her face in his palms, slanting his mouth over hers, and kissing her deeply, their tongues tangling in a lusty dance. Whitney gave as good as she got, savoring the scent, feel, and taste of him.

When he finally broke the kiss, he rested his forehead against hers, and between choppy breaths said, "I love you too."

Tears immediately flooded her eyes as she drew back and stared into his brilliantly blue ones. Love, warmth, desire, caring, and adoration, it was all there reflecting back at her. And just as quickly as her heart seemed to stop, it was soon overflowing with love for this beautiful, incredible man. The father of her child.

"I didn't say it—"

"Shh!" he said softly and kissed her again, cutting off her words. "I love you, and it's something I want—no—*need* you to know. You're not in this alone. We're a team."

Whitney gave him a tremulous smile. "I'm glad."

He had said he'd never marry again, and she was okay with that. She'd rather have his love than be married to someone else.

Myles thumbed the tears from her cheeks, his touch gentle and gaze tender. "So what do you want to do now?"

It took a moment for her to remember what they'd been talking about. "You mean about your psychotic ex-wife?" she asked as they settled back on the couch, his arm around her, her tucked in at his side and their fingers entwined.

He surprised her by saying, "I think we should file charges against her. She shouldn't be able to get away with what they did."

"What about Evan Campbell?" she asked.

"He claims that despite Holly giving him the twenty-five grand, he wasn't the one responsible for using your eggs in the fertilization process. The only thing he will admit to is having contact with Blake, our surrogate, during the process and the pregnancy. But he insists they're just friends, and the private investigator can't find evidence that any money was exchanged between the two."

"What do you think really happened?"

His expression hardened slightly. "I think he switched the labels on the containers with the eggs, and that's how my sperm fertilized your eggs. It's the only thing that makes sense—unless the entire staff was in on it. But he won't admit to it because that would be fertility fraud, which is a class B felony, punishable by three to five years in prison and a fine of up to fifty grand."

Whitney stared absently at their entwined fingers. "You were once a defense lawyer. Do you think the prosecutor would have a strong case on either of them?" She could only imagine the kind of press a case like this would bring. National, for sure. And they'd pore over every sordid detail and drag the poor surrogate through hell. Their lives would be a living nightmare.

"Because of the money, they could probably make a conspiracy case stick against both. There's also a strong circumstantial case that Campbell tampered with the eggs since someone else performed the embryo transfer. As to his motive, it's Holly's word against his, because she swears he promised that all our attempts would fail."

Whitney raised her gaze to his. "I feel so torn. On the one hand, what they did was wrong. Criminally and morally. But on the other hand, if they hadn't done what they did, we wouldn't have Haylee, and I wouldn't have you in my life. I'll forever be grateful for you both. In the most twisted way possible, your ex-wife gave me the two people I love most in the world."

"We're lucky it turned out as well as it did." He dropped another kiss on her mouth. "Look, I still have a few connections in the DA's office. I'll talk to them about the situation."

"What I'd like best is if they could both be dealt with without the story going public. And I don't want them going to jail. Our jails are crowded enough."

Myles hummed in agreement, his gaze intent on her. He regarded her for so long that she let out a self-conscious giggle. "What?"

"I was just thinking that you've never been married, and I've been married twice, and I—"

"Babe, before you say another word, I'm not looking for marriage."

He raised a brow at her. "Really?"

"Honest to God, and hope to live to hold my great-grands," she said, making a quick cross-her-heart motion with her hand. "No seriously, I'm happy with what we have, so don't ever be afraid that I'll wake up one day looking for an engagement ring or that marriage is something I'll demand as proof that you love me. A marriage certificate won't change how much I love you, just like that legal document couldn't save either of your marriages."

"Just when I think I can't love you more," he whispered, caressing her cheek with his thumb.

Whitney wrinkled her nose at him. "That's because I'm infinitely lovable."

His eyes darkened, and his expression smoldered. "Since I don't have to be home until this afternoon, why don't we go upstairs so I can show you how infinitely fuckable you are, too."

He didn't need to ask her twice. Whitney shot up off the couch, grabbed his hand, and led him to her room, where she'd make sure he showed her everything.

Epilogue

Three Years Later

"Myles, would you please come and get your daughter! I'm trying to get dressed, and she's getting into my makeup." Whitney then turned to Haylee. "What did Mommy say? You don't need mascara."

Of course, when Haylee was misbehaving, she was *his* daughter.

"But Mommy, I want to look like you," her daughter whined, long spiral curls framing her sweet oval face.

Whitney's spine turned the consistency of a limp noodle in the face of her daughter's big pleading brown eyes—eyes fringed with lashes to spare. As Myles's mother had predicted, Haylee was growing into a beautiful mix of Whitney and Natalie.

"Haylee, sweetheart, you don't need makeup. You're beautiful without it. It's Mommy who needs the help."

Having caught the tail end of their conversation, Myles entered their bathroom and gently snagged her around the waist, pulling her to him. "Mommy doesn't need it either, princess."

Whitney laughed quietly as she gazed at her lover, her best

friend, and the father of her child. "I think we've established that you have almost no objectivity when it comes to the females in this house," she lovingly chided him.

Smiling, Myles leaned down and kissed the mound of her stomach. "How are my babies doing? Are they ready for today?"

"A few minutes ago, they were kicking up a storm," she said, rubbing her eight-months-pregnant belly.

At the beginning of the year, they'd learned she was pregnant with twins, news that hadn't come as a surprise to their respective families given that twins ran on both sides.

And if that wasn't enough, they'd later learned they were having a boy and a girl, and there was no one more eager to welcome them into the world than their older sister. Well, with the exception of Whitney. She wanted nothing more than to be able to hold them in her arms. She also desperately wanted her body back.

Their father also couldn't wait to meet them, constantly rubbing her belly like it was Aladdin's magic lamp, as if that would hasten their arrival.

"I'm the one who calms them down," he said with a wink at her. Myles had appointed himself the Pied Piper of all their children. "Come on, princess," he said, extending his hand to their daughter. "Let's let Mommy finish getting ready."

Haylee appeared undecided, her eyes still on the array of makeup products on the counter.

"You can have a chocolate chip cookie before we drop you off at Aunt Natalie's, okay?" Myles coaxed, taking her small hand in his.

Her expression immediately transformed, pleasure putting a beaming smile on her face. "Daddy, can I have two? You said next time I could have an extra one if I was a good girl at school."

Apparently, getting caught red-handed with her mother's

makeup case when she'd repeatedly been told not to touch it
and to stay out of their bathroom didn't count.

"Yes, you can have two. Now come on."

"Wait, Daddy!" Haylee shouted, using her indoor-voice shout
because, as every parent knew, there were several decibels between the two. "I have to say goodbye to the babies."

Turning from the mirror, Whitney faced her daughter and
stood still for what had become routine since her stomach
popped four months ago.

Haylee reached up and gently patted the baby bump. "Bye,
babies. I luv you. And stop kicking Mommy, okay?"

The kid took her older sister duties seriously. Lucky twins.
Lucky her.

Myles's eyes met hers, and Whitney knew he felt it too, the
I'd do anything in the world for you love they had for their daughter, and the two children they'd yet to meet.

After they left, Whitney resumed putting on her makeup.
Today, they were attending Cam's wedding. He'd finally found
a woman he wanted to spend forever with. Those were his
words. The man was whipped in the best way possible.

And as the bride was from the area, the wedding was being
held in LA, which meant Kennedy, Nate, and Aurora had flown
in from New York. Whitney had invited the entire gang to
stay with her, but none had wanted to burden the mother with
two buns in the oven.

Kennedy and Nate had married two years ago and had a
one-year-old daughter, and Aurora had married six months
later and had a nine-month-old son. Both couples had traveled
with their children, who would be staying with Aurora and
Nate's parents during the wedding.

Finished with her makeup, Whitney returned to their bedroom and changed into the dress laid out on the bed. Myles
had sold his house two and a half years ago, and he and their

daughter had moved into hers. The living together thing had been a bit of an adjustment—for Myles, mostly. Even though he had no desire to keep his house and rent it out, he'd refused her offer to have his name added to hers.

As she'd said to him, "You're it for me. I'm not going anywhere, and what's mine is yours. This is as much your home as it's Haylee's and mine." Unfortunately, that still hadn't been enough to sway him, but she wasn't giving up. One day he'd see it her way.

In the meantime, they enjoyed a wonderful but hectic life. They'd made a conscious decision to start trying for a baby a year ago. Thankfully, her endometriosis hadn't made conceiving an issue. She'd gotten pregnant within two months of them "trying," which had simply meant them continuing to enjoy a fantastic sex life.

The most difficult part of them melding their lives was coordinating their schedules. Before her pregnancy, she'd embarked on the rigors of a four-month, thirty-six-stop world tour. During the time, she'd flown home six times, and Myles and Haylee had flown out to visit during her concerts in Melbourne, Australia, and Johannesburg, South Africa. God, how she'd missed them between the visits.

When she arrived downstairs, dressed to the nines in a one-of-a-kind April Rose creation, evening bag in hand, her daughter sported her *Dora the Explorer* backpack on her back, all traces of makeup gone from her face.

Myles's blue eyes darkened as he took Whitney in. "Hey, gorgeous."

"Mommy, you look beautiful." Haylee pronounced it *bow-tee-full*.

"Thank you, sweetheart." Whitney leaned down and kissed her on the cheek. She then straightened and pressed a lingering kiss on Myles's lips. "And thank you, my love. You look pretty dashing yourself."

"Come on. The sooner we get out of here, the sooner we get to come home."

The lustful look in his eyes made it clear just what all the rush was about, as they'd have the house to themselves, which was something that would soon come to an end once the twins arrived. His sister frequently took Haylee for the night, but she'd need at least another pair of adult hands to deal with two infants. Which meant they wouldn't be alone for some time in the foreseeable future.

Whitney laughed dryly. "It's a wedding, not dinner at a restaurant."

"Everyone knows you can't stay out too late. You're sleeping for three."

You're sleeping for three had become code for *let's get you naked and in bed.*

"Come on, honey, the reception will be over at ten. That'll give us plenty of time to come home and—" she glanced at their daughter, who was avidly following their conversation "—um, sleep."

"Yes, sleep," he said, mock serious. "And you know how much we both need our sleep. These days, you need it more."

Suppressing a laugh, she elbowed him gently in the side. As if she needed any reminders of just how happy he was to be the beneficiary of her increased pregnancy-related libido and breasts.

Forty minutes later, they were headed to the wedding venue. As far as she was concerned, mid-November was the perfect month to hold a wedding. Today the temperature was a picture-perfect seventy-one degrees, and Whitney was looking forward to snuggling up under the covers with Myles when it cooled down overnight.

"You'll never guess who I ran into yesterday," Myles remarked, his tone casual.

"You're gonna have to narrow it down for me. I forgot to attach the tracking device to you before I left."

She and Haylee had spent the majority of the day with Kennedy, Aurora, and their kids. Haylee had played the role of their more worldly (and somewhat bossy) cousin, insisting she was old enough to change their diapers...until things got ugly. That was when she'd screwed up her face and turned the smelly task back over to the adults.

Myles huffed a laugh. "My ex-mother-in-law. She was happy to inform me that Holly remarried this past summer. To some real estate mogul."

"Are you surprised that she got married again?"

His ex-wife hadn't been charged for what she did. Myles could have filed civil charges against her, as he was the wronged party in what she'd attempted to do, but they'd decided against that. Her punishment was forfeiting her half of the settlement. Evan Campbell pled guilty to fertility fraud, and to avoid a prison sentence, he had to agree to surrender his medical license and agree not to work in health care. The last they'd heard, he'd moved to Nevada and was working at one of the casinos.

"Not really, I guess. Once she decided she didn't want to be single, she was determined to find a husband."

Whitney shivered. "I'm so glad I'm not like that." Then she chuckled. "When I was younger, the one thing I didn't want was to have a child out of wedlock. Now look at me." She stared at him lovingly. "I'm about to add two more to the mix and I wouldn't have it any other way, because what we have is as close to perfection as it gets."

Myles tore his eyes off the road for a moment, love shining in his eyes as he glanced at her. "Yeah, what we have is pretty damn special."

★ ★ ★

The next five hours beat out every Hollywood event she'd attended that year, and that included the Grammys and Oscars, both of which she'd been nominated for. While once Myles had dreaded being her plus one at those kinds of events, he'd learned to embrace the role, dutifully posing with her on the red carpet and doing what was asked of him when instructed.

Myles, look over here for the camera.

Myles, how are you preparing for the new baby?

Myles, can you stand on the other side of Sahara and angle this way?

Myles, will there be wedding bells on the horizon?

And not once had he told them to shove it or to go and fuck themselves, and she couldn't have been more proud.

The bride and groom made a stunning couple, and Cameron looked as happy as Whitney had ever seen him. Aurora's husband couldn't keep his eyes off the new mother, who glowed like a sunbeam. And Kennedy and Nate looked like a couple of newlyweds, tanned and relaxed from their recent anniversary trip to the Bahamas.

They were all doing well, and not just in the romantic relationship department. Oasis's net sales had increased twenty to thirty-five percent year over year in the last three years, and she and April (who'd given birth to her second child—a girl—two years ago) collaborated to start a company specializing in wedding apparel. It was being marketed under April's company, April Rose Designs, and the line was called Bloom. The bride was wearing one of their gowns today.

As planned, Kennedy and Aurora opened an office in Los Angeles, and it seemed that month after month, year after year, the need for their services only grew against a backdrop of strikes and allegations of sexual harassment that hit the entertainment industry. In the spring, they'd be opening an office in Chicago.

But as much as she'd enjoyed celebrating Cameron's wedding with so many of the people she loved, Whitney was happy to be home, face scrubbed free of makeup, pajamas on, off her tired, aching feet, and in bed, being spooned by her gorgeous man.

"I haven't had that much fun at a wedding since Kennedy and Nate got married," she said with a contented sigh.

Myles let out a rumbling laugh. "That's because you helped plan the damn thing."

Whitney giggled, remembering how much fun she, Kennedy, and Aurora had planning the wedding. The official wedding planner had been too through with them, but in the end admitted they'd made her job easier. "Okay, maybe I'm a little biased, but admit it. We did a great job."

Myles kissed her behind the ear as his hand continued to rub her stomach. She could feel him growing hard against her butt. "You're great at everything you do. Well, your lasagna could do with a bit more garlic, and your parallel parking abilities are sadly lacking," he teased.

"I'm a fantastic cook and a great driver," she said, tongue in cheek. She'd grown into a better-than-average cook, and she'd all but given up on parallel parking as she barely ever had cause to use it.

Myles chuckled as he nuzzled her neck. "How's the swelling?"

"I did pretty good tonight," she said, wiggling her toes. She'd only danced a few times, mostly with him. Her ankles and feet made it through the entire event like a bunch of champs.

"What about your hands? Any swelling there?"

Whitney's brow furrowed. She held her left hand out in front of her, displaying it to him. "I haven't had problems with my hands. At least, not yet," she added, fearing she'd spoken too soon.

It happened so fast. She had no idea what Myles was doing

when he reached over and slid something on her finger. Realization came when he moved his hand away. It was the combination of the coolness of the metal against her skin and the sight of the diamond twinkling in the dim lighting of their bedroom.

Whitney gasped loudly, her eyes wide and her mouth agape. She turned awkwardly to face him. The look in his eyes—pure delight and infinite love—had her stumbling in search of words. "Wha— Why— Is this an engagement ring?" she asked, confused, dazed, and incredulous all at once.

It couldn't be. Not after all these years. Not after they'd agreed that they didn't need to validate their relationship with a piece of paper known as a marriage certificate. Maybe this was an *even though we're never getting married, I'll love you until the end of time* ring.

Yes, that must be it.

"Whitney, sweetheart, will you marry me?" His voice was soft and his tone reverent. His eyes were filled with so much love and adoration, it made her heart ache.

Palming his clean-shaven jaw, she replied softly, "Honey, you don't have to do this. It's all the weddings we've been going to, isn't it?"

Myles's fingers circled her wrist, stilling her hand. "No, it's because I want to marry you."

"But you said—"

"That I'd never do it again. I know." He shook his head, chuckling wryly. "It took me years to realize that I pledged to love and cherish two women until death, and the one woman I will love and cherish until the day I die, I haven't. That's not just wrong. It defies logic."

Whitney blinked back the tears welling in her eyes. This man of hers. He never failed to show up and show out, and she loved that about him. "But I don't need that from you. I know you love me and that we'll always be together."

"Now, if you don't want to marry me, that's one thing. But if—"

"No, that's not what I'm saying," she protested.

"Then what are you saying? Do you want to marry me? Because I want to marry you more than anything."

Whitney searched his familiar blue eyes and could only see the love she knew was reflected in hers. She swallowed hard. "Let's do it after the babies are born. I don't want to get married in a muumuu."

Myles chuckled. "I'm going to take that as a yes."

She gave a fervent nod. "One hundred percent yes. And since we're doing it and I'm only ever going to do this once, I want one with all the works, sparing no expense."

"I wouldn't expect anything less for you," he said, an indulgent smile on his face.

"There's one thing I want you to do."

"Anything."

"Let me add your name to the house. That will be your gift to me."

Myles sighed. "It means that much to you, doesn't it?"

Whitney nodded. "Consider it the ultimate act of commitment and trust."

He kissed the finger wearing the ring and then her lips. "Done. Now, it's time for you to get that sleep I was talking about earlier."

Whitney's smile was covered when his mouth came down on hers. She knew they would sleep great that night.

★ ★ ★ ★ ★

About the Author

Beverley Kendall discovered her love of books while growing up in the then small city of Barrie, Ontario, Canada. With her love of books and romance, she always wished that everyone would find their happily ever after. She currently writes sexy historical, new adult and contemporary romances. As the mother of one too bright and mischievous young boy, she pulls full-time duty on all fronts. When she's not writing full-time, running The Season review website or mothering, she's probably reading or sleeping and dreaming of a time when she'll have time for her favorite hobbies: knitting, crocheting and sewing. Beverley has lived on two continents, in three countries, two provinces and four states. She stopped her nomadic existence and settled in the southeast. All things artistic feed her creative passion, but none more than writing.

Visit her at: beverleykendall.com.

TOKEN

Kennedy Mitchell is brilliant, beautiful and tired of being the only Black woman in the room.

Two years ago, she was plucked from reception for a seat at the boardroom table in the name of 'representation'. Rather than play along, she and her best friend founded Token, a boutique PR agency that helps diversity-challenged companies and celebrities.

With famous people getting into reputation-damaging controversies, Token is in high demand and business is booming, but when her ex shows up needing help repairing his reputation, things get even more complicated and soon Kennedy finds herself drawn into a PR scandal of her own.

AVAILABLE IN PAPERBACK AND EBOOK NOW